"My God, Vanessa, you look wonderful!"

At his spontaneous, sincere exclamation she hugged him even harder. Trent crushed her in his arms. He couldn't seem to get her close enough.

At last he drew back infinitesimally to gaze down into her face. Her thick fringe of eyelashes swept down, veiling her in mystery, while her tender, sensitive lips parted ever so slightly.

His eyes fixed on her trembling, vulnerable mouth, Trent struggled to regain his self-control. He had sworn he wouldn't take advantage of Vanessa's fragile emotional state in any way. He'd vowed not even to hold her hand unless she reached over and took his first. Yet here, not even a minute after she'd arrived, he was holding her clutched to him and bending eagerly, irrevocably downward to taste those irresistible lips for the very first time.

Dear Reader,

Sophisticated but sensitive, savvy yet unabashedly sentimental—that's today's woman, today's romance reader—you! And Silhouette Special Editions are written expressly to reward your quest for substantial, emotionally involving love stories.

So take a leisurely stroll under the cover's lavender arch into a garden of romantic delights. Pick and choose among titles if you must—we hope you'll soon equate all six Special Editions each month with consistently gratifying romantic reading.

Watch for sparkling new stories from your Silhouette favorites—Nora Roberts, Tracy Sinclair, Ginna Gray, Lindsay McKenna, Curtiss Ann Matlock, among others—along with some exciting newcomers to Silhouette, such as Karen Keast and Patricia Coughlin. Be on the lookout, too, for the new Silhouette Classics, a distinctive collection of bestselling Special Editions and Silhouette Intimate Moments now brought back to the stands—two each month—by popular demand.

On behalf of all the authors and editors of Special Editions,
Warmest wishes,

Leslie Kazanjian
Senior Editor

ANNE LACEY
Intrepid Heart

Silhouette Special Edition

Published by Silhouette Books New York

America's Publisher of Contemporary Romance

For a man from Michigan, DWIGHT V. SWAIN,
the best writing teacher in the whole U.S.A.,
with my love and everlasting appreciation

SILHOUETTE BOOKS
300 East 42nd St., New York, N.Y. 10017

Copyright © 1987 by Anne Lacey

ISBN: 0-373-09422-1

First Silhouette Books printing December 1987

All the characters in this book are fictitious. Any
resemblance to actual persons, living or dead, is
purely coincidental.

SILHOUETTE, SILHOUETTE SPECIAL EDITION and colophon
are registered trademarks of the publisher.

America's Publisher of Contemporary Romance

Printed in the U.S.A.

ANNE LACEY

lives in Baton Rouge, Louisiana, where she enjoys exploring antebellum homes up and down the Mississippi River as well as frequently revisiting two favorite river cities, New Orleans, and Natchez, Mississippi. She is admittedly an adventurous lady, having lived in Arkansas, Oklahoma, Arizona, Mississippi and several places in Texas. She has traveled extensively in the United States, Europe and Canada and keeps a bag packed at all times for unexpected trips.

CANADA

Catt Island

Davidson Island

Isle Royale

LAKE SUPERIOR

MINNESOTA

Copper Harbor
Prophet Islands

MICHIGAN

LAKE HURON

WISCONSIN

LAKE MICHIGAN

Grand Rapids

Detroit

Lansing

ILLINOIS

INDIANA

OHIO

Underlined places are fictitious.

Prologue

Help, somebody! Help!"

"Vanessa's drowned! Help!"

"Let me through, kids!"

"Hey, are you a lifeguard, mister?"

Trent Davidson ignored the questions being flung at him while his eyes took in the small, slender, very wet girl lying on her stomach before him.

She's twelve, maybe thirteen, he realized. Even before he reached her side he was aware of her long, coltish legs, as well as the softly curving back and waist.

Rapidly Trent flipped the girl onto her back and swung his long body over to shadow her. Then, as he prepared to begin mouth-to-mouth resuscitation, he finally looked down at her. Even with her face mottled and blue, she jolted him.

My God, she's a beautiful kid! he thought before covering her tender, vulnerable mouth with his own.

Forcing air into her lungs, he watched her chest rise. Again and again he repeated the motion. Come on, kid—breathe, dammit! he thought desperately.

He was dimly aware of the growing babble of voices behind him. Then one rose higher and sharper than the others. "What the *hell*? What's happened to my sister?"

Trent recognized the voice even as he continued to breathe into the girl's mouth and watch her budding chest rise. That heavy Southern drawl belonged to Clark Hamilton, a guy about his own age with whom Trent had gone waterskiing on a couple of occasions. So this gorgeous kid was Clark's little sister....

Suddenly she gasped and then began, mercifully, to breathe. A minute or two later, the poor kid got sick to her stomach.

Trent held her head and thought he'd never been so glad in his life to see somebody throw up.

But apparently the young girl found it all horribly embarrassing. When she could sit up, she threw Trent a humiliated look, her cheeks flushing brick red, before she collapsed into the arms of her relieved big brother.

Trent saw a lot of the Hamilton family during the rest of that summer. Young Vanessa's parents were so grateful to him for saving their daughter that they invited him over to their summer lake house quite frequently. Although he enjoyed their hospitality, Trent found them a rather strange family.

Mrs. Hamilton was a tall, handsome Southern matriarch who clearly doted on Clark but was less devoted to her daughter. Often, when Mrs. Hamilton looked at Vanessa, Trent saw the shrewd, appraising glance of a Michigan horse trader studying a mare for sale. Obviously Mrs. H. had big plans for Vanessa, but Trent didn't even want to speculate on what they might involve.

Mr. Hamilton was a successful businessman but apparently a rather ineffectual family man. Tall and gray-haired, he usually wore a bourbon flush. He adored his little girl, customarily calling Vanessa "sweetheart" or "honeybunch."

Clark was the archetypal big brother, who had christened his sister with the nickname "Nessie." Except for being a chronic tease, Clark was a nice guy, seemingly without the complexities of his parents and sister.

Then there was Vanessa, around whom the whole family seemed to revolve.

She was only a kid, but she could be charming, perceptive and even a little bit wacky at times, Trent noticed. Above all, she gave promise of becoming a spectacular beauty when she was fully grown. Vanessa asked Trent a thousand questions each and every time she saw him, and he was both amused and touched to realize that his rescue of her had apparently inspired a girlish crush on him.

Any other thirteen-year-old would have bored the hell out of Trent, since he was ten years older, but from the very beginning Vanessa was utterly unique. She had a bright, quick mind and an active imagination. Half the time she lived in some never-never land where she was a magic princess and everyone else existed to do her bidding, and the rest of the time she endured the mundane world where pimply boys a year older sought her out. She was also surprisingly intuitive. Vanessa regularly caught Trent off guard, either by reading his mind or just by divining his intentions.

On the last night of that very special summer, Trent and Vanessa sat together in the porch swing after dinner. There were other guests—several politicians among them—and as the talk had turned to the next election, Vanessa and Trent had sidled out separately.

Trent was leaving the following day to return to Auburn University, where he was a graduate student in pharmacology. Vanessa and her family would return at the end of the week to their home in Atlanta.

"Trent, you're all alone in the whole world, aren't you?" Vanessa asked him, her dark eyes swimming with sympathy as she tried to visualize this calamity.

"In a way," he replied, a trifle amused by Vanessa's flair for the dramatic. "Both of my parents are dead."

"That's so...terrible!" Her soft Southern voice broke at the thought.

"It really isn't—not to me," Trent reassured her. "You see, my mother died before I was three, so I don't remember her at all, and my father was always so old he was more like a grandfather. At the same time that Dad was teaching me all about herbs and plants, he was also preparing me for his inevitable death. Later, when he did become seriously ill, he hated the confinement and limitations of the disease as much as the pain. I couldn't want him to go on suffering. I was just lucky to have had him for as long as I did."

"But after you get all those college degrees, you're going to go back up to that island in Michigan, aren't you? And you'll be there in your dad's lab all alone, and you'll go home after work and you'll still be all alone." Long black eyelashes swept down to veil Vanessa's marvelous eyes; she was a youthful Scarlett O'Hara in her cunning. "Oh, you'll get terribly set in your ways, Trent. Why, you'll forget all your table manners and become an old bachelor who's impossible to live with!"

He appeared to seriously consider these dire predictions. "I suppose that could all happen, Vanessa. So what would you suggest?"

She leaned forward eagerly, her piquant face alight. "I think you should marry somebody before you go way back up there to live. That way you won't get so lonely and—and you'll have someone to look after you when you get sick!"

Trent had never been sick in his life, so he couldn't help but smile even as he continued to play along with her.

"Hmmm . . . that does sound good. Do you have a possible wife to suggest for me?"

Vanessa drew a long, deep breath. She's a cheeky little thing, he thought admiringly. "Oh, Trent, I love you!" she blurted out, and he saw the suddenly imploring look on her face. "Tell me—oh, but you must tell me the *truth*—do you love me, too?"

"No," he replied honestly, telling Vanessa the truth as she'd requested. But then, before anguish and humiliation had completely drenched her dark, expressive eyes and swamped that soft and lovely face, he added softly, "But I will when you grow up, Vanessa."

Then he leaned over and kissed her on the cheek.

NEW YORK CITY, FOUR YEARS AGO . . .

"Trent! Oh, Trent, I can't believe it's really *you*!"

"Vanessa!"

Trent was so amazed, startled and suddenly exhilarated that all he could manage to say was her name.

He would have known her anywhere in the world. She had grown up to be just as beautiful as he'd expected. No, he realized, she was even more beautiful than he could have imagined. Thick, rippling dark curls framed a heart-stopping face, and her expressive eyes, looking up at him, brimmed with emotion.

She was slender, barely medium height, and so utterly lovely that she absolutely took his breath away.

Trent had not thought of Vanessa very much during the past eight years. He had been so busy, so involved with other people and compelling projects. A couple of years back she had finally quit writing to him because, Trent knew guiltily, he had stopped responding to her numerous cards and letters. He had been living on the island with Helene Rosenni then, and Helene had been very demanding of his every free moment. He and Helene had finally broken up the previous spring.

Now, looking down at the lovely, youthful face before him, all the hubbub of the busy New York hotel lobby faded away, and Trent had the first intimation that he might have made a terrible mistake in neglecting Vanessa. Fortunately, she didn't appear to hold it against him.

He had continued to envision her as she'd once been—simply a bright, pretty child. But all the while she'd been growing up to become the most beautiful young woman on earth. How old was Vanessa now? Twenty-one, of course, for Trent was thirty-one.

"Oh, I'm forgetting my manners, Trent. You must come meet my husband, Bailey Ashton," she said smoothly. "We're just passing through on our way back from Europe. I live in Washington now." She extended her hand toward a group of men across the room.

Husband. For a moment Trent was so shocked that the word didn't even register. Why, Vanessa was much too young to be married, he thought. Perhaps not from a legal standpoint, but most young women wanted to complete their education and begin a career before choosing a life's partner.

The last news Trent had had of Vanessa, she'd been a sophomore at Newcomb College in New Orleans. When had she quit?

She'd always been interested in marriage, he recalled, but why had she tied herself down so soon? She never even gave me a chance to know her as a grown-up, Trent brooded.

He looked down into her dark brown eyes, still filled with emotion as she stared up at him. It didn't make sense.

Dazed, he let his eyes follow her gesture across the room to the cluster of older men. The one nearest them was stolid, balding and obviously middle-aged. Questions lashed Trent's mind, cutting him like lasers. Then he remembered the speculative way Mrs. Hamilton used to look at Vanessa, and he swallowed hard.

In a fog, Trent allowed himself to be led across the lobby. "You probably haven't heard, Trent, but—but my daddy died last year," Vanessa said in a suddenly low and trembly voice.

No, Trent hadn't heard—and now, apparently, Vanessa had found herself a new daddy—a congressman from Georgia, no less. Numbly Trent heard himself being presented, and he automatically shook the hand of the forty-five-year-old man who had stepped forth to fill the void in Vanessa's life. Why, this guy even had her father's bourbon flush, Trent thought in astonishment.

"Vanessa's told me all about you," Bailey Ashton said, giving Trent's hand a hard squeeze. "Several times, in fact. Thanks for saving my baby for me."

I thought I had saved her for a young man, you smooth bastard, Trent thought savagely. I *should* have saved her for myself!

Still thunderstruck, he couldn't think of anything to say aloud. Fortunately, Bailey Ashton, at ease with the social niceties, kept the conversation going.

"You're a pharmacologist, aren't you?"

"Actually, I'm a pharmacognosist, although my academic degrees are in pharmacology," Trent said stiffly.

Ashton blinked. "Well, what the heck is that?" he drawled.

"Bailey, I told you," Vanessa said quietly. "Trent's a man who specializes in the study of medicinal plants."

"Oh, sure, that's right," Ashton said, chummily clapping Trent on the back. Trent saw the congressman's eyes scan the room, any momentary interest in Trent quickly fading.

But Vanessa still had one important, all-consuming question. "Is your wife here with you, Trent?" she asked, a funny little edge to her voice.

"I'm not married, Vanessa," he replied in surprise. "I never have been."

Now Vanessa was the one who looked flabbergasted. She stood frozen next to the self-important man to whom she was now married, and Trent saw the dawn of deep misery in her eyes.

"But I thought—oh, I'd heard that . . . that you were engaged," she said in a thin, strained voice.

Trent couldn't imagine how she'd heard that. Although in the first throes of his infatuation with Helene he had bought her a small ring, it was more a "promise ring" than the real McCoy. Helene had given the ring back to Trent when they'd broken up, flinging it straight into his face. Trent had thought, in retrospect, that all Helene represented was two years of sexual infatuation and sheer utter idiocy. Until today, he hadn't imagined just how dearly he was going to have to pay for those years.

For a long, stark moment, Trent and Vanessa stared at each other while pain and regret vibrated almost visibly between them.

Ashton nudged her. "Baby, we gotta get going."

So Vanessa and Trent flashed each other the stiff smiles of casual acquaintances and said how very nice it had been to run into each other again, even on this cold and wintry day—a day, Trent thought, wearily massaging the bridge of his nose, that had suddenly turned a whole lot colder, a great deal bleaker.

THE ALASKAN WILDERNESS, TWO YEARS AGO...

Congressman Killed
Wife Survives Crash

(AP) A private plane piloted by Congressman Bailey Ashton, 47, crashed early yesterday in the Alaska wilderness not far from White Horse.

Both Ashton and his mother-in-law, Claire Hamilton, 52, were killed outright, according to the congressman's wife, Vanessa Ashton, 23.

Although Mrs. Ashton suffered a number of broken bones, she managed to alternately walk and crawl halfway down the slope until she reached the camp of a group of amateur mountain climbers....

ATLANTA, GEORGIA, ONE YEAR AGO...

Vanessa Ashton Still Hospitalized

Doctors at Pinewood Hospital here in Atlanta confirmed yesterday that Vanessa Ashton, 24, plucky young widow of the late Congressman Bailey Ashton, has been hospitalized for most of the previous year due to clinical depression.

"Mrs. Ashton has proved either unresponsive to conventional medications or unable to tolerate their side effects," said her primary physician, Dr. Rolf Zellar.

Depression among survivors of traumatic accidents is "so common it is almost predictable," Dr. Zellar added. "The survivor always wonders, Why? Why did I make it and why didn't they? Of course, in Mrs. Ashton's case, she had numerous physical injuries as well. Long periods of helplessness and hospitalization often create depression in otherwise healthy people and may aggravate it in those already depressed."

Mrs. Ashton's doctors have confirmed that they are now seeking alternate drugs that would not have the side effects of more traditional medications. They have contacted researchers in herbal medicines in Indiana, Michigan and California....

DAVIDSON ISLAND, MICHIGAN THREE MONTHS AGO...

Trent stared down at the letter that lay in the center of his desk, surrounded by stacks of pharmacy journals, books and pamphlets. He was actually afraid to open it.

By now he knew just how desperately sick Vanessa had been, much sicker by far than her doctors had led friends and reporters to believe. But Clark Hamilton knew, and he was frantic for his sister.

The letter from Dr. Rolf Zellar had been waiting for Trent when he'd returned to his office after lunch. It was almost two o'clock, because Trent had taken an after-lunch stroll around the small inland lake that lay at the far end of the island. His dog, Boots, had accompanied him and had been in no hurry to return. Meanwhile his assistant, Olga, had placed the letter on Trent's desk when she'd sorted the day's mail.

Now he regarded it as a threat, much as a coiled rattlesnake would have been. *What if Vanessa had gotten worse, not better?*

Anxiously Trent paced the length of his simple office. It was a large room, filled with strong, sturdy furniture that he had built himself, sawing and hammering, sanding and staining the pieces during the long, lonely winter evenings, while snow fell silently outside, piling up in deep drifts and sealing him into a quiet white world.

Enough! He had to know the truth about Vanessa sometime. Rapidly Trent strode back to his desk, snatched up his letter opener and slit the cream-colored envelope.

He drew out a sheet of bond paper with a fancy letterhead and began to read the typed words:

Dear Dr. Davidson:
It is my pleasure to tell you that Mrs. Vanessa Ashton has had a remarkable and wholly efficacious response

to your compound H-320B. In fact, Vanessa has asked me to tell you that this is surely the second time you've saved her life.

Trent dropped the letter and rubbed at his suspiciously burning eyes. Even after he'd subdued them he could still feel the muscles of his throat working convulsively.

She was going to be all right! That beautiful little girl he had known and loved and who had grown up to become the most beautiful woman in the world was going to be all right!

Sometimes life gave you a second chance, after all.

And this time I won't blow it, Trent vowed.

On impulse, he snatched up a scratch pad and dashed off a quick note to her. "I'm getting dreadfully set in my ways. You'd better get well soon and come marry me," he wrote. He scribbled "Love, Trent" at the bottom and addressed an envelope to Vanessa Ashton.

He hoped the silly note would make her laugh—or provoke a smile at the very least. And maybe Vanessa would even see through his teasing words to a deeper truth as well.

He and Vanessa loved each other. They always had.

Of course, there was one slight problem: they really didn't know each other at all.

Chapter One

Attention, all passengers. This ferry will dock on Catt Island in approximately five minutes.''

Five minutes! As soon as she heard the captain's announcement over the loudspeaker, Vanessa Ashton darted away from the rail. She had been standing outside on the upper deck of the ferry, where she could watch the churning blue waters of Lake Superior and view the passing bank with its heavy forests, small fishing villages, coves and inlets. The unfamiliar countryside and waterways had fascinated her, but now she swung her shoulder bag down the length of her arm as she hurried off toward the ladies' rest room. Five minutes!

She wanted to look just as good as she could. After all, she was about to see Trent again! Lord, how many years had it been?

She knew, of course. Vanessa never lost track of anything that concerned Trent. More than four years had passed since they had faced each other so awkwardly in the lobby of that expensive New York hotel. Almost five years, in fact. She'd been barely twenty-one then, and now she was almost twenty-six.

When she'd first gotten so sick, she would have welcomed a visit from Trent. But by then he'd been sealed in for the winter on his island off Michigan's Upper Peninsula. Then, after the spring thaw, when he could have come to Georgia—and, indeed, had offered to do so—Vanessa had not really wanted to see him. Or, more accurately, she hadn't wanted Trent to see *her* in such a sorry emotional state— depressed, crying and looking like hell. But all that was behind her now. She was well at last, Vanessa felt certain. Her broken bones had knit back together quite nicely, and as for the other—those ghastly "recall episodes" and the teeth-grinding nightmares—they were all over, too, she vowed.

Unfortunately, though, she still didn't look completely well. Vanessa peered anxiously at her reflection in the wavy rest room mirror. Her face looked skinny and pale, which made her eyes seem huge. She was still about ten pounds under her usual slender weight, and now that Vanessa was able to notice things like that, her thinness troubled her.

"Trent will think I look like a plucked chicken," she'd complained yesterday to Clark when he'd arrived to drive her to the airport. The suit she'd been wearing had been too loose, its baggy skirt too short to be fashionable. Why, her legs looked about as shapely as broomsticks! How long had it been, anyway, since she'd bought herself some decent clothes?

"Trent is going to think you look marvelous," Clark had retorted. "Believe me, you do, too, compared to a year ago, Nessie."

She had waved a fist dangerously close to his nose. "You call me that revolting name one more time—"

"Okay, okay," Clark had said, surrendering.

Not that she really would have hit Clark, of course. Not after all she'd put her poor brother and his wife, Kitty, through. As if paying regular visits to the hospital hadn't been enough already, Clark and Kitty had also had her underfoot for four months once she'd finally left the hospital. Everyone from internist to neurologist to psychiatrist had insisted that Vanessa not stay alone, and she simply had been too tired and worn out to argue anymore. So she'd served out the time, day by dreary day, as though it were a prison sentence, reporting dutifully to the medical center once a week for more physical therapy to strengthen her arm after its two operations and for meetings with a circle of doleful people in group therapy with Dr. Zellar. By now Vanessa was thoroughly sick to death of all of them— doctors, therapists, fellow patients, even her anxious, loving, *hovering* relatives.

At last ... at last ... she'd been set free, and now she was on her way north to see Trent. Joy from the two events mingled and bubbled up from a deep wellspring of happiness within her. Eagerly Vanessa stepped back from the mirror to get an almost full-length view of herself.

At least she wasn't still wearing the tacky suit in which she'd fled Atlanta yesterday. As soon as her plane had landed in Grand Rapids, Vanessa had asked a cabdriver to take her to the nearest large shopping mall. There she'd acquired the attractive outfit she was presently wearing: casual slacks, a cowl-neck sweater and a long, unstructured jacket. Not only did the new clothes lift her spirits, but they looked more suitable for a long ferry ride—and helped conceal her thinness as well.

Okay, the bod looks properly clad, she decided. Now, how about the mug?

To her own highly critical eyes, Vanessa thought she looked exactly like someone who'd been quite sick. Although the dark wings of illness had finally lifted, their shadow continued to linger. Her skin still felt too taut and looked too dry. Tiny new lines had formed around her mouth and eyes, and Vanessa worried that these were wrinkles and might not ever disappear. Then, too, her eyes remained darkly circled. In the harsh rest room light she could see those circles quite plainly.

"Damn!" she muttered aloud, rummaging in her large shoulder bag for a tiny waterproof case of cosmetics. Finally locating her concealer stick, she drew it recklessly across the skin beneath her eyes.

Travel and wind had rubbed off the rest of her makeup, so Vanessa hastily reapplied blusher to her cheekbones and gloss to her lips. Her eyes, at least, needed no artifice, for which she was grateful.

Vanessa turned her attention to her hair. She didn't think all her brushing and use of conditioners was helping a bit; it still looked dull and dry. I should have had it cut, Vanessa thought desperately, dragging a brush through the long, windblown locks. For more than a minute she brushed and brushed, trying to elicit just a little shine.

At last, defeated, she stopped. Oh, I look just terrible, Vanessa thought bleakly. Trent's such a handsome man, and what he's getting is an absolute scarecrow—a caricature of my former self! He'll be ashamed to be seen with me. Oh, God, *why* did I come?

Tears threatened for a treacherous moment, but Vanessa refused to give in to them. Glumly she left the bathroom, taking a flight of steps down to the lower deck, where she scanned the approaching shore. The ferry was bearing down on land hard and fast now, cutting a path through the churning white-tipped waves.

With anticipation, Vanessa scanned the island they were approaching, attractive with its towering pine trees, colorful buildings and a small, well-protected harbor. Off to the left lay a large public marina with boats bobbing gently. At the breakwater where the ferry would dock, five, maybe six, people stood waiting.

As the ferry drew closer, Vanessa was able to pick out Trent quite easily; he towered over the others. At the sight of him her heart gave a great leap, then settled into a steady yet romping gallop.

Trent. He was thirty-six now, but somehow he just never changed at all, not to her. He was still the tall, dark, handsome prince of all her girlhood fantasies—the one person on earth who slew the dragons and carried her home, safe and well again. He was her hero, her rescuer, her guardian angel, as well as being the sexiest and best-looking man she'd ever laid eyes on.

Vanessa could still remember vividly the terror and despair with which she'd sunk into that vine-choked lake almost thirteen years ago. She still remembered the heavy brown waters closing over her desperately struggling head. Then there had been only empty black nothingness until she'd opened her eyes to find Trent's navy-blue eyes staring down worriedly into her own.

And then, much more recently, when she'd gone down into another swirling dark nothingness of despair, Trent had saved her once again. This time he'd offered an almost magic potion that had relaxed her tense body and allowed deep healing sleep while at the same time lifting her spirits.

Don't forget his note, too, she reminded herself, thinking of that dear and funny message written in his almost indecipherable scrawl. She still carried that note with her everywhere, and it had become her talisman, reminding her that she was still young and attractive, with a whole wonderful future ahead of her.

Of course, Trent had invited her here—to spend the summer continuing her recuperation—out of a misplaced feeling of pity. She absolutely knew that. Even though she'd leaped eagerly at Trent's invitation, she had reminded herself a thousand times that she must not get her hopes up romantically. *He just feels sorry for you,* she said to quench the excitement and exhilaration that kept springing up, fountainlike, inside her.

Trent had seen her now. A smile lighted up his whole face, and his hand rose, waving to her. Why, he looked positively radiant! Was he really that glad to see *her*?

Spontaneously Vanessa's own hand moved. She waved madly to Trent, then shouldered her way ahead of the few other passengers, who yielded good-naturedly, smiling at her obvious state of excitement and impatience.

The minute the gangplank clattered down she was there waiting, and when the signal to disembark was finally given, Vanessa dashed past the ferry workers. Then she was running toward Trent's outstretched arms, forgetting that she had ever been weak, sick, scared and hospitalized. All that mattered now was being alive and being here with him. Finally, all of her problems were over.

Vanessa looked beautiful—absolutely, breathtakingly beautiful! Throughout the whole long morning and the endless afternoon, Trent had warned himself not to expect too much, not to get his hopes up, to remember that Vanessa had been through a number of quite severe ordeals and could not possibly have emerged from them unscathed.

By the time he'd finally reached the ferry landing it was late afternoon, and Trent was sweating despite the fact that the weather had cooled off markedly for late May. His heart pounded in his ears, and his pulse raced. He reminded himself to anticipate some frail, tragic-faced, lank-haired zombie, even though Clark thought that Vanessa had come "a long way back."

But then there she was at last, looking incredibly like the lovely girl he'd seen several years ago in New York, and Trent simply couldn't get his arms around her fast enough.

Vanessa ran straight into them, just as warm and wriggly as Boots had been when he was a puppy. But she certainly smelled better than Boots ever had, her aroma one of sun and fresh air as well as a light, hypnotizing fragrance that was obviously something potent and expensive.

"Vanessa! My God, Vanessa, you look wonderful!"

At his spontaneous, sincere exclamation she wriggled some more and hugged him even harder. Trent crushed her in his arms. He couldn't seem to hold her close enough.

"Trent! Oh, Trent, I'm so happy to see you!"

At last he drew back infinitesimally to gaze down into her face. It was glowing, framed by masses of dark, shining hair. And her eyes—her large, dark, expressive, gorgeous eyes—enthralled him. She was laughing and crying all at the same time, and delight shot through Trent like adrenaline. He couldn't resist dropping light kisses on her nose, cheeks and forehead. Immediately Vanessa went up on tiptoe, her arms gliding around his neck.

Trent reveled in her touch and laughed aloud for the sheer joy of it. At the sound, Vanessa's face changed subtly. Her thick fringe of eyelashes swept down, veiling her in mystery, while her tender, sensitive lips parted ever so slightly. It was an invitation any man would have recognized.

His eyes fixed on her trembling, vulnerable mouth, Trent struggled to regain his self-control. He had sworn, both to Clark and to whatever deities inhabited the heavens, that he would not take advantage of Vanessa's fragile emotional state in any way. He'd vowed not even to hold her hand unless she reached over and took his first. Yet here, not even a minute after she'd arrived, he was holding her clutched to him and bending eagerly, irrevocably downward to taste those irresistible lips for the very first time.

Her warm mouth glided beneath his like satin. Indescribable sensations of touch and taste ignited instantly within him. Trent's own mouth opened, clinging to hers, savoring her enchanting coral lips until he felt completely drunk with joy and desire. Kissing Vanessa was like biting into the lushest tropical fruit on earth.

Good God, was he completely crazy? Alarmed, Trent drew back, peering down at her almost fearfully. But when he saw the rapturous expression on Vanessa's face, he began to breathe again.

Her eyes were closed, her lips still slightly parted. She seemed to glow with sheer bliss. Trent felt stunned, humbled, touched, charmed and captivated—all at the same time.

Never before had such a torrent of emotions washed over him, and he felt certain at that moment that he could never, ever let Vanessa go. Somewhere inside him, a fierce, instinctive sense of masculine possession awoke. This woman—this beguiling child-woman-enchantress—was *his*. Passionately he longed to protect her from every known danger—and from every other man.

Paradoxically, at the same instant, his desire crested, and Trent wanted to lie down with her, kiss every sweet inch of her body and do to Vanessa exactly the things he would kill any other man for doing. He struggled to reconcile the two fierce feelings—protectiveness and desire—that warred for supremacy in his breast.

My God, how was he *ever* going to stay away from her all summer?

But he must. He and Clark had agreed that it was crucial for Vanessa to be allowed to recover completely, free from pressure. Trent forced himself to step back.

Slowly Vanessa's eyes opened, and she looked up at him. Irresistibly he sank again into those dark mysterious depths. "Oh, Trent, how lovely!" she exclaimed ecstatically.

She didn't look in the least as though she'd been harmed by the kiss, Trent thought in relief, trying to be his usual practical self once again.

Now Vanessa leaned toward him, pressing soft but significant kisses on his chin and the corners of his mouth, which was as high as she could reach. "Oh, Trent, thank you for inviting me here for the summer—"

She wasn't helping his condition a bit, yet Trent just stood there grinning down at her. Good God, he had to do something—say something.

"I should thank you," he finally replied, his voice gruff from his own high-tide feelings. Then, taking refuge in the typically male preoccupation with luggage, he added, "Is that little satchel on your shoulder all you brought?"

Alarm shot through her rich brown eyes. "You mean my other bags haven't come? I sent three ahead."

"Oh, those. Yes, they arrived Wednesday. Three of them." He felt like the typical absentminded professor as he heard himself babbling on about luggage, for God's sake! This wasn't like him at all, Trent thought in bewilderment.

But Vanessa didn't seem to notice. Her eyes shining, she linked an arm through one of his and peered up at him expectantly.

"Now what? How do we get to your very own island, Trent?"

"The only way to Davidson Island," he answered, smiling down at her, "is by motorboat. I'm docked just around the bend, in front of the harbormaster's office."

"Oh, good! I can't wait to see it—to see everything! You know, Trent . . ." Vanessa's voice dropped, taking on the intimate tone of a very personal confidence. "I've been dying to travel for months now, so this is absolutely perfect. I flew from Atlanta to Grand Rapids and spent the night there, then hopped a commuter plane to Copper Harbor and took the ferry out here to Catt Island. Now the last leg of my journey will be by motorboat. Why, it simply couldn't be better!"

"You must be tired," Trent said solicitously, realizing that somehow, without his even realizing it, his fingers and Vanessa's had gotten tangled up together. Her small hand, clutching his much larger one, felt as warm as her lips.

"Oh, I'm not tired," she said in gentle contradiction. "I want to see everything," she repeated, almost dreamily, "especially your very own island."

Trent loved the Southern lilt of her voice. Strange, since those dragged-out, die-away accents had irritated the hell out of him when he'd been a student at Auburn. Of course, nothing about Vanessa had ever irritated him.

"If you can wait to see Davidson Island for just another hour, we'll grab dinner while we're here." Trent spoke rapidly, instinctively enfolding her little hand in his. "You might as well get used to our one and only restaurant, because I eat over here a lot."

"You do?" Vanessa said in surprise. "I thought your housekeeper, Mrs. Pushka, cooked most of your meals."

"She does," Trent confirmed, "but she's getting old—she's seventy-five now. She's still determined to work, though, so I try to make things a little easier for her: I get my own breakfast and I tell her business brings me to Catt Island at dinnertime a couple of evenings a week. I also insist she take Sunday off completely."

"Well, I can certainly get my own breakfast, too," Vanessa said swiftly. "I was doing it at Clark's house, anyway, since he and Kitty always rushed off to work. Why, I could fix yours as well, Trent."

"You didn't come here to be a galley slave, Vanessa," Trent said emphatically. "But I'll tell you what—if you're an early riser, we can get breakfast together."

"I'd like that," she said brightly, smoothing her dark hair back with one small hand. "What time is early?"

"Seven-thirty or eight," Trent lied. He usually sat down to breakfast before seven, but what was the big rush, after all? The brush of her shoulder against him as they walked along close together sent tremors of excitement rushing through him.

"I think I can manage that," Vanessa said with a cheerful smile. "Now, where's your favorite restaurant?"

"It's not a matter of being my favorite restaurant, it's the *only* restaurant," Trent said ruefully. "Fortunately, it grows on you."

Her perfume was also growing on him. He felt positively light-headed and ten years younger. How very, very beautiful she was....

Vanessa looked around with great interest as they strolled down the island's main street. "Why, it's a regular little town, isn't it? Shops, stores—oh, I see a laundry and the post office and even a church steeple. Who lives here, Trent? Mostly retired people, I suppose. Or fishermen? Say, how many people do you employ on Davidson Island? And you mentioned the harbormaster, Trent. What does he do?"

She hadn't changed! She was still the same Vanessa he remembered, Trent thought exultantly, listening to her sweet Southern voice skip from subject to subject. She was still interested in *everything*—and still kept up the smooth flow of warm Southern-belle chatter she'd been raised to. Disasters, depression, doctors and drugs...none of them could alter her intrepid spirit.

And she certainly still asked a ton of questions!

Chapter Two

Sally's Café looked as though it suited its plain and simple name, Vanessa thought. There was a handprinted menu tacked on the front door, and inside were square tables covered with red-and-white checkered cloths and secluded booths set back against the wall. The aroma was inviting, and there seemed to be quite a lot of customers, couples seated at tables as well as lone men straddling stools at the counter.

When Vanessa and Trent entered, everyone turned to stare at them, but the chorus of greetings that immediately rang out made Vanessa feel welcome. "Hello, miss . . . good evening, Trent," the occupants called, and Vanessa beamed at all of them. How nice that everyone was so friendly! Of course, she supposed, on a sparsely populated island like this there would be more than a slight interest in one's neighbors.

"Table or booth?" she threw over her shoulder to Trent as she threaded her way through a narrow aisle between tables.

"Booth. We'll have a little more privacy there," he said in a voice for her ears only, his breath warm against her neck.

From behind them rose a softly sibilant sound. "Why do I get the feeling that *we're* the topic of conversation?" Vanessa said, laughing, as she slipped into a booth.

"Because we are, of course," Trent replied readily. "A new face is always welcome on a little island like this one. We get so tired of looking at each other."

I'd never get tired of looking at you, Trent Davidson! Vanessa thought passionately. "Well, of course, I'm also with the island's most eligible bachelor," she teased gently.

"The *only* bachelor," he shot back. "You don't get a lot of choices on this island. But I doubt if I'm regarded as very eligible."

"Oh?" she prodded.

"I'm more like a lost cause," Trent admitted ruefully. "I think you were probably right about me years ago, Vanessa. I'm definitely in danger of becoming a crusty old bachelor, thoroughly disagreeable and set in my ways."

We'll just see about that, Vanessa thought to herself. She glanced up and found Trent's expression as he watched her both wistful and amused. Had he read her mind? she wondered. If not . . . what? Did that wistfulness concern her at all?

He continued to stare until Vanessa grew edgy. "Do I have dirt on my nose?" she asked Trent, suddenly self-conscious.

"Nope, no dirt. But you must have the longest, thickest eyelashes in the world," he replied softly, and Vanessa felt her cheeks grow warm with pleasure.

Before she could think of a reply, Trent reached for the menus, which were propped up behind the napkin holder. "Are you hungry?" he asked in a matter-of-fact way.

"Starved!" she replied automatically, then realized to her surprise that it was actually true. For months Vanessa had had to force herself to eat, but suddenly she was ravenous.

"Hmmm . . . let's see what I can recommend."

While Trent studied the menu, Vanessa studied him. Her eyes lingered on his thick, dark, wavy hair, and she yearned to reach over and touch it. Trent didn't seem to change like other people, unless one cared to carp about those two or three silver hairs at his temples. Vanessa found them distinguished. His angular face was still vigorous, youthful and unlined, a face that promised to wear very, very well.

His heavy eyebrows were jet black above deep-set, dark blue eyes. Short, very thick lashes blinked as he gazed at the menu.

His features were well-defined, chin, nose and jawline all hinting at inner strength and virile masculinity.

His wide mouth was wholly uncompromising, Vanessa mused. It had always revealed Trent's moods even more readily than his eyes. A straight, set line was its customary demeanor, and an accurate barometer of his disciplined nature and determination to achieve. But the corners of his long mouth had always tended to turn up when he was pleased or glide downward in a gesture of displeasure.

Trent's mouth was certainly on its downward keel now as he read off the restaurant's choices to Vanessa: "Smothered steak, grilled whitefish, baked chicken with potatoes . . . oh, God—liver and onions!"

Vanessa smothered a grin and knew she must never, ever set liver in front of Trent Davidson, not if she valued her life!

Now his mouth quirked up, indicating that, in his opinion, the selections were improving. "Chicken pot pie, ham steak, fish and corn chowder, fried chicken—"

Trent paused, practically smiling, and Vanessa knew in that moment that he absolutely adored fried chicken. Silently she sent up a small prayer of thanks that Southern fried chicken was one dish she could cook really well.

"Then we get into assorted salads and sandwiches... well, Vanessa, choose whatever you like. At least I can promise you that the dinner rolls and the home-baked pie will be fantastic!"

Trent's eyes were alight, his voice enthusiastic, and his mouth had now definitely formed a smile. Vanessa's eyes followed its curves longingly.

She still felt utterly disoriented by that heart-stopping kiss he'd given her at the ferry landing. It had been absolutely unforgettable, an electric kiss that had made her lips tingle and sent a warm current racing through her body, jolting her fully back to life and away from all those dark, lonely places where she'd wandered lost and alone for so long, always missing him so....

Trent's lips had been just like the man himself, strong and soft at the same time, and they had fit over hers as if designed expressly to bestow kisses on her. For years Vanessa had dreamed of Trent's kiss, had longed for it and had lain awake during innumerable nights, trying to imagine just how exciting it would be. Instinctively she had always known that his kiss would make her blood race and her legs feel weak. What she hadn't anticipated was the joyous, sunlit feeling of having come home at last that welled up from deep within her.

Yes, despite all her extravagant imaginings, the reality of Trent's kiss had been even better—and that must surely set some kind of record for the miraculous, Vanessa thought.

Her mind leaped ahead to what it would be like in a day or two, or a week or two, when she and Trent kissed more lingeringly, more completely, letting tongue and teeth play as well as lips!

"Good evening, miss."

A very young waitress materialized at their table, sending Vanessa a look of unabashed curiosity. The girl was no older than fifteen or sixteen, and with her straight blond hair and scrubbed, freckled face she appeared even younger. "Hello, Dr. Davidson," she said to Trent. "Would you and the...er...lady like to order now?"

"I'm ready," Trent replied with a smile. "What will you have, Vanessa?"

She knew she delighted him when she ordered fried chicken and hot rolls. Three cooked vegetables came with the dinner special, and already that was more food than Vanessa expected to eat. Still, Trent insisted on ordering a salad for each of them. The house dressing was delicious, he told Vanessa, and she nodded, agreeable to anything that pleased Trent. "Now, what would you like to drink?" he asked.

Wine was what Vanessa would have liked, but she was supposed to avoid alcohol for a while yet. "Iced tea?" she said tentatively, and felt relieved when the waitress nodded. Although Vanessa had traveled a lot, especially during her marriage to Bailey, none of her trips had included the Great Lakes region. She hadn't known if they would serve something that she considered a uniquely Southern beverage.

Trent ordered a glass of white wine, then turned attentively to Vanessa as the young waitress left with their orders. "What are you thinking about?" he asked her softly, and she shared her thoughts.

"Oh, Americans have gotten to be a rather homogeneous crew, despite all those Yankee tales you heard down home on the ol' honeysuckle-draped verandas."

Amusement flashed in Trent's dark blue eyes. "Isn't 'down home' what you and Clark used to say?"

"Now don't y'all be tacky, Trent, honey," Vanessa retorted, continuing the syrupy, exaggerated accent, and was rewarded by his shout of laughter. But, to her chagrin, every eye in the café turned in their direction.

"Seriously, one concern I have for you is the climate," Trent said, a little frown of worry slipping between his eyebrows. "What's the temperature in Atlanta today? Eighty? Eighty-five?"

"I don't know. I wasn't there today," Vanessa said in pert reply.

"Okay, smarty," Trent warned, his voice an amused growl.

"But yesterday, when I left, would you believe it was ninety?" Even as she spoke, Vanessa found herself staring at the faint hollows beneath Trent's cheekbones. She was fascinated by the slight indentations at his temples. He had such marvelous bone structure; no wonder he was so handsome.

"That's hot!" Trent exclaimed. "Of course, you're acclimated to it, humidity and all. But how are you faring with our cooler temperatures?"

"Oh, I'm doing okay," Vanessa replied easily. "Today was fairly warm, not that I was exactly ready to do a striptease on the deck of that ferry. But I've always preferred a temperate climate. Even snow doesn't particularly bother me. Why, the two winters when my folks took Clark and me to Aspen they all called me the original snow bunny."

She was exaggerating a little bit, Vanessa realized, but only because she didn't want Trent to think of her as some frail hothouse flower.

"Clark told me about those skiing trips," Trent remarked. "And I guess I was forgetting that you also climbed halfway down a snowy mountain in Alaska, in spite of cracked ribs and a broken arm."

Unconsciously Vanessa began to rub her once-injured left arm, then realized what she was doing and stopped. "Please, Trent. I really don't want to talk about... Bailey and Mother," she pleaded, her throat tightening with anxiety.

"I'm sorry," Trent said roughly, obviously abashed. "I should have realized—"

"There's no way you could have realized," Vanessa chimed in, not wanting to drop any reproaches, even implied ones, on this beautiful, wonderful man who was finally back in her life once again.

Awkwardly she went on. "Some people like to talk about...about something traumatic for the rest of their lives. But I'm not that way. In fact—" Vanessa stopped, drawing a deep breath. "I am heartily sick of the whole topic! For months and months everyone kept urging me to 'express your emotions' and 'get in touch with your feelings' and 'ventilate the anger and grief.' Oh, I know some of that is worthwhile. But, Trent, a person could spend her whole life just exploring her own head! That's not for me— there are too many busy, exciting, real-life things I want to do and see!"

She stopped, aware of his spreading smile. "Are you laughing at me, Trent?" Vanessa asked, just a trifle suspiciously.

"No. What you see is profound relief! Nessie, allow me to congratulate you. It's wonderful to find you still so unchanged. That's something I was afraid of, I guess—that you might have changed..." His voice trailed off.

Vanessa sat back in the booth and basked in Trent's approval. She just wished he hadn't called her by that old, hated nickname: "Nessie." Me and the Loch Ness monster, Vanessa thought grimly. At twelve, Clark had christened her with the despised moniker, and Vanessa's pleas that he abstain from using it had only given him a greater, more perverse glee. "Yeah, and you *look* just like the Loch Ness monster, too!" Clark used to shout.

But Trent, bless him, obviously didn't know she disliked the nickname.

Now she leaned across the table, confiding in him. "Dr. Zellar used to say I was 'a strongly integrated personality,' but I couldn't figure out if he was actually complimenting me or just calling me a hardhead. Oh, Trent, don't laugh like that! Everyone is staring at us again.''

Suddenly his hands reached across the table to grip both of hers and send that warm riptide of feeling coursing through her again. "I adore that hard head of yours, Vanessa! Now, may I ask just one question about the plane crash? Actually, it's about the aftermath of the crash.''

"All right, Trent,'' Vanessa said, torn between feeling ridiculously happy that she pleased him so and slightly wary of what he was about to ask.

"Does your arm hurt a lot? When I first saw you standing on the ferry today I noticed you were rubbing it.'' Both his voice and his dark blue eyes reflected his concern.

"It just hurts when I get tired,'' Vanessa said evenly, then felt her eyes crinkling with a small smile. "And it's absolutely infallible as a weather barometer. Now I can always predict storms.''

"I have some liniment I think will help,'' Trent said thoughtfully. "It doesn't exactly smell like roses, but since wintergreen is one of its dominant ingredients, it's not too bad.''

"Will you rub it in for me, Trent?'' Vanessa asked, deliberately giving him the old 'wide-eyed and innocent' look. She was flirting, of course, and Trent obviously knew that she was, but he didn't seem to mind a bit.

"My pleasure! I'll be delighted to become your personal masseur.'' His large, strong hands tightened over hers, increasing the warm torrent of feelings swirling inside her, until Vanessa felt almost treacherously weak. *What was this overwhelming effect he kept having on her?*

Then, suddenly, Trent's eyes looked beyond her, as if he saw someone approaching. He turned his attention back to Vanessa, his expression a trifle wary. "Here comes Sally,'' he said, and squeezed Vanessa's hands warmly before releasing them.

"Oh. You mean there really is a Sally of Sally's Café?" Vanessa asked, not bothering to glance over her shoulder.

"Sure is. Oh, good. She's just been stopped by another table of folks. You'll meet Olga, Sally's oldest daughter, either tomorrow or the next day. She's a pharmacist who works with me. Sally's youngest daughter, Karen, is our waitress."

Trent's voice, telling Vanessa about Olga and the others, was carefully casual . . . too much so. Vanessa knew at once that the connection went beyond the casual, knew intuitively, as chills zigzagged down her spine.

"Is Olga married?" she asked Trent nervously. "I—I guess I'm especially curious about her because you used to mention her in your letters. I know she's worked for you for quite a number of years."

"No, Olga has never married," Trent said offhandedly. Too offhandedly? Vanessa wondered. She began to feel something close to panic. Oh, God, had she come all of this way only to find Trent intimately involved with yet *another* woman?

Vanessa remembered keenly the Helene Rosenni episode of seven years ago. How could she ever forget it? When she had first learned from Clark that Trent was deeply in love with some girl, living with her—that he'd even bought her an engagement ring—Vanessa had felt as if she'd been stabbed to the heart. In addition to her mental anguish she had actually hurt physically as well. For weeks her chest and stomach had ached until she'd been unable to eat or draw a really deep breath. Night after night she had cried herself to sleep.

In retrospect, Vanessa knew that it was that wound that had triggered her impulsive marriage to Bailey a couple of years later. She'd already believed that Trent was married and gone from her life forever. Then, with her father's death, she'd had another severe blow to absorb, another beloved man to relinquish. Vanessa had been dazed, numb from the losses. In that state of mind, relying on both her mother and Bailey for comfort, she had tried to please them by doing as they wished. Vanessa had known Bailey was crazy about her, and she had suspected—correctly, as it turned out—that he would be doting, indulgent and very good to her.

Still, in her heart of hearts, Vanessa had always known she would never have given Bailey an earnest thought if she'd only known that Trent was not married.

Now could Olga be a part of the picture of his present life? Vanessa wondered almost desperately.

Perhaps Trent realized her frightened thoughts, for he looked directly at Vanessa, and when he spoke his voice was grave. "Olga is a good pharmacist, and she's been a loyal friend as well. Unfortunately, she has a rather...uh, possessive personality. Frankly, Vanessa, I sometimes wish she'd resign and leave these islands. I think Olga would have better luck in finding what she wants in a larger place."

"She's in love with you, isn't she?" Vanessa probed.

Now she saw profound and unmistakable discomfort moving across Trent's face. Even more revealingly, his mouth twisted down. "I guess she might be. It's strictly one-sided. Here's Sally now."

Vanessa swung around to see a large blond woman in her fifties bearing down on them.

Trent's introductions were smooth, but there was a hint of something in his voice that might have been apprehension. Vanessa felt sure she wasn't imagining it even as she reached out to shake hands with Sally Hedlung.

The older woman looked at Vanessa levelly and greeted her in a friendly fashion, but the expression behind her pale blue eyes spoke volumes. They sized her up, showing something akin to alarm. Vanessa's heart quickened. Yes, *something* was definitely going on here, undoubtedly something to do with Olga, who was in love with Trent.

But, of course, how could she blame Olga for that? Vanessa thought frankly. She, of all people, was bound to understand why a woman would find Trent lovable.

Meanwhile, her small hand was being swallowed by Sally's work-roughened one. An almost painful squeeze ended with a too-quick release. Then Sally was making polite, if rather pointed, conversation. "Will you be visiting long, Mrs. Ashton?" she asked Vanessa.

"Just till I wear out my welcome, I guess," Vanessa answered obliquely. She darted a look at Trent and saw that his expression was one of relief. Did he not want the Hedlungs to know that she'd been invited for the whole summer?

"I'm sure you'll be welcome for a long time," Sally said, her regret only faintly masked. "I hope you enjoy your dinner, Mrs. Ashton, and that we'll see more of you while you're here in the Prophet Islands."

"Call me Vanessa, please," Vanessa said firmly to this woman who was so many years her senior.

"Thank you," Sally said tonelessly. Then she turned to Trent again.

He wore the familiar grim expression of a male determined to get something unpleasant over and done with, Vanessa noted. With her keen instincts now triggered, she began to hone in on the probable truth.

There definitely had been *something* between Trent and Olga, she decided, even if it was something Trent now regretted. But Olga's mother had no doubt kept hoping for quite a different sort of outcome. Probably she'd wanted Trent to marry Olga, and saw the appearance of a "rival" on the scene as cause for alarm.

"Did you notice that fried chicken is back on the menu, Trent?" Sally was asking Trent, striving for a near-jocular voice.

"I certainly did. Thanks! In fact, Vanessa and I both ordered it for dinner."

"Good! I'll go make sure that what you get is crisp and hot," said Sally. "Nice to have met you, Mrs. Ash—Vanessa."

"Nice to have met you, too," Vanessa echoed. Well, if it hadn't been exactly *nice*, she thought, it had at least been educational.

"Oh, Trent—" Sally turned back. "Send my Olga home early this Friday, if you can. It's her sister Kristen's birthday."

"I'll try, Sally. But you know how wound up in her work Olga gets sometimes," Trent warned.

"She works too hard!"

No doubt Sally had not meant for her words to sound accusing, but they still emerged that way.

"I agree!" Trent shot back as if stung. "I wish you could persuade Olga to spend less time on my island and more on this one, Sally. Then she'd have sufficient time for rest and relaxation. More time to spend with her family, too."

Sally's round face sank into tired lines. "I'll talk to her, Trent."

She walked away rapidly, and Vanessa noticed for the first time that Trent was gripping the edge of the table. His cheeks looked faintly flushed, as if from anger. Then he turned back to Vanessa, and she saw the expression disappear. "I'm sorry about that," he said softly.

Vanessa managed an offhand shrug. "No problem."

"Soon everyone will know you're here." He continued to look at Vanessa as if debating something with himself.

Although a rampant curiosity surged through her, Vanessa knew not to ask. In her experience, personal questions always tended to make men clam up, and at any rate, this was none of her business.

At just that moment Karen returned with their salads, and they each turned to the food with relief, commenting on its crisp tastiness and sharing the salt and pepper shakers. Vanessa wondered at her sudden voracious appetite. Perhaps it was the fresh air or the stimulation of travel. But more likely it was Trent's exciting presence. As he looked up from spearing a plump tomato slice, his navy eyes glowing with obvious pleasure, Vanessa felt warmth and security wash over her in a comforting wave.

When their dinner arrived, Vanessa ate heartily, a little chagrined to discover that the best fried chicken and hot rolls she'd ever tasted had been cooked in Michigan, not Dixie.

"I'll bet Sally could open a franchise operation and make a fortune with this food." Vanessa sighed ecstatically, before taking another bite of fluffy roll smeared with home-made strawberry jam.

"Probably—but Sally wouldn't want the bother," Trent said. He offered Vanessa the one roll that remained, and she seized it hungrily.

Midway through her lemon meringue pie, Vanessa's stomach absolutely refused to accommodate another bite. What a shame, she thought, pushing away her dessert plate. The crust had been flaky and delicious, the filling perfect in its tart sweetness, the meringue piled high and delicately browned.

"Had enough dinner?" Trent teased.

"I certainly have! I've had enough for myself and three other hungry people. Oh, Trent, do you suppose Sally would possibly part with some of her recipes? Do you know how she makes this..."

Vanessa's voice trailed off at the expression in Trent's eyes. They were alight with tenderness and anticipation. Why, he looked as if this was as important to him as it was to her! "Let me take you home now, Vanessa," he said.

"Oh, yes," she replied simply, but emotion tightened her throat, thickened her voice. *Home with Trent.* She had almost despaired of its ever happening, but sometimes miracles actually did occur and dreams really came true.

Trent's boat was a sleek, gleaming thirty-footer, white with teak trim, and Vanessa thought it was absolutely beautiful.

"Motorboat, my eye!" she yelled in mock indignation over the roar of its powerful engine and the rush of the waves as Trent backed away from the pier. "I thought you meant a little putt-putt thing where you yank a cord and go chugging off. Lord, this—this *yacht* is positively gorgeous!"

"Cruiser," he called back to her, amused.

"What?" Vanessa said, snatching at her long black hair, which was whipping around her face.

"This is called a cruiser. We need larger craft on the Great Lakes because of the likelihood of sudden storms and high waves. Here you can't run around in a rowboat or a canoe or one of your little Southern putt-putts without risking your life."

"Oh. How fast can this cruiser go?" Vanessa asked. "And how far before you have to refuel?"

Trent recited all the pertinent statistics—speed, miles per gallon, safety features—as he guided them carefully out of the harbor. Momentarily Vanessa fell silent, admiring his hands, which were competently spinning the wheel around.

"Is this the same boat you used to explore the Canadian shore one summer, Trent? You wrote me about that trip," she said reflectively.

"No, I had a different one then. This baby's only a couple of years old. Now, any more questions, or can I head us toward home?"

"Uh-oh," Vanessa moaned. "I know I drive people crazy with questions, but how else can I ever learn anything?"

"I was just teasing. I really don't mind the questions," Trent called back to her. "I think they're a sign of an inquiring mind."

"Great! Because I certainly inquire," said Vanessa in relief. Then she swung back to the rail excitedly. "What are those lights you're turning on? Running lights? Is that the right term?''

"Sure is. See, you know more than you—"

Before Trent could even finish his sentence, Vanessa was off on a whole new series of questions. "How long will it take us to get to your island? Seven minutes? Well, that's certainly not long! Don't feel you have to break any speed records just because I'm aboard. And don't laugh like that at me, either! I know how you guys love to show off. Listen, I'd rather take a whole ten minutes and actually *make* it there.... Oh, Trent, look! What are those lights floating over there? Is that a buoy?''

The wind carried her eager words back to him, and Trent relaxed, grinning and enjoying the almost forgotten feeling of being keenly awake and entirely alive. For a long time— so very long, it seemed now—his life had been almost boringly predictable. It had been perfectly satisfactory. No major problems. But the keen edge of excitement and anticipation had been missing. He'd actually started feeling a little tired and rusty and had tried to accept it as a natural part of getting older. Of course, his brain cells were still as active as they'd ever been, but they no longer moved with the lightning speed he'd once used. In recent years there had been no need for lightning speed.

A single hour in Vanessa's company had certainly changed all of that! He was going to have to stay on his toes just to keep up with her, he realized, and the thought of a whole summer together filled him with excitement and exhilaration.

As twilight deepened, the waters of Lake Superior grew black and murky. Vanessa shivered, suddenly chilled despite her elation. Trent, busy at the wheel of his cruiser, didn't appear to notice. But when Vanessa glanced at him next he motioned her to come closer, then dropped his thick wool jacket over her shoulders.

"Thanks!" she said over the rush of wind, feeling snugly enfolded in the overlarge garment. It still felt warm from Trent's own body heat.

How handsome he looked right now, she thought, with color in his cheeks and the wind ruffling his hair. Beneath Trent's white turtleneck sweater the muscles of his arms and shoulders moved easily yet powerfully, and Vanessa stared at him, entranced. She kept wanting to pinch herself just to make sure she wasn't dreaming. Was she really, truly here with him? Having an elusive dream finally come true took a little getting used to.

"Just another minute or two, Vanessa," Trent called, and she knew he'd noticed her attention riveted on him and had probably attributed it to impatience. "Just keep watching the horizon on the right."

Vanessa turned and squinted intently in the direction Trent indicated. First she saw only a distant speck; then, as it rapidly increased in size, she was able to discern distant green-clad heights. "Is there a forest, Trent?" she cried.

"Sure is, honey. We've got a little bit of everything!"

Now she could see more as Davidson Island began to loom up in the distance, looking for all the world like an enchanted island out of a Disney movie. Vanessa hugged her arms around her waist with excitement as she hurried back to the rail. "What do you mean, 'everything,' Trent?" she screamed over her shoulder to him.

"A lake. An old copper mine. High sand dunes..."

"Oh!" Vanessa exclaimed, watching as the bright green island drew nearer until its toylike trees began to more nearly resemble actual trees. Soon she was even able to identify the trees as pines—not the kind of pines that grew in Georgia, but "cousins" still familiar enough to be recognizable.

Trent cut the cruiser's engine and they began to coast in toward the shore. The engine's lull made it much easier for them to hear each other speak. "Oh, Trent, what a glorious, wonderful island!" Vanessa exclaimed. "Are there any wild animals here?"

"You bet! Deer and elk and bear; beaver, muskrats—rabbits, too," Trent said to her encouragingly.

"Bear?" exclaimed Vanessa, instantly apprehensive.

"Just a few black ones that lumber about. Don't worry, they're as scared of you as you are of them."

"That I doubt," Vanessa said dryly. But she flashed Trent a halfhearted smile that said she wouldn't have hysterics over a few bears. She could tell from the disgusted look on his face that he was kicking himself for even mentioning them to her. "So what else lives here, Trent?"

"Birds!" he answered, relieved. "Just wait, Nessie, till you see all the various species of birds. Huge flocks of Canada geese breed here—"

"Romantic place, huh?" she flung back, laughing.

"For sure!" Trent agreed, but when Vanessa glanced at him next, she discovered that Trent wasn't laughing. Instead, she intercepted a deep blue look that swept down the entire length of her body. Suddenly a wild thrill shot through Vanessa. How long had she waited for Trent to see her as the woman she'd become and not as the little girl he'd once known? Their eyes met and locked in mutual awareness and a sudden foreign heaviness began to infuse Vanessa's limbs. Her respiration increased perceptibly. For just a moment apprehension and dread stung her. Trent wouldn't just automatically *assume*—? Or would he? No, of course not! Still, he was a man—all man. So she should probably be careful not to—

Oh, the hell with it! thought Vanessa in absolute exasperation with herself. This was *Trent*, for heaven's sake! Surely nothing could happen between them that would be painful, unpleasant or disagreeable in any way. But she didn't want to risk this magical enchantment to common, ordinary reality.

It was Vanessa's opinion that reality usually left a lot to be desired.

Mercifully, Trent appeared to have sensed her apprehension and was seeking to alleviate it now. He began talking rapidly about the island, as if to reassure Vanessa that his look of hearty, even lustful, male appreciation was not meant to frighten her.

"There's a small vineyard and grape arbor, too," he continued. "One day you'll have to try the Davidson vintage. Frankly, it hasn't won any prizes yet, and Mrs. Pushka used to say it tasted like vinegar, but I think my winemaking has improved since then. There are large gardens, too, for both vegetables and flowers. Greenhouses. The laboratory where I also have my office. And, of course, there are beds and beds of lady's slipper and ginseng, as well as a couple of hundred other herbs."

"Lady's slipper and ginseng were what you put in that tonic I took, right?" Vanessa asked.

"They were two of the active ingredients. There were others as well," he replied.

"Oh, I want to see them, Trent—all of the herbs and every other single thing!" Vanessa declared fervently.

"You will. I promise. Now sit down, will you, till I can get us docked. I don't want a bump knocking you over on your nose when you've come so far."

Obediently Vanessa plopped down in a seat on the starboard side of the cruiser as Trent docked skillfully with hardly a noise or a bump. No sooner had he tossed the first line over a post than Vanessa was scrambling out and rushing headlong down the pier.

She looked excitedly left and right. Finally she looked up, far up, where a hint of a house could just barely be glimpsed through the thick foliage and trees.

"Hey, wait for me," Trent called.

His words came just a moment too late. As Vanessa reached the path that led up to the house, she suddenly

found herself confronted by a small, fierce-looking dog.
White fur bristling, he growled deep and low in his throat.

"Trent!"

At Vanessa's terrified cry, Trent turned sharply, then
laughed with relief. "Oh, that's just Boots, my terrier. He
won't hurt you."

Already Vanessa had begun a frightened retreat, but
Boots matched her step for step, still growling ominously.

"Trent, he acts like he's going to tear out my throat,"
Vanessa wailed, her voice trembling with terror. "Oh,
please—!"

Trent tossed one last coil of rope over the post by the pier,
then dashed to her rescue. He managed to catch Vanessa in
his arms, glower at his dog and command sharply, "Stop
that, Boots!" all at the same time.

Vanessa clung to Trent unashamedly, and for the next
minute or two he simply held her. She pressed closer to his
warmth and strength, her face nestled against the long column of his neck, her nose gratefully inhaling his clean masculine scent. "It's okay, Vanessa. It's okay," he murmured
soothingly.

Boots gave a whine, and Vanessa heard Trent snap out
another command to "Sit!"

Finally she dared loosen her death grip on Trent. Still held
in the protective circle of his arms, Vanessa twisted her head
to look warily at the dog and saw that Boots was sitting as
commanded. The dog's head was tilted to one side, his
expression lugubrious as he studied the strange new creature that was presently enjoying the affections of his master.

"Boots doesn't bite," Trent assured Vanessa, but she
looked up at him skeptically.

"I really think Boots was about to make an exception to
that," she replied, her voice thin.

Trent laughed and caught her close once again, envelop-
ing her in a cocoon of safety and warmth. Oh, how she

loved the strength of his body and the glide of his vibrant skin against hers!

"Boots is just a trifle overzealous in protecting *his* island," Trent explained. "You see, he's really convinced that all of this belongs to him. But about the worst he can do in a pinch is lick you to death. Here, Vanessa, come see for yourself."

She still hung back, clutching at Trent instinctively. "He scared me so!"

"I know. I'm sorry, honey. I should have warned you he'd come charging down here, barking his head off. Now will you trust me, please?"

Vanessa knew she had to try. But she was still so afraid that she squeezed her eyes almost closed as Trent drew her a few steps nearer. "Bend down with me," he instructed, then called to his dog, "Boots, come."

With an answering whine, the dog crept closer. "Vanessa, this is Boots. He's very vocal, but he's loyal, too, and really quite a dear fellow when you get to know him. Now stretch out your hand and let him get your scent."

Vanessa obeyed, although her slim white hand was still shaking badly.

"Boots, this is Vanessa. You will love and protect her," Trent continued, making introductions as if between two people.

Suddenly Boots ducked his head, dipping it under Vanessa's shaky palm. "You can pet him now," Trent added unnecessarily, for she had already understood and responded to the animal's own initiative.

"Hello, Boots," she said, her voice still not quite normal but only quavering a trifle now. "Why, you're really pretty friendly after all!"

Boots licked at Vanessa's palm, and his tail began to wag. With a sigh of relief, she rocked back on her heels. "Will he know me now?" she asked Trent, still half fearfully.

"From this moment on, to Boots you are a friend," Trent intoned. Then he stood up, drawing Vanessa with him. "Now, shall we go see the house?"

Boots led the way, trotting ahead of them while Vanessa and Trent followed, walking arm in arm up the narrow stone path.

The path soon took a bend, leaving the area of the dock and rising gradually upward. Vanessa stopped and looked slowly all around. In the fast-fading light she saw that the stone path was bordered with plants and vines, bushes and shrubs. Flowers bloomed in a mad profusion of colors. Tulips of every hue edged the walk along with hundreds of orange-red tiger lilies. White daisies dipped their dainty heads and nodded to Vanessa as if in welcome. Just ahead lay a narrow stone bridge that spanned a merrily trickling silver stream. A gentle hill lay beyond, and there, again, all was a riot of flowers and brightly colored plants.

Wisps of evening mist were beginning to cloak the appealing scene, and Vanessa felt herself irresistibly drawn to all the beauty around her. Now, more than ever before, she felt as though she had stumbled by some remote magic into one of her beloved childhood fables. Surely fairyland itself could not be lovelier!

Only the tug of Trent's voice and his own irresistible presence were stronger than the island's lure. "Like it?" he asked her softly.

"Oh, Trent!" Vanessa breathed, completely bedazzled. She leaned back against him, and he swept one long arm around her. She felt its sinewy strength and trembled with her own vivid awareness of his long, hard, whipcord length.

"Trent, why didn't you tell me Davidson Island would be like *this*?" Vanessa breathed, turning to stare up into his angular face and trying to read his eyes, which were an even deeper blue than the waters of Lake Superior, shadowed now in the twilight.

"You really do like it, don't you?" Trent said with surprise.

Vanessa gulped and nodded. For the first time in her life, she understood what was meant by being rendered speechless.

"Come on," Trent said, his voice low and matter-of-fact although his eyes brimmed with joy. "Come see the stream and the bridge."

He led Vanessa up over the narrow stone bridge and would have continued beyond, but she balked. "Stop! Let me look! Oh, Trent, how utterly lovely!"

"I'm relieved," Trent admitted. "I was afraid you might not like it here, Vanessa."

She turned astonished eyes on him. "Not like it? Do you think I'm *crazy*?"

"Some women find it too isolated, lonely, rustic—and that's just in summer. I won't even begin to tell you what Helene thought of this place in the winter."

"But—" Vanessa glanced down at the sparkling silver stream. "I don't understand! Aren't there all sorts of things to do here in the winter? What about—well, cross-country skiing, that's always sounded like fun to me. Or—or even fishing. Yes, fishing through a hole in the ice! I've never done that, either." She turned back to him, perplexed. "What about you, Trent? Do *you* get lonely? Do you find the island too isolated and rustic?"

"Frankly, no," he said, his arm gliding down her shoulders until it stopped and tightened around her waist. Although exciting warmth and keen awareness of him followed with his touch, she made herself concentrate on his words rather than the feelings he was evoking.

"Actually, I don't think I've ever felt lonely in my life," he continued reflectively. "But then I grew up here, remember? I learned to entertain myself and to spend most of my days alone while I was just a small child. I'm used to my own company and quite at peace with it. But Helene's violent reactions to the island made me question my perspective."

"I think Helene suffered from a limited imagination," Vanessa retorted, seeing no reason to be particularly gracious toward her predecessor.

Trent chuckled and hugged her even closer. "Actually, you're right!"

"Why, I think anyone with just a few interests could entertain herself quite well," Vanessa continued, warming to her topic.

Trent stared at her in silent admiration.

It certainly doesn't hurt one bit for him to look at me like that, Vanessa thought.

"Come on to the house," Trent urged, tugging on her hand. "Catch a deep breath to carry you up the hill."

"Oh, pooh!" Vanessa said, laughing off Trent's solicitous concern, her Southern accent deepening as she teased, "Why, I could run right up this little ol' hill."

To prove it, she walked briskly beside him, following the stone path around a stand of large, thick trees. As they stepped into a clearing, Trent's house sprang into view above her.

It was a two-story structure, built of native stone and wood and vaguely Alpine in design. Although small enough to seem cozy, the house would nevertheless have enough rooms for a fairly large family, Vanessa realized. She loved it on sight and exclaimed admiringly, especially at the spectacular view of the Great Lake the front porch afforded.

"Wait till you see the inside of this place before you get too excited," Trent warned her. "One friend said my Victorian living and dining rooms belonged in a haunted house, and I think he was just being kind!" Trent opened the heavy front door and flicked a light switch. Lamps immediately glowed.

"Umm..." said Vanessa as Trent stood back to let her enter the hall. Then he opened a door to the right, and she followed, discovering herself in a formal living room. She gazed slowly around her at the ornate carved rosewood furniture, cushioned in red velour and set on floral carpets. Instinctively her nose crinkled. "It's rather marvelously *ghastly*, isn't it?" she asked, trailing her hand along a marble-topped table.

"Truly," Trent agreed, shooting her a winning smile that sent Vanessa's heart into flip-flops. "I consider this room a real test of taste. By the way, you just passed with flying colors, but you'd be surprised how many lovers of Victorian furniture there are."

Vanessa laughed at that, but as she walked slowly all around the room, she voiced an obvious question. "Why don't you sell this stuff or donate it to some museum, Trent, and get some really good things of your own? Or are these cherished family heirlooms with which you hesitate to part?"

"No, not really. They belonged to my father's first wife, Clarissa, and came with her from Detroit. So they're at least a century old," Trent explained.

"A *century*?" Vanessa stopped her exploring to stare at Trent incredulously. "You're joking!"

"No, not at all. My father was almost sixty when I was born. If he were still alive he'd be ninety-six today."

"My God!" Vanessa exclaimed. Then, as a sudden thought occurred to her, she burst out laughing.

"What is it?" Trent asked, leaning his arms across the back of an overstuffed chair and watching her closely.

Vanessa felt color rise in her cheeks. "I can't tell you!"

"Of course you can. You can tell me anything, Vanessa. Now what is it?" Trent coaxed. "You look like you're about to strangle."

Vanessa gave up and laughed with sheer abandon. "Trent, I just thought what—what a very long and virile life *you'll* probably have!"

"I figured it must be something like that," he said, amused. "You looked very naughty. But, yes, to answer your assumption, I'm rather hopeful that various... ah...attributes of my long-lived parent have also been transmitted to me. Now, come see the dining room next. It's Clarissa's legacy, too."

"Whatever happened to Clarissa?" Vanessa asked.

"She died of cancer."

"You mean your poor father was widowed *twice*? Oh, how awful! It's just dreadful to be all alone."

They crossed the hall, and Trent opened another room reeking of lemon wax and disuse. Vanessa made a brief inspection of the claw-legged table and chairs and the heavy, dark sideboard that would require a winch to move. "At least the rest of the house can only improve," she sighed. "Good Lord, Trent, no wonder you keep the doors to these rooms closed!"

"I never use them; that's why I haven't bothered to redecorate," he explained. Then he added on a teasing note, "And what if the rest of the house doesn't improve?"

Vanessa could feel his hand resting now on the small of her back. Although the area it encompassed was small, her skin radiated with sheer warmth.

"If the rest of the house isn't better, then I'll camp out on your boat," she threatened. "Or else I'll stay on the bridge. Yes, that's it! I'll have you roof over the bridge, and I'll live all summer long with that fabulous view and the little singing stream."

"I knew that bridge needed something," said Trent, rubbing his chin thoughtfully. "Perhaps a roof is it. Yes, Vanessa, I think you're exactly—"

His words were drowned by her squeal of delight. She had just entered the huge family room.

Trent followed her, then leaned back against a wall and watched while Vanessa scouted it thoroughly. Modern, comfortable sofas, chairs, tables and especially his spacious bookcases crammed with volumes, were all noted and exclaimed over.

She looked as appealing as a child on Christmas morning, Trent thought, and he watched her with the same sort of pleasure a proud parent might feel. Only Vanessa was no longer a child. Rather, she was a woman so utterly beautiful that just looking at her made him feel light-headed and overheated. It was a good thing she kept him talking nonstop, Trent thought ruefully, because with much time to contemplate and admire Vanessa's physical charms, their effect on him would probably become embarrassingly evident. That shining black hair of hers, how would it look all spread out over his pillow? And her huge, lustrous eyes, would they close or stay open if he made passionate love to her?

You'd better stop thinking that way, Trent warned himself sternly. Instead, he forced himself to reflect on the few faint reminders of Vanessa's illness. The circles beneath her eyes, which had never been there before. The pallor of her skin and the rather obvious thinness of her body. Of course, Vanessa had always been exquisitely slender, and Trent definitely preferred women that way. More voluptuous women like Olga, with her large breasts and hips, had never really appealed to him. Still, Nessie could definitely use a few more pounds, he thought.

She'd been through hell: that's what he mustn't—couldn't—forget.

"The furniture?" he said, responding belatedly to Vanessa's latest inquiry about where he'd gotten such fabulous stuff. "It was made from trees felled right here on the island. And that, by the way, is the only reason I'll allow virgin timber to be cut."

"Yes, but for whom?" Vanessa repeated, running her hands over the arm of one low sofa. "Who was the carpenter? The workmanship is superb!"

"Thanks," Trent said, pushing away from the wall and taking a modest bow.

"You?" she gasped. "Why, Trent, you mean you build furniture in addition to everything else?"

"Not much to it, though it does involve a lot of time. The winter nights and a lot of my weekends are long and quiet. I can only stand books and TV so long—finally, I have to *do* something," he finished.

"I know what you mean. I'm a pretty active person myself," Vanessa said, coming over to stand in front of him. Immediately Trent's hands went out to span her slim waist while his eyes scrutinized her pale, perfect skin and the pearly teeth glistening behind her soft, inviting lips.

His body still hadn't gotten the message. It didn't understand that he couldn't have her because she'd been so ill. I guess I've spent too much time alone in recent months. I *know* I've been celibate far too long, Trent thought, annoyed by his aroused senses and the surging male hormones that continued to ignore his stern instructions.

"What else have you built, Trent?" Vanessa asked softly, and he felt her small hands press lightly on his shoulders. Even that delicate touch of hers made him tingle all over. He swallowed hard.

"I've built a few things for your room," he said negligently.

"Oh, I want to see!" Vanessa cried, childlike.

"Just up the stairs, the first door on the right," he instructed, and then he thrilled anew when Vanessa instinctively reached for his hand.

They were at the foot of the staircase when the door leading from the kitchen creaked open, startling them both. They swung around as one, then stopped.

A tiny, birdlike woman stood there, her face an ancient mask of wrinkles, her hair snow-white and thinning. "Oh, my goodness!" she exclaimed in surprise, and stared as if spellbound at Vanessa. The younger woman froze, impaled by that scrutiny. "I didn't know anyone was here!"

"I find that hard to believe, Frieda," Trent commented dryly, "between the boat roaring in and Boots barking. Why, you probably watched us through your binoculars when we walked up here from the dock."

"You show some respect, young man!" Mrs. Pushka said, scolding Trent as though he were five or six years old, Vanessa thought. She glanced down to conceal her own grin at hearing Dr. Trent Davidson being so addressed—and in his very own home, at that! "Course I watched you. When somebody lands on this island I want to know whether to fire up the teakettle or load a couple of shells in Myron's rifle."

Trent drew Vanessa back to his side. "Myron was her late husband," he remarked.

"Course I knew, too, that you'd gone to fetch a very special lady, 'cause you told me. I still have my wits about me, you know—or maybe you don't! But, my goodness, I didn't dream the lady would look like this pretty little thing, or that she'd put me so much in mind of your own mother, Trent."

Vanessa felt Trent's start of surprise. "Why, I never noticed any particular resemblance." To Vanessa he added, "I have a number of photographs of my mother."

"You'd have had to know Tracy," Mrs. Pushka said firmly. "She had the same way of moving and smiling—and of liking this island, too. Well, my dear, since Trent has obviously forgotten all the manners I once taught him, I'll introduce myself. I'm Frieda Pushka."

"Vanessa Ashton," said Vanessa, holding out her hand to the old woman.

The old woman's bony hand squeezed hers almost as hard as Sally Hedlung's had. The women around here certainly do have a grip on things, Vanessa thought, wincing.

"So you think I'm like Trent's mother?" she asked, pleased by the comparison.

"A bit. Course you're younger than Tracy was—prettier, too, I'm bound to admit. But she had a sweet nature and a strong, loving heart. I still miss her. Still think of her every single day. She sure brightened up this island—and what she did for old Dr. Davidson you'd have had to see to believe!"

"I'd like to know more about her," Vanessa said politely. "We'll have to have a long talk soon." She liked this blunt, plainspoken old woman and hoped that she, too, would be able to earn Mrs. Pushka's approval.

She saw Mrs. Pushka glance down at her hand, linked with Trent's. Then the old woman smiled up at Vanessa. "It's gonna be nice to have you here." Mischief danced in her shrewd gray eyes. "And you're sure going to put Olga Hedlung's nose out of joint!"

Chapter Three

Slowly Vanessa strolled around the spacious and charming bedroom that would be hers for the summer. The furniture, all of sturdy, solid white pine, looked brand new. Despite the room's size, it was ultrafeminine, even delicate, and Vanessa was astonished by Trent's numerous decorative touches.

Fluffy, festive pillows trimmed with antique lace were piled high on the double bed. Their colors were a perfect match for the luxurious bedspread of violet and cream. The same color motif was repeated in the drapes, which were also trimmed with rich-looking lace. A chaise longue, obviously newly upholstered in deep purple brocade, provided an ideal resting place over by the windows.

There was a small fireplace to help warm the room on bitter winter days, and on the narrow mantel sat a valuable French clock, which Vanessa had examined at length. She knew little about home furnishings, having always relied on professional decorators, but even her inexperienced eye could recognize the value of the clock, with all its gold leaf.

Fresh flowers, mostly roses, filled a large vase on a low dresser, and there was even a smaller bouquet in the adjoining bathroom. Vanessa bent her head to inhale deeply of the roses' scent, then made yet another circuit of her room. Already she loved it.

A sudden yawn surprised her, reminding Vanessa of her deep weariness. She'd packed more activity into the past two days than she'd been accustomed to doing in a week. But, thank God, she was rejoining the living once again and returning to all the busyness of normal life.

Where was Trent? Vanessa found herself wondering as she turned toward the bed, which suddenly held an almost irresistible allure for her. He'd brought her up here and shown her around. Then, having gotten her more or less settled, he'd excused himself to go confer with Mrs. Pushka on the week's menus. A few revisions needed to be made in light of Vanessa's prohibition against alcohol, he'd mentioned.

"I'll be back up to tuck you in," he'd promised, chucking Vanessa under the chin as though she were a small, cherished child.

Now, yawning once again, Vanessa thought that Trent had better hurry or he'd find her fast asleep. Carefully she removed the heavy bedspread and folded it neatly, then turned back the sheets and the light blanket. She kicked off her scuffs, dropped her rose-colored robe across the foot of the bed and then, wearing only a blue nightshirt that celebrated the Atlanta Braves, she crawled between the cream-colored sheets.

"Ahh..." Vanessa stretched out, relaxing every muscle. At just that moment, Trent knocked on her door.

A soft "Vanessa?" accompanied the knock.

"C'mon in, Trent," she invited drowsily, sitting up in bed and bunching the pillows behind her back.

"I'm sorry I took so long," he apologized, a troubled expression furrowing his brow. "Mrs. Pushka isn't the easiest person in the world to get rid of when she's in a talkative mood. Then I had to go hunt up the liniment. I found it...finally." Triumphantly he held up a medium-sized green bottle.

Vanessa hadn't forgotten Trent's promise to massage her arm with his own wintergreen preparation, and she welcomed any opportunity to bring him nearer her. She patted the opposite side of her bed invitingly, then caught herself abruptly. He might get entirely the wrong idea! "Shall I stay here, Trent, or do you want me to get up?" she asked nervously.

But already he was dropping down where she had first indicated. "You stay right there," he said soothingly. "Just give me your arm and let me know if I get too rough."

No, he wasn't getting the wrong idea. Relieved, Vanessa rolled up the sleeve that covered the upper part of her left arm, while she smiled into Trent's blue eyes. "Don't worry. I always yell when something hurts."

His dark hair spilled over his forehead, and a faint flush rode his high cheekbones. Vanessa's heart skipped a beat, and she felt warmth rippling through her at Trent's mere closeness, for he had yet to touch her.

She studied his angular features and admired his straight black eyebrows. Then, feeling that she might be overdoing her scrutiny, Vanessa glanced down. But that proved a mistake of sorts, too, since Trent moved at just that moment, his powerful thigh muscles rippling within the confines of his dark slacks. Suddenly her mouth felt dry.

Trent uncapped the bottle he held. A pungent smell abruptly filled the air and left Vanessa gasping in surprise. "How do you like my wintergreen concoction?" Trent said, flashing her a mischievous grin.

"Frankly, it's never going to replace the French perfumes on my dresser," Vanessa said, and Trent laughed.

"However, if it helps my achy old arm, then I guess I can put up with it," she added.

Abruptly Trent's face sobered. "I hate to think of you ever hurting, Vanessa, or of you having been hurt, either...." he said softly. He drew a breath, then went on, more cheerfully, "So hold your nose and here we go."

A warm trickle glided over Vanessa's upper arm, surprising her. She had been braced for a dash of icy lotion, the kind most often applied to her in the hospital. With a smile and an uplifted eyebrow, she questioned Trent.

"Microwaves are wonderful," he said, grinning. "Now relax and let me rub it in slowly and thoroughly."

He has marvelous hands, she thought wonderingly as they began to lightly stroke, press and knead. They might even be the hands of a healer, if such a thing existed. They were large, competent and businesslike; nevertheless, they had an instinctive knowledge and delicacy of touch that left Vanessa wanting to close her eyes in bliss.

Instead, she forced herself to talk, since it wouldn't do to just lie back and purr. So she chattered on inconsequentially, wondering at the same time if Trent, who would so gladly spare her pain, had any awareness that *he* had been her first experience with deep adult pain.

"This room is wonderful, Trent. I especially love these soft pastels. I think violet and cream are probably my two favorite colors. Why, I couldn't like the room better if it had been designed exactly for me."

"It was designed exactly for you," Trent admitted, his fingers making a gentle circular motion just below her shoulder. "I tried to remember various colors I'd seen you wear, and the particular shades that *you* made so beautiful."

"Trent!" Vanessa whispered. Briefly tears stung her eyes, she was so touched. "Did you build all of this furniture, too? It looks quite new, but some of the pieces seem mellower...richer—"

"Those are the older pieces," he interrupted gently. "Dad built this bed and the chaise longue for my mother. I built your nightstand, the bookcases and the dresser to match."

"I noticed a trunk in the back of the closet," Vanessa said.

"Yes. Tracy's things are packed away there. You might want to take a look at them someday," he offered.

"Oh, I will. I want to know more about your mother."

"I didn't dream she was anything like you. Not until to-night, when Mrs. Pushka said so," Trent said reflectively.

"Oh, it means so much to me that you'd let me use Tracy's room," Vanessa said, her emotions surging once again.

"It's not Tracy's room now. It's Vanessa's. Perhaps it will always be." Slowly yet deliberately, Trent looked up at her.

At the tender expression on his face, Vanessa caught her breath. What did Trent mean? Surely he hadn't actually been serious when he'd written that dear little note to her saying that she should come back and marry him! No, of course not. They scarcely knew each other, despite ties that went way back over the years. But, oh, wouldn't it be wonderful and marvelous if—

Superstitiously Vanessa refused to finish the thought. Still, it brought awe and delight to her. Excitement at her old, old dream of winning Trent, of marrying him, made her tingle to her toes. She was so thrilled that she scarcely knew what to say. She certainly couldn't say what was uppermost in her mind. Lamely she fell back on the obvious and mundane.

"What did you and Mrs. Pushka talk about?" Vanessa asked.

"You, of course. She's a nosy old thing, in case you haven't guessed. She also has absolutely no love for Olga. They got into a wrangle almost ten years ago, and neither has ever shown the slightest interest in apologizing and making up."

Trent continued to work as he talked, his hands kneading and caressing, sending heat through her pores and deep into her skin. Vanessa glanced down into his gleaming dark hair, and she felt her throat tighten anew with gratitude and love. And she felt something else as well, as she watched Trent work: an arousing, stirring, slowly building hunger, something she'd never felt with any other man. Suddenly she wanted to stretch sinuously and sink back on the pillows, pulling him down into her arms. How strange and wonderful it was to feel this way. . . .

Meanwhile, Trent continued to talk. "Frieda wanted to know when and where I'd met you, Vanessa. She seems to attach some deep metaphysical significance to the fact that I once squeezed water out of you after you'd been lying around on the bottom of a lake."

Vanessa made herself remember that long-ago afternoon on a Georgia lake. "Well, I attach deep significance to it, too!" she said emphatically. "The last thing I remember was thinking I was dying. The next thing I remember is looking up and seeing *you*." She paused momentarily, her thoughts far away. "You know, Trent, the only other time in my life when I thought I was dying—but this time I didn't even care—was when all the drugs were giving me hives and headaches and making me more depressed than ever. Thank God, you were around for me then, too."

"I'm glad I was. Now I'm just thankful it's all over." Abruptly Trent's hands dropped. He capped the bottle and set it on Vanessa's nightstand, and they looked at each other for a long, wordless moment, staring deep into each other's eyes. Vanessa wondered if Trent was even half as captivated as she.

Nervously she cleared her throat. "Trent, there's an old Chinese saying that I heard about recently." She ducked her head, avoiding his eyes. Suddenly she felt unaccountably shy. "Maybe it's Japanese. Anyway, they believe that if you save a person's life you become responsible for that person from then on." Vanessa drew an uneven breath. "You've saved my life twice. Does that make you twice as responsible for me, I wonder?''

"No, Nessie—because sometimes I can't even be responsible for myself.'' Trent laughed.

Impossible! Vanessa didn't believe him for a moment. Other people might be mixed up, screwed up, might fail, flounder about and just generally prove undependable. But Trent Davidson absolutely wasn't one of them. Why, he'd always headed arrowlike toward his goals, achieving them in swift order and moving on to accomplish even greater things.

But she wasn't going to argue with him tonight, Vanessa decided. Certainly not with those banked fires flickering in the depths of his blue eyes, and not with the adorable little upward quirk of his mouth while he studied her as if she pleased him so very, very much.

Suddenly she grew aware of Trent's breathing. It had grown heavier, deeper, and now his scrutiny was on her lips. An inner trembling seized Vanessa. Spontaneously she reached out toward him, gently dropping one hand on the sleeve of his white turtleneck sweater. That small gesture of acceptance and affection was enough.

Trent's head moved forward quickly, shadowing Vanessa's. His own strong, warm hands, smelling of spicy wintergreen, quickly framed her face. Then his mouth was descending inexorably toward hers.

Vanessa's chin came up, her face tilting to receive his kiss until their mouths were tightly sealed. Thrills shot through her, and all apprehension fled. Unfamiliar yearnings clamored, creating a bittersweet ache. Instinctively she leaned closer to Trent, her body reacting to the electrifying feelings he aroused in her as his hands caressed her face. Her blood, rushing through her veins, seemed to pulse with a need.

Trent tore his lips away from hers only long enough to whisper her name: "Vanessa!'' His tone of voice was incredulous, shaken by amazement, and the sound of his breathing filled her ears.

His mouth covered hers again hungrily. Desire was heating Vanessa's blood, thundering in her head. Her fingers twined in Trent's hair. Until today she had never even felt its touch. Now she felt the crispness of the blunt-cut ends and the softness where it sprang naturally from his scalp. Oh, what were all these brand-new feelings that Trent alone evoked within her?

She knew, of course, but only from romantic allusions and earthy novels. Certainly, nothing she had ever shared in a king-size bed with Bailey Ashton had any relation to this, to Trent. Sex with Bailey had always been something to be gotten through as quickly as possible, and those nights when he was clearly not in the mood had always filled Vanessa with relief.

Sex, in her opinion, was the most disappointing and overrated activity in the universe.

Yet a part of her had always sensed, too, that it might be different with Trent. That same womanly instinct whispered that since Trent was the exception to every other unpleasant certainty in life, why wouldn't he be to this one, too?

But she didn't *know* and fear of further disappointment and disillusionment slashed through her suddenly. It was maddening. Infuriating. But oh, so real! She froze, and then her hands began to push at Trent's shoulders.

With a groan, he drew back. And now Vanessa swayed, feeling herself bereft and alone once more. Her own breathing was uneven, her chest rising and falling rapidly.

Still, relief swept her as she realized that—as always—Trent was in control of his desires and emotions. He was still his wholly reliable and responsible self, whatever words he might utter to the contrary. Although Vanessa knew he was aroused from the ragged sound of his breathing and from the bright, hot light still leaping in his eyes, Trent was no

savage who must yield to primitive desires just because they
gripped him. He was a mature, sophisticated man, and while
Vanessa had no doubt but that he was entirely experienced
and worldly-wise, she also knew he didn't want to frighten
her.

And yet, until she had suddenly been seized by the not-
irrational fear of disappointment, how sweet it had all been!
The taste of Trent still clung to her mouth, and she ran her
tongue over her lips, the better to savor his kisses in memory. He smiled at her gesture.

"Enough!" Trent said, leaping up from her bed.

Now Vanessa dared to tease him a little. "Is that all you
have to say?"

"You're woman enough to know what I want to say, you
little witch!" Trent ran a distracted hand through his hair as
though he was still not quite back to reality. "Seriously,
Vanessa, if I get out of line, just haul off and knock my head
off. I'm sure you've had to do that to plenty of other guys."
He glanced at his wristwatch. "Now it's time you were
asleep."

"You sound like I'm a little kid up past my bedtime,"
Vanessa said, pouting.

"Well, your big brother Clark gave me so many instructions I practically need a checklist."

"I promise to tell Clark that you're tending me very well
indeed," Vanessa retorted, but she was overtaken by a yawn.

"Sleep as late as you want tomorrow," Trent urged, his
hand going to the light switch. As the room was plunged
into darkness, Vanessa heard him draw another ragged
breath. "I'm so glad you're here, Vanessa. I used to wonder if—if we would ever have a chance to be together
again."

Trent stepped back, and the door clicked shut behind him,
leaving Vanessa alone in the room, pleasantly shell-shocked
by his words. *Trent had wondered about them, too,* she
thought with delight.

Oh, yes, it was finally going to be all right! At last her life was on course. From now on everything was going to be absolutely perfect!

Trent ran a hand through his hair, then shook his head, unable to shake off the nagging feeling of uneasiness that had settled over him. "There must be something wrong with *you*, fella," he muttered to himself in exasperation.

He knew he was moving too fast, too soon. He'd made a number of mistakes already, mistakes that might have seriously affected the welfare of a very confused and depressed woman, if indeed such a woman had stepped off the ferry today.

Fortunately, Vanessa was healthier than he'd dared hope, and she'd proved strong enough to weather his blunders, to cope with his barely tethered physical desires. Indeed, remembering the glow that had suffused her beautiful face at their kisses, Trent knew he'd gotten some unexpected luck he probably didn't deserve.

But there was always the danger of pushing her too far, triggering a reaction, as evidently he had when he'd felt her stiffen suddenly in his arms. It was time he got himself and his physical needs in hand.

The real issue was him, not Vanessa, he decided, firmly putting aside that bit of apprehension still lodged in the pit of his stomach.

Trent strode downstairs and crossed to the kitchen door, calling Boots inside for the night. The dog came happily, his tail wagging. He followed Trent back into the family room, where he sprawled at the foot of his master's armchair.

Automatically Trent began to speak aloud to the animal, a habit he'd acquired years ago during cold, silent winter nights. "I'm borrowing trouble again, Boots. Sometimes I think that's an occupational hazard of overeducated PhDs.

"If I want to worry about something," he continued softly, "then Olga's a more likely topic, don't you think?"

Boots cocked his head to one side and whined in response.

With Vanessa staying on the island now, Olga was certainly a present concern. Trent knew he'd be a fool not to be concerned about how she'd react.

Olga was the island equivalent of the girl next door. Trent had first met her when the elder Dr. Davidson had belatedly sent his son to attend church on Catt Island. The "medicine man," as he'd commonly been known, had not been a true believer in either churches or public schools, but neighborhood pressure had finally been brought to bear. As a result, Trent had been ten before he'd ever spent much time in the company of other children.

Olga had been a plump, neat, prissy little girl, impaling him uncomfortably with her pale blue stare. She'd always had that very light coloring that Trent had never found particularly attractive—translucent ivory skin, with white-blond hair, eyebrows and lashes.

Trent didn't know what he'd ever done to arouse Olga's devotion, but midway through his high school years it had become obvious to everyone that she was smitten. Trent had only to greet Olga, and her pale skin would flush fiery red.

In school she was a smart though not a brilliant student, but she studied so much that her grades were nearly perfect. She had a reserved nature and a wintry air that sometimes prompted other kids to refer to her as the Snow Queen. But Trent knew Olga was not a frigid woman, for she would sometimes turn a heated gaze on him that could have boiled water.

Not wanting to encourage her, Trent avoided her as much as he could in high school, and was merely polite to her when he could not. For several years he escaped her orbit by attending the University of Michigan at Ann Arbor before pursuing his doctorate at Auburn, his mother's alma mater. Olga attended a small church-owned college in lower Michigan. But when Trent returned to the island to reopen his dad's old lab, he was somehow not surprised to discover that Olga had become a registered pharmacist.

Everyone on Catt Island had confidently expected Trent to hire Olga. He would have preferred not to, but there were few pharmacists willing to work on an isolated island, and Trent had also feared offending the close island community if he didn't. Still, his acceptance of her had been less than enthusiastic.

He'd found her to be a dedicated and zealous employee, and for the most part he was able to ignore his suspicion that she still thought she loved him. Early on, through quiet innuendos, Olga had suggested her willingness to do whatever Trent might wish, and he'd made every effort to make it clear that their relationship was to remain solely a professional one.

Olga had never completely given up, not even when Helene had moved onto the island and stayed for almost two years. Occasionally during those years Olga's pale eyelids had been red and swollen; occasionally, too, Trent had detected the looks of animosity she'd shot Helene's way, but Olga had never voiced her jealousy and resentment to Trent. Why should she? He had never encouraged her, had never responded to her, had never led her on in any way.

Unfortunately, that was no longer the case.

A worried sigh escaped Trent, and Boots crept closer, rubbing his cold nose against Trent's hand in wordless consolation. "How did I let it happen, Boots?" Trent asked, stroking the dog's knobby head as, once again, he tried to understand the irrational act that had been so out of character for him.

It had happened eighteen months ago, during frozen January's short, dark days and unremitting gloom. There had been so much snow and ice that it had seemed as if the world would never be warm again. Trent had been working too hard, worried to distraction over Vanessa, who lay gravely ill in a hospital far away, not responding to conventional medications. He'd been in the midst of final tests on his herbal compound H-320B, which was still so new it was just a number and had yet to acquire a name.

Late one afternoon, after several nights virtually without sleep, Trent had fallen asleep on the couch in his office. When he'd awoken shortly after nine, he'd been grateful to see that Olga had tossed a blanket over him.

Coming fully awake then, he'd realized Olga was there, looking at him, her face glowing with her concern for him. He'd felt so cold and alone, and suddenly Olga's almost maternal presence had seemed warmly comforting.

In retrospect Trent realized he'd been at low ebb without knowing it. Half-asleep, still depressed, he'd had little inner strength to resist the solicitous woman who'd had a hot dinner waiting for him, who'd poured him a brandy and snuggled up beside him on the sofa, urging him to relax and let her rub his stiff shoulders.

Then, when Olga had finally leaned down to kiss him, something in him had snapped. He'd so badly wanted to relax, to let go of the pressures and responsibilities and let someone else carry the burdens just for a little while.... And as her soft lips had touched his, a tiny, cynical voice in Trent's mind had said, "Oh, what the hell?"

He'd been seduced, but that was no excuse. And he'd paid with a guilt that had made the episode a wholly unsatisfactory experience. Even with the warmth of three drinks like fire in his belly, Trent had not been able to enjoy the experience. Later, he'd actually been surprised that he'd been able to offer her what she so badly wanted. Ordinarily he couldn't have so thoroughly ignored his instincts, but his need to connect somehow with another human being, to break out of his self-imposed isolation, had been overwhelming. So, for that one brief night, Trent had taken Olga back to the house and into his bed.

Morning had brought him only shame, regret and remorse. He'd felt a level of guilt unusual for a man who had long ago accepted his own strongly sensual nature. But, no matter how willing, even eager, Olga had been for their encounter, he'd known her desires were based on feelings for him beyond pure physical desire—feelings he could never return.

Now Trent winced again, remembering the coal-hot agony into which that night had plunged him. Skittishly his memory bounced over the next awful scene connected to that appalling one-night stand. Although Trent had almost felt he'd rather shoot himself, or Olga, or both of them, he'd had to face her with the truth instead. He'd shattered her happiness, dousing the wedding light in her ice-blue eyes that, briefly, had made her look almost pretty.

It hadn't been easy for Trent to tell Olga that he didn't love her and didn't even want an ongoing affair with her. As he'd watched her face go still and white, her pale eyes stunned by shock, he'd felt like the worst sort of bastard.

Any other woman would have screamed accusations at him, dissolved in tears and finally fled the island, hoping never to see again the man who had given her pride such a beating. But Olga was not like other women. She had elected to stay on, and although she had never referred to that night and its traumatic aftermath, Trent could always sense her watching him, waiting... still hoping things could change, still wishing that, by loving, she would finally be loved.

Trent had told Olga it could never happen again, but her own desires made her unable to listen to harsh reality. He had lived with the guilt ever since. And now, he realized, he should have told Olga himself that Vanessa was coming. She would have been angry and hurt, but probably less so than if she heard it from others. Trent had mentioned to her that an "old friend" would be visiting him soon, but in his heart he'd known that Olga had automatically assumed the friend would be male; they always had been before. Of course, now Trent could depend on her mother and sister to tell her differently.

Trent sighed. "Well, Boots, I guess I've handled this whole thing badly from start to finish."

Boots made a noise deep in his throat that sounded suspiciously like agreement.

What a glorious, spellbinding place!

Excitedly Vanessa leaned out her bedroom window on the morning following her arrival. From her second-story vantage point it seemed as if she could see forever—orchards and greenhouses, long hedges planted from bushy shrubs, neat rows of green-, yellow- and white-topped plants waving in the breeze. Just around the corner of the window lay an old-fashioned barn. By sticking her head out into the crisp, sunshiny day, Vanessa could see at least half of it, including a huge apple emblem painted on one side.

Michigan must be proud of its apples, she thought. She'd seen that same fat red apple symbol on several different structures since she'd been in the state.

Absently Vanessa reached for her coffee and instead succeeded in almost turning it over. Rapidly she righted the rocking cup, then brought it to her lips to sip the last lukewarm drops. Mrs. Pushka had brought her the coffee about fifteen minutes earlier.

"Trent thought you might sleep in till nine or later," the old woman had said, wagging her head wisely. "I knew you'd be too excited, and sure enough, I soon heard you moving around overhead. Come on downstairs as soon as you're ready for a bite of breakfast."

"I thought Trent and I were supposed to get our own breakfast," Vanessa had protested.

"No need for that," Mrs. Pushka had sniffed. "Long as I'm up on my feet and wide-awake, I might as well be cooking. That's my job, after all—not that Trent makes it easy for me." She heaved an elaborate sigh. "He's got strong ideas about what he will and won't eat. I made him eat everything when he was a kid, like it or not. But once he got bigger than me, he put his foot down. Wonder he doesn't die from scurvy!''

Mrs. Pushka went off, muttering about people who rejected grapefruit juice and cabbage, leaving Vanessa with a fragrant cup of coffee. Mrs. Pushka was an old dear, Vanessa thought. She might be bossy and, to Trent, an occasional pain in the rear, but Vanessa knew she and the tough old woman were going to get along swimmingly.

And thinking of swimming... Vanessa set down her empty coffee cup and peered ahead. Beautiful blue Lake Superior would definitely be too cold for swimming, but she wondered if maybe the water in Trent's inland lake was warmer.

Despite the accident that had once almost claimed her life, Vanessa was not afraid of water at all. Oh, sure, in the wake of the accident she'd been nervous at first, but Clark had cured her quickly by unceremoniously dumping her off a pier and yelling, "So, swim or sink!"

Trent had been there visiting with them that day, and he had been appalled at Clark's technique. But swim Vanessa had. Really, there was nothing like having an older brother to make a girl courageous—although the best thing about her memory of that particular day was recalling how Trent had dried her off when she'd finally clambered out of the lake—and how he'd hugged her and praised her for being so brave.

That was one of those moments when Vanessa knew she would have readily died for him.

Of course, now she would much rather *live* for him—and, dare she hope—even live *with* him one of these days. Remembering his kisses of the previous night made her feel like a giddy teenager again, ready to hug herself and twirl about the room, humming some lush, sentimental love song.

She focused her attention once more on the view. Was that the laboratory over there? The plain building, long and low, put her in mind of a concrete cellblock. It certainly wasn't very pretty, Vanessa thought critically, but of course a laboratory wasn't necessarily supposed to be.

A movement over in that direction caught Vanessa's eye. A tall, buxom blond woman, wearing a white lab coat over a pair of black slacks, stepped along briskly. She carried a large basket on her arm, and a pair of shears in her hand glinted silver in the sun. As Vanessa watched, the blond woman stopped and began efficiently snipping away at a large green bush.

Undoubtedly this was Olga Hedlung, Vanessa realized. The woman's pale hair, almost white in the blaze of sunlight, resembled the hair of the two women Vanessa had met yesterday at the restaurant. Vanessa was tempted to call out or wave to the other woman, but just at that moment she heard Trent's footsteps coming up the stairs. "Vanessa! Are you ready for breakfast?"

A thrill raced through her at the sound of his voice. Vanessa closed the window and swung around. "Yes, Trent," she called. "I'm on my way downstairs right now."

Chapter Four

Why did he continue to feel that something was wrong? Trent wondered. For the first time in his life he was unable to sort out his own conflicting feelings because, at the same time that he sensed something amiss, he actually felt happier than he ever had. And there was no question in his mind that the reason for his happiness was the eager, excited young woman at his side, asking one question after another.

How lovely Vanessa was today! Trent marveled, stealing another glance at her. A cool breeze, driving off the Great Lake, had tinged her face faintly pink, but pure pleasure had set her aglow. Although she had dressed quite simply in jeans and an oversized polo shirt that reached almost to her knees, she looked fresh and fashionable.

Trent loved looking at Vanessa's hair, too. The dark curls spilled down her back, pinned carelessly at the nape of her neck but still resisting any major attempt to control them. Her big, lustrous eyes shone, and her inviting mouth smiled up at him. Each time Trent looked at her he felt his heart soar aloft like a kite in a high wind.

She was without doubt the most beautiful woman he'd ever seen, and his fierce, almost desperate hunger for this all-grown-up Vanessa remained a source of wonder to him.

"You've heard about ginseng, of course," he replied to her most recent question. "I have several acres of the stuff, because ginseng preparations sell so well. It's known as the 'universal tonic,' and is especially favored by Oriental gentlemen who feel their sexual potency may be waning. It's not an easy herb to cultivate—takes six years just for a plant to mature. That's why it's so expensive."

"How interesting," Vanessa mused. "What's over here, Trent?"

"These are beds of dill," he answered. He shot her a teasing grin. "Did you know dill will keep a goblin from your door? Just stick up a sprig and you'll soon notice a great absence of ghosts and witches and such."

"Now where did you ever hear such a story?" Vanessa asked, chuckling.

"I think it came from Rumania, possibly Albania."

"Transylvania, more likely," Vanessa shot back.

Trent laughed heartily, as he wondered exactly what this exhilarating feeling that surged through him really was. Vanessa seemed to have opened up a whole new vein of feelings within him, feelings so strange and new that Trent had no previous experience by which to judge them.

In his thirty-six years Trent had, of course, had relationships with several different women. With each one there had first been attraction, then hot pursuit. Sexual satisfaction had lasted for a while, but finally a gradual disinterest and disenchantment had set in. Helene had lasted longest, but in the end he'd grown bored with her, too.

Fortunately his boredom had coincided with Helene's almost frantic need for streets, sidewalks, rush-hour traffic and people, plenty of people. She simply couldn't abide being alone, and the nature of Trent's work dictated that she spend a good deal of time entertaining herself. Helene hadn't been fond of reading or watching TV; she hadn't been interested in hiking or sailing or communing with nature. What she really liked were cocktail parties, lunches with her sorority sisters and big, fancy evening bashes where she could wear a formal gown and dance all night with a handsome man in a tuxedo.

Helene was now married to a banker who was very much into social events and charity fund-raisers, Trent had heard recently. Knowing Helene's ways as he did, he thought it sounded like a perfect match, and he hoped she was happy. In spite of their initial mutual attraction, she'd never really been happy here with him. Never, even for a moment, had he seen on Helene's face the glow that lighted Vanessa's lovely features right now. God, she was so gorgeous; she absolutely set him on fire!

At the same time, Trent had never felt such an overwhelming desire to protect a woman as he felt toward Vanessa. In her young life she'd had such a difficult time, and she was such a delicate, vulnerable woman. Her fragile-looking hand was tucked through Trent's arm right now as they strolled along a stone path bordered by raised beds of herbs, and he was more keenly aware of her touch than he'd ever been of another's. That light, gentle pressure distracted him, and he had to fight the compelling desire to pull Vanessa close and feast on those tempting lips.

Earlier that morning, when she'd first appeared on the stairs, he'd brushed her lips with his and had found his breakfast immeasurably sweeter for that brief taste. But he had determined anew not to threaten Vanessa, frighten her or take advantage of her in any way.

He knew how easy it would be to have her. The way she twinkled up at him adoringly was like a green light, and Trent knew she was still grateful to him for saving her life when she'd been a kid. And now that his herbal compound had wrenched her out of crippling depression, she had a second reason for gratitude.

For a sudden, passionate moment, Trent felt almost resentful of his "miracle" discovery. He didn't want Vanessa's *gratitude*. But, of course, if he hadn't invented it, Vanessa might still be struggling to regain her health, and he wouldn't be experiencing the pleasure of her company right now. He remembered, too, how he'd been stirred by a certain perverse pride at breakfast, when Vanessa had topped off a surprisingly large meal of bacon and blueberry pancakes with a teaspoonful of his own herbal medicine. She swallowed only teaspoonfuls now, he'd noted, remembering that the initial dose he'd recommended had been several tablespoonfuls at each meal. For just a moment he'd been suffused with pride in his work and sheer pleasure at his own creation.

Undoubtedly time would settle his turbulent emotions, he assured himself. He'd been a little out of control—taken by surprise—yesterday, but there would be no such repetition today. Even if he did long to hold her, to stroke her...to gently raise that shirt she wore and unveil her breasts...to taste her sweet flesh....

"Trent, you haven't heard a word I've said," Vanessa burst out suddenly.

"What? I'm sorry," he blurted, jumping guiltily.

"Well, I guess I'm just not interesting enough to hold your attention," she declared, dropping his arm and swinging her pert nose into the air.

For a moment the fear of having offended her stabbed through Trent. Then he saw the mischievous glint in those matchless brown eyes.

"Forgive me, Nessie." He laughed and swung his arm up over her narrow shoulders to hug her close. "I do tend to wool-gather at times, but believe me, I'm very much aware of being here with you."

"How eloquent." She smiled at him, her softly parted lips and small pearly teeth fascinating him anew.

Impulsively Trent ducked his head and kissed her velvety soft cheek. Immediately sensations drenched and overwhelmed him: her natural scent, the enchantment of her skin's perfect texture, the brush across his temple of a strand of her silken hair. He saw her eyes widen in sheer delight. Well, so much for good intentions.

"Where shall we go now?" he asked abruptly, feeling absolutely unsteady and practically undone by a seething current of desire.

"Anywhere you say, Trent," Vanessa replied docilely.

At just that moment the incongruous feeling struck Trent again. His stomach knotted. *Something was wrong*.

But *what*, for God's sake?

Sometimes the expressions on Trent's face surprised her, Vanessa thought. She kept encountering looks that seemed, from her previous and limited knowledge of him, quite uncharacteristic. That smoldering passion was one, of course. That rather dreamy, indulgent look when he'd lost track of her conversation was another. Still, she'd had no sense of his having actually retreated from her; that was why she'd dared to needle him as she'd done.

Vanessa suspected that Trent's awareness of her was a sensual, perhaps erotic one—maybe even a fantasy in which she figured prominently. She wanted him, too, but the thought of Trent's *wanting* her—in a hard, real, masculine way—raised her anxiety level.

Although imagining herself and Trent together in one of her fantasies could make her knees start to quiver and her heart pound, the legacy of Vanessa's marriage to Bailey had made her uncomfortable with physical intimacy. Although she'd cared about Bailey, appreciating the comforting security he provided, their lovemaking, fraught with his insecurities about growing old and losing his "baby" to a younger man, had never been passionate or romantic.

Maybe poor Bailey should have tried some of Trent's ginseng! Vanessa thought humorously, but immediately felt ashamed of herself.

So now, with Trent, Vanessa naturally felt pulled two ways. While part of her gloried in his rapid response to her, another part remained wary.

She supposed she was sending him mixed messages, too. Oh, well, they'd have the whole summer to sort it out together. Vanessa pushed the troublesome thoughts to the back of her mind and forced herself to ignore the warm weight of Trent's arm over her shoulder and the fragrant aroma of his after-shave.

"So where's your lab, Trent?" she asked, taking in the rich green world that surrounded her.

Vanessa and Trent had already strolled around the grounds, Boots tagging along, and she was amazed at how large Davidson Island actually was. She was also surprised by the number of structures that had been built here. From Mrs. Pushka's small cottage, situated directly behind the main house, to the barn and greenhouses that Vanessa had spotted earlier, they had walked to see drying sheds for herbs and guest quarters that housed employees when violent snow or ice storms prevented their leaving the island.

The people, by contrast, were few: just Mrs. Pushka and Trent's three lab employees, although hourly workers came frequently from the mainland to tend the extensive grounds and harvest the herbs.

"Okay, I guess it is time to show you the lab," Trent said.

Vanessa didn't miss the reluctance in his voice, and she wondered at it as Trent led her toward the long cellblock-like building. But just as they were about to step inside, a jarring and ungodly clatter arose from the direction of the house. Vanessa gave a start of surprise, and Boots, at her side, went into frenzied barking. It was like being on a desert island and thinking oneself quite alone, then suddenly hearing a siren, she thought.

"What on earth is that?" she asked, her voice sharp.

"That, my dear, is lunch," Trent replied, smiling down at her indulgently. "Mrs. Pushka has baked a cheese soufflé which she hopes will please you. She's banging two pots together because she wants us back at the house immediately—or she warned me, the soufflé will be tough as rubber. She does issue quite a few orders around here, I'm afraid."

"Looks like she has you well trained," Vanessa said, teasing him again.

"She tries. What she really lives for is to see me married. And now that you've arrived, she's ecstatic with hope once again. Maybe she knows what happens to crusty old bachelors and fears for my ultimate table manners."

As Trent spoke lightly, laughingly, he guided Vanessa firmly away from the area of his laboratory, and she couldn't help but wonder if their halting on the lab's very doorstep, only to return to the house instead, was mere coincidence.

Somehow she didn't really think so.

The lunch of soufflé, green salad and hot whole wheat bread left Vanessa feeling stuffed and sleepy. She was certainly eating far more here in the Prophet Islands than she had for months, but everything tasted so fresh and good. When she saw the younger woman yawn, Mrs. Pushka suggested that Vanessa take a nap. And when Vanessa agreed, Trent looked up in rather obvious relief.

"While you sack out, I'll dash over to the lab and read my mail," he said, still in that oh-so-casual tone of voice that immediately aroused Vanessa's suspicions.

"All right," she replied evenly.

"Rest as long as you like," Trent urged. "Then, if you feel up to it, we'll take a bicycle ride to the far end of the island."

"Oh, I'll be up to it," Vanessa assured him.

Trent smiled with pleasure and squeezed her shoulder gently as he passed her chair on his way out of the room.

Meanwhile, Mrs. Pushka moved slowly around the table, removing the dishes and serving platters. When Vanessa saw a tremor run through the old woman's liver-spotted hand, she was immediately on her feet to assist. Mrs. Pushka protested, but only halfheartedly, for she seemed eager to talk.

"I think Trent is trying to avoid introducing me to Olga," Vanessa suggested, bearing away the remains of the superb soufflé.

"Humph!" the old lady sniffed. "Wouldn't surprise *me.* Men always think they can carry off that sort of thing, and mostly they can't. Women are lots better at intrigue."

"Well, it's certainly unlikely that Trent can prevent Olga and me from meeting," said Vanessa realistically. "What's he afraid of, anyway?"

"Oh, I think he's afraid that Olga will say something to hurt your feelings." Mrs. Pushka dumped her load of dishes into the sink with an ear-jarring clatter. "That woman can be downright rude."

"I can deal with rudeness," Vanessa protested.

"Course you can," Mrs. Pushka affirmed. "You'll have to 'scuse Trent for thinking you're practically helpless. Usually his instincts are pretty good, but he's worried about your health. And his experience with Helene—well, any time she broke a fingernail she carried on like she'd cut off her hand."

"Helene—" Vanessa began.

"Was not like a real person," Mrs. Pushka interrupted firmly. "She was more of a windup doll. Helene walked, she talked, she ate plenty, and she did a lot of lolling around in bed." Mrs. Pushka dropped her voice conspiratorially. "I'm not sure Trent ever wanted her for anything else."

Vanessa couldn't resist giggling. "Mrs. Pushka, you're terrible!"

"Probably," the older woman agreed matter-of-factly. "Anyway, I believe there's another reason why Trent's afraid for you and Olga to meet."

"Oh, and what would that be?" Vanessa said, setting her own dishes down more gently than Mrs. Pushka had done.

"It's just a suspicion, mind you. But last winter... no, I guess it was two winters back... things between Trent and Olga changed somehow. Trent was never overly fond of Olga—though she's tagged around after him about like Boots does ever since she was a girl. But along about then he started avoiding Olga like she'd caught plague. And Olga, she got even paler and quieter and quit working late and hanging around the house here on any little excuse like she used to...."

"You think he slept with her?" Vanessa said flatly, but it wasn't really a question. Why wouldn't he? Olga was a voluptuous woman. They'd worked together in constant proximity here, and they were both unmarried.

"That's my suspicion. Course, I don't really *know*," Mrs. Pushka continued. "I think Olga caught Trent in a weak moment and later he was plenty sorry. That woman's been running after him for years—and that's just how long he's been running away from her, too."

Mrs. Pushka opened the refrigerator door and began stacking butter and various leftovers inside as Vanessa handed them to her. "What do you think?" she asked Vanessa after a minute in her blunt fashion.

"Oh, I think you're probably right."

The words were oddly hard for Vanessa to enunciate. Her throat muscles ached, and tension made her voice sound unnatural. Her own reactions astounded her. Why, she was actually jealous! she realized in amazement. Had she grown

possessive of Trent so very soon? Or was this just a contin-
uation of what she'd always felt for him?

Probably the latter, she thought. This whole matter was
none of her business, why did she feel this strange, almost
frightening sense of betrayal?

"Course, this conversation had better stay our little se-
cret," Mrs. Pushka said, her voice almost apologetic.

"Of course," Vanessa agreed, suddenly weary. In silence
they finished cleaning up, rinsing the dishes for the dish-
washer. Then Vanessa excused herself and retreated to the
beautiful, quaint, rather old-fashioned bedroom Trent had
designed for her. *I definitely belong here,* she thought ruefully. Me and my little ol' Victorian ideas. Me and my sexual unresponsiveness, too, she thought sadly.

A truly modern woman would rather die than admit she
didn't enjoy sex! But Trent was a modern man, and he
would be unwilling to settle for anything except a real
woman.

A few tears began to trickle down Vanessa's cheeks, but
the sound of her own sniffling annoyed her.

So quit your damned blubbering and go fight for him! she
urged herself, and immediately began to feel better. She
would start with a nice restorative nap, which would put a
little color in her face and a gleam in her eyes. With her
overly thin body, she certainly needed every other weapon
she could muster.

At first Vanessa was afraid she wouldn't be able to fall
asleep, but soon she dropped off and began spinning a long,
very involved dream in which she and Trent, Bailey and
Olga were all mixed up in a series of complex and complicated relationships.

"I'm all right," Vanessa argued to all of them in her
dream. *"Why, I'm just as much a woman as anyone else!"*

Abruptly she awoke and turned her head to glance at her
bedside clock. It was ten after three. Trent has probably
been waiting for me, she thought, leaping out of bed.

Still, she lingered long enough to brush her teeth leisurely and give her hair a hundred strokes; then she slipped back into her clothes, since she'd chosen to nap in her lacy teddy.

Sometimes men appreciated a girl more when they had to wait a while for her, Vanessa reflected. It was a Southern notion that smacked of sexism, she knew, but still, she'd rarely known it to fail.

The bicycles Trent produced were both blue and basic. Of course, there was scarcely any need for expensive high-speed racing bikes, since Trent had said they would be following ancient and sometimes rough Indian trails.

"How do you know this is an Indian trail?" Vanessa called to Trent, who was pedaling along in the lead, Boots racing beside him. "It looks like any ol' cow trail to me."

"Cow trails amble off in all directions," Trent shouted back to her. "Cattle are totally incapable of traveling in a direct, straight line. But human beings do, and this path is a direct dead shoot over to the old copper mine."

Vanessa had to strain her ears to catch the last of his words. Between the wind blowing and Boots, who chose just that moment to bark at a small brown bird and send it fluttering into the air, it wasn't easy for her to hear Trent.

But she could *watch* him as she pedaled along. She could admire his broad shoulders and straight spine. She could follow the shift of his slim male hips as he moved on the bike seat. He was so very well built! she thought admiringly; she doubted she could find a better physique on a beefcake calendar. She'd never known any man as all around attractive as Trent.

Actually he wasn't a classically handsome man, at least not like Vanessa's brother, Clark. Clark, the devil, knew how his appearance caused feminine heads to turn. But Trent had apparently never known just how very desirable he was. His manner with other people was always natural and relaxed and without the driving need for continual conquests that some good-looking men exhibited. Still, through the years, enough other women had found Trent desirable to give Vanessa a severe case of heartache.

Of course, Trent's quiet life here on the island would not appeal to certain women, Vanessa knew, although she herself looked around with ever-growing interest. From the sandy shoreline on their left, where the great blue inland sea tugged rhythmically, to the thick, heavy forest on her right, the island was beautiful and unspoiled. With each scenic vista that came into view, Vanessa loved it more.

They pedaled for perhaps a mile or two, until Vanessa's legs began to protest the unaccustomed exercise and she was finding it more difficult to breathe. Mercifully, Trent called a halt before she had to tell him she was winded.

"We'll leave the bikes here where the trail ends," he advised her. "From this point on we have to hike."

Dutifully Vanessa followed him into the forest, where he propped his bicycle beneath the broad, sturdy trunk of a large shade tree, since the ground was too uneven to support the kickstand. Vanessa did the same with her bike, then bent down to give the excited Boots an absentminded pat. The terrier was a whirling dervish at her feet, barking eagerly in anticipation.

"Trent, these woods look awfully dark and scary," Vanessa commented as he led the way into their dim, shadowy interior.

"They aren't, Nessie. Just stay close to me. Here—" He extended a large warm hand to her, and Vanessa grabbed hold of it gratefully.

Carefully she began to pick her way through thick underbrush as he led her along a narrow trail. "Are there snakes?" she asked breathlessly.

"Only small nonpoisonous ones," Trent assured her. "We're too far north for any dangerous reptiles."

"I still hope we don't see any," Vanessa said with a little shiver. "Now, what about those black bears you mentioned yesterday?"

"Oh, they'll just go running off if they see you, unless—" Trent paused thoughtfully.

"Unless what?" demanded Vanessa.

"You do have to be careful not to disturb a mother bear with a cub. If Mama thinks her baby is threatened, she can turn mean in a hurry. But usually that's the only time you need to worry." While Trent talked, he continued to lead Vanessa on a gradual uphill climb.

"What do you mean *usually*?" said Vanessa, seizing on the exception in Trent's smooth delivery.

"Oh, come on, worrywart!" Trent laughed. "No bear is going to eat you—I wouldn't let them—and you'll be glad you came when you see the old copper mine and the inland lake."

He was right. The primeval forest, as hushed and peaceful as a cathedral, gradually began to work its charm on her. The pungent smell of spruce and fir trees evoked pleasant childhood memories, reminding her of festive holidays. Birch and aspens, identified for her by Trent, swayed above occasional fallen trunks of white pine. Bright carpets of wildflowers softened the forest picture of tall, stern wooden sentinels. Gradually Vanessa's fears melted away, and although she continued to relish the security of Trent's strong hand over hers, she no longer clung to it like a lifeline.

The copper mine was situated at the top of a heavily forested hill, and Vanessa would probably have missed seeing its entrance if Trent hadn't pointed it out to her. "Just stick your head inside and take a quick peek," he instructed. "It's not really safe to go very far inside. Tunnels that run off in all directions are just barely shored up, and old mine shafts are just waiting to cave in."

The mine was dank and cold, a forbidding place with a musty smell, and Vanessa withdrew quickly. Then she was struck by a thought that made her smile.

"Trent, I'll bet *you've* explored this mine plenty of times," she said.

He threw her a startled look. "Actually, I have. I probably made two dozen expeditions down there until Dad found out and blistered me good. But how on earth did you know that, Vanessa?"

"I'm moderately psychic, I think," she informed him. "Of course, I also had a brother who was a terror, so I know how boys think."

"Well, the first time Dad ever showed me the mine I got the selfsame lecture that you just heard from me—the old place is treacherous and unsafe."

"So you just naturally had to check it out for yourself," said Vanessa wisely.

"Absolutely! I mean, a guy can't take just anybody's word for something as exciting as that. But ultimately I got caught. It was one of the few times Dad ever spanked me. Mostly he was too busy to pay much attention to me so a spanking—wow! I'd really caught his attention for once." Trent's mouth quirked up, recalling the adventure and its aftermath.

"That's the kindest thing I've ever heard anyone say about corporal punishment," Vanessa retorted. "I can't decide if it's humorous or pathetic."

"Humorous, definitely. Though I guess you'd have had to know my dad. Matter of fact, I'm sorry you didn't. Frankly, I don't think he cared much for kids, but what sixty-year-old really wants the responsibility of raising a lively little boy all alone? And I was definitely a high-energy type. Soon after the mine episode, Dad set me to work learning herbs, then growing and gathering 'em. 'You're beginning to show some promise, boy,' he said after a while, and that may have been all that kept him from killing me.

Now, Vanessa, just follow me down the hill, and you'll soon be basking on the sunny banks of Lake Davidson, where moose, among other things, like to browse. Sometimes, if you lie in the grass and stay very still, you can watch them when they come out of the woods to drink."

He led her along a challenging trail with panoramic views of forest and sparkling water. Once Trent stopped and bent down, showing Vanessa a dainty cluster of diminutive calypso orchids that had sprung from the rich mold of the shady woodlands.

Now this is more like it, Vanessa thought privately when their winding path ended at the bottom of the hill and a small, lush lake came into view.

Suddenly Boots took off like a launched torpedo, barking as he ran. Vanessa's gaze followed the dog to a brambly-looking area far on the opposite side of the lake. "What's over there, Trent?" she asked curiously.

His hand tightened slightly over hers. "Another verboten area, honey. There aren't many on the island, but I did want to point them out to you first thing so you'll remember to stay away."

"Why? What's there?" she asked, intrigued.

"Bog! Sticky, slimy bog," he answered emphatically. "There are briars, leeches and quicksand, as well as several poisonous plants: water hemlock, hemp dogbane and green false hellebore. They all have medicinal value, which is the only reason I tolerate them, but—"

"Say no more," Vanessa interrupted hastily. But a small, wistful sigh escaped her. She had always imagined Davidson Island as being absolutely perfect, probably because it belonged to Trent and *he* was absolutely perfect. Now she was disappointed to find that the island wasn't Eden. Why was so much of life like that—just plain disappointing? No one had ever been able to give Vanessa an answer, and sometimes it made her feel quite sad.

"Have a seat, Nessie. Let's rest for a few minutes before we have to start back," Trent suggested.

Dubiously Vanessa looked down at ankle-high grass and weeds. "Go on," Trent urged. "The ground's dry."

She dropped down and he followed, sitting beside her. Then he whistled for Boots, who was probably chasing a rabbit. "I don't want him getting too wet and dirty," Trent muttered to Vanessa. "He's come back stinking of the bog before, and I always have to bathe him in very strong soap before he's acceptable house company again." Trent stared across the lake at the dog, who hesitated, obviously torn between the joys of the bog and loyalty to his master.

"Here, Boots! I mean it now," Trent yelled.

Whining a little, Boots reluctantly rejoined them and sprawled, panting, beside Vanessa. After a minute she reached up to stroke the dog's head, and Boots whined again, this time in pleasurable contentment.

As Boots nosed forward, Vanessa rocked back a little and discovered that Trent's chest was directly behind her. When her shoulders and head touched that strong yet comfortable pillow, he slipped an arm around her neck and rested his hand lightly over her vulnerable throat. After a moment, his thumb—a little rough, but warm and wonderful-feeling, too—began to glide slowly up and down.

Vanessa closed her eyes, oblivious to the dog's cold nose, which was now poking at her knee. She felt only Trent's touch, his warmth, his nice clean manly smell. And she was in paradise once again.

Chapter Five

Trent saw that sad, passionate, lost look flash across her face before she managed to hide it, and it tore at his heart. He hadn't seen that look often in the short time that Vanessa had been on the island with him. Usually she was her chipper and chirping self. But at odd moments that desperate look flashed, and each time he was reminded once again of all that Vanessa had endured just to survive and come through as she had.

And each time he'd seen that look, Trent had felt the almost overwhelming desire to hug and cradle Vanessa—not in a loverlike way, not now, but rather as he would comfort a lost and frightened child. He wanted to carry her off to safety in his arms. Promise her—yes, even vow to her—that he'd take care of things now. She would be cherished and protected from today on, and nothing would ever dare hurt her again.

Of course, he couldn't do it. For one thing, he wasn't ready to commit himself to Vanessa after so short a period of reacquaintance. But mostly he couldn't make any such promises because he just wasn't God, and it wasn't in his power to assure Vanessa a smooth, uneventful and painless life from now on. Though he might wish it for her with all his heart, he certainly couldn't guarantee it.

An adult's life, he knew, must always be built on the realization of uncertainty. Why, even the weather forecasts here on planet earth couldn't always be accurately forecast, as Trent, a longtime resident of a regularly storm-lashed area, certainly knew. His own mother, a young woman everyone remembered as lively, intelligent and delightful, had perished in an unexpected squall when she was returning to the Prophet Islands after a weekend shopping expedition.

Tracy Davidson had left the energetic whirlwind toddler Trent safely in the care of Mrs. Pushka since, as he had grown up hearing, Tracy had laughingly said that she didn't want to chase Trent through every single department store she visited. But Trent had definitely been on her mind, for she'd made the trip specifically to buy new clothes and toys for her rapidly growing three-year-old son.

Perhaps that was why, years later, it had been so satisfying emotionally for Trent when he'd rescued Vanessa from drowning. Because there had been no one to save his mother when waves engulfed the ferry on which she was traveling and capsized it, plunging Tracy into the icy waters of Lake Superior. But Trent had been given the opportunity to save another lively and lovely young woman from the same fate.

So now, while he couldn't promise Vanessa safety and peace, he could at least offer her his strength and friendship as reinforcements. He could slip an arm around her as he did now, while they sat beside the placid inland lake, and feel some of the tension drain from her body as she relaxed against him.

Gazing down into the sweet-smelling cloud of midnight-black hair, Trent had a thousand questions of his own that he longed to ask Vanessa. Some of them concerned the life she'd led in Washington, where she must have met many national and international figures in the political arena.

Mostly, though, he wondered about her relationship with Bailey Ashton. What had it been like, that marriage to her middle-aged husband? Since Vanessa clearly did not care to discuss it, Trent wondered if he would ever know.

As they sat beside the lake and he watched various expressions flit across her delicate, classically beautiful features, the memory of her sad and passionate look remained strongest.

Was *that* it? he wondered. Was that what kept bothering him about Vanessa? Was it that look that sent the uncomfortable feeling slicing through him, a sensation of acute alertness, as if he'd missed something of significance?

Now the lost look had passed, and she turned to Trent gratefully and thankfully, as if in relief. And—he could almost predict this—she immediately began asking her next million and one questions.

Now, beside the lake, she asked him about the Indian-fighters and fur traders who had trod the same trails they'd followed today. Then she asked Trent all about the Michigan copper industry, whose heyday had ended in the early 1920s. Fortunately, Trent was well versed in the history of his native state; if he hadn't been, the inquisitive Ms. Ashton would soon have found him out.

So Trent patiently answered all her questions. Then he told her the names of various trees that bordered the lake, and pointed out familiar herbs growing in the wild. He purposely kept his voice and his touch casual, reminding himself not to startle or frighten Vanessa. It was important that she grow accustomed to him and trust him, and Trent certainly intended to do nothing that might cost him that trust.

"Ready to go back?" he asked Vanessa at last when she began stirring a trifle.

"Yes," she agreed.

Briefly Trent let his lips trail along the delightful curve of her neck; then he pressed a light little kiss on the nape. A shiver ran through Vanessa—delight, Trent hoped.

They rode home slowly, Boots trailing tiredly after them. Back at the house, Trent stowed away both bicycles in the old barn, then came inside through the back door, which was used far more often than the door at the front.

He found Vanessa in the hall, talking with Mrs. Pushka. At the sound of Trent's footsteps, she turned to him excitedly. "Clark called. He just wanted to be sure I arrived here all right. Oh, what a fussbudget he is!"

"I'm sorry you missed his call," Trent commented.

"Well, I'm not!" Vanessa declared. "He's been acting like I'm a half-wit and he's my guardian ever since I got out of the hospital. Now I think I'll go up to my room for a shower. Thanks so much, Trent, for the lovely afternoon."

The face she lifted to him was radiant, and Trent longed to bend down and kiss her—but knew he couldn't limit himself to a merely friendly kiss.

Since he felt Mrs. Pushka watching them, he settled for a smile instead. Vanessa flashed him one in return, then turned and ran up the stairs.

As soon as they heard Vanessa's door close, Mrs. Pushka turned to him, beaming. "Oh, Trent, what a wonderful girl she is!" the old lady exclaimed, in a manner wholly uncharacteristic of her.

Trent was more than a little surprised. Mrs. Pushka and Olga had heartily disliked each other for years, and Helene had been terrified of the outspoken old woman. Altogether, it hadn't exactly made for a smoothly running household.

"I'm glad you and Vanessa like each other," Trent replied sincerely.

"Why, Trent, that sweet girl just loves you to death!" his longtime housekeeper exclaimed enthusiastically.

Fear fluttered in his stomach. Yes, there it was again—that jarring flash, that haunting, inexplicable knowledge that something... something was most assuredly *wrong*.

As the next few days passed happily and uneventfully, Trent was better able to disdain the worrisome feeling. After all, unsettling emotions to the contrary, everything was "splendid, wonderful and marvelous!" He had only to ask Vanessa, who had made that extravagant exclamation.

For the first time in years, Trent ignored his work, telling himself that this was a well-deserved vacation. The actual truth was that he could scarcely tear himself away from Vanessa's side. She was so excited, so happy, always bubbling over with more questions and filled with fun. As if she were a rare and miraculous plant that bloomed before Trent's eyes, each day seemed to find her more beautiful than the last, and more content as well, joking and laughing up at him until Trent felt utterly transformed.

He took Vanessa all around Davidson Island in the cruiser and then far out into Lake Superior until they set foot on the Canadian shore. He also took her to meet various friends who lived on islands similar to his own.

Vanessa accompanied Trent when he went back to Catt Island on mundane errands, usually grocery shopping for the newly energized Mrs. Pushka, who kept coaxing Vanessa to eat by preparing delicious entrées and fancy desserts like fresh strawberry pie and chocolate mousse.

"Vanessa, you must tell me what *you'd* like to do," Trent kept urging her, but she always insisted that she was perfectly agreeable to anything and everything. Even when Trent suggested that they rent a few movies to watch in the evenings on his VCR—since network television on their far-flung island was not always reliable—Vanessa seemed to have no particular choices.

"Oh, I'll watch anything that moves," she told Trent laughingly.

He soon discovered that brother Clark phoned Vanessa every third or fourth day, and that the absolute best moments of all came every night when he knocked on Vanessa's door. Then, for a leisurely quarter of an hour, Trent massaged his wintergreen liniment into her still-weakened arm. Vanessa vowed that it ached less with every passing day.

On those occasions, Trent tried to control his physical reactions and keep himself strictly in line, but they were always his severest test. Vanessa looked positively adorable propped up alone in bed, wearing that silly Atlanta Braves nightshirt that Trent dreamed of sliding slowly off her smooth shoulders.

But he was so determined not to frighten her again that he forced himself to concentrate on the business at hand: rub her slim arm thoroughly and deeply, but don't make her tender skin raw, he ordered himself; massage in liniment skillfully and try not to notice the arm's soft, creamy-smooth texture.

Finally, Trent was always rewarded with a good-night kiss, freely given and lovingly bestowed. For just a few moments, Vanessa's lips would cling to his while he gamely resisted the almost overpowering urge to crush her in his arms and claim a thousand hungry kisses.

The very moment she began to draw back, he would release her promptly. "Thank you, Trent. It was such a lovely day!" she'd usually exclaim.

"Mine was lovely because you were in a part of it, Vanessa," Trent would reply, and that usually won another of her sweet, flashing smiles.

He tried not to notice that her lips clung to his a little longer each night. He tried not to care. But the truth was that Trent rarely thought of little else.

"Vanessa, this is Olga Hedlung. Olga, I'd like you to meet..." As Trent made the introductions he'd dreaded, he wondered what on earth he'd been worried about. Although Olga looked as rigid as if she'd swallowed a ramrod, she extended her hand to meet Vanessa's. Her head even jerked in a silent nod. Vanessa, of course, began chattering away. Had she ever met a stranger in her life? Trent wondered; he didn't think so. Vanessa always assumed she was among friends. "It's so nice to meet you, Ms. Hedlung," she said, with every appearance of sincerity. "Trent's written me so much about you through the years. I really know what your work and dedication have meant to him."

Okay, maybe she was laying it on a bit thick, Trent mused. Still, Vanessa certainly sounded nice.

"I met your mother and sister the day I arrived," she continued. "They're charming! We ate dinner at your mother's restaurant, and what fabulous food! I've been gaining weight like mad ever since I came to the islands, and I definitely started off on your mother's hot rolls and lemon pie."

Olga actually managed a half-thawed smile. "I'll tell Mother you enjoyed your dinner, Mrs. Ashton. She'll be pleased."

Another polite lie, Trent knew. Sally would have been far more pleased if Vanessa had strangled on a wishbone and died. Still, for all their mutual exaggerations, this introduction was going more smoothly than Trent had dared hope.

"Do call me Vanessa, because I can tell we're practically the same age."

Even Olga recognized that particular generosity. "Thank you. Of course, you must call me Olga, too."

"Perhaps you'll show me around the lab a bit," Vanessa went on smoothly, looking all around with her unflagging curiosity. "I know Trent needs to check his mail and probably do a number of other things, too."

"Yes. It would be helpful if he'd check the results of his latest experiments," Olga shot back. Her voice wasn't malicious, but the glower she aimed in Trent's direction was unmistakable. "We're really not accustomed to Dr. Davidson's being gone from the lab for such long periods of time."

"One week?" Trent said, glaring right back at his lab assistant.

"Actually, I think it's been eight days," Olga said with fanatic precision. Her colorless face looked as cold as a churn filled with frozen milk.

Damn her, anyway! But before Trent could quell his anger and make an appropriate reply, Vanessa was already apologizing for him.

"Oh, it's my fault, Olga. Trent's been nice enough to keep me company since I'm so new to the islands and still scared of my own shadow. He's been showing me all around.... My, how *interesting* this laboratory is. What are all these various gadgets and gizmos?"

That Vanessa's pleasant, innocent voice and her incessant curiosity worked their magic even on the unsmiling Olga amazed Trent. But since Olga's life had so long been centered almost exclusively on her work, she couldn't resist the opportunity to show off to such an eager audience.

"If you'll step over this way, Vanessa, I think you'll find what Dr. Davidson and I have been doing with lady's slipper to be interesting. Timothy is extracting some of the active ingredients right now, and Perry, Dr. Davidson's other assistant, is working with mandrake. See his gown, gloves and mask? He has to exercise such unusual precautions because mandrake is so poisonous."

"My goodness, whatever are you going to do with it?"

Trent whipped into his office and closed the door. Of course, there remained some danger in leaving the two women alone. Still, he didn't think that Olga would go on the attack in the presence of Timothy and Perry, two young men who also lived on Catt Island with their families. She wouldn't want to lose face with her co-workers and neighbors.

Trent also thought he could trust Vanessa not to drink a mandrake cocktail should Olga offer her one....

He zipped through the day's accumulation of mail as well as inquiries from his three subordinates, scribbling "Yes," "No" or "File" on numerous papers and tossing the rest of them into the wastebasket. Then he sat down at his desk to concentrate on various new statistics Olga had compiled for his review.

Quietly his door opened, and Trent glanced up to see Olga standing there alone. She let the door glide shut behind her, then leaned against it. Her face held a challenge.

"Where's Vanessa?" Trent asked sharply.

"Timothy has her viewing evening primrose under the microscope." Olga shrugged. "Then he'll stick some pretty flower slides under her nose. Vanessa's so childlike, she's easily entertained."

Trent felt his face flush as if he himself had been the recipient of her insult. "Vanessa is in her midtwenties," he retorted. "She exhibits a childlike exuberance and curiosity that I, personally, find charming. But she's no child."

Olga shrugged again, "Perhaps I used the wrong word. She is certainly very beautiful...like a doll, a very expensive doll. Yes, I think your Vanessa is a doll. There's no character or substance to her. She's just a giddy little clinging vine."

"That's enough, Olga!" Trent warned her, feeling the color continue to rise in his face.

"Helene I could understand. She had some sophistication—and her main attraction was obvious—"

"Olga, I warn you, don't say any more!" Trent exploded.

He saw her hand tighten on the doorknob. But when she spoke next, her voice remained cool, just as cool as the pale blue eyes impaling him. "If you ever decide that what you want is a real woman, I'll still be here, Trent."

"You won't still be here if you don't shut up right now!" he threatened.

Wordlessly Olga tilted her head in a cold nod of agreement and eased quietly through the door. As it closed behind her, Trent ran a shaking hand through his hair and vowed to forget the unpleasant scene just as quickly as possible.

But forgetting proved difficult; Olga's words continued to rankle, festering deep inside of him. As much as Trent loathed admitting it, even to himself, some element of what she'd said rang true.

He wasn't a man to dwell on the past. As a result, Trent tended to forget occasionally that Vanessa had ever been sick. It was particularly easy for him to forget a week later on a languid summer night.

Trent and Vanessa had shared another delicious dinner, since Mrs. Pushka was still performing her Julia Child act, whipping out three full meals each day and turning a deaf ear to Trent's remonstrations. Right now the old woman was cleaning up the kitchen, having firmly rejected both Trent's and Vanessa's pleas to help her.

"You young folks just get out of my way," Mrs. Pushka had snapped when Trent had grown insistent. So now he and Vanessa sat together in the front porch swing, watching the sun set over Lake Superior in spectacular rainbow colors.

Memories tugged at him as the wide old swing glided gently to and fro. "Trent, we seem fated to sit in front porch swings," Vanessa said to him, as if she had just read his mind.

He laughed and nodded, remembering vividly another summer evening when he'd sat in a swing with Vanessa. On that occasion she'd proposed to him. *I probably should have accepted*, Trent thought. What a world of grief I might have spared us both—especially Vanessa.

On the other hand, he could scarcely have promised to marry a thirteen-year-old, Trent thought ruefully. And how could he have held a child of that age to her pledge?

Now, like the child she'd once been, Vanessa sat curled up beside him in the swing. Several minutes of quiet passed before Trent realized she was unnaturally silent.

"What would you like to do tomorrow, Vanessa?" he asked, breaking the silence between them and hoping—really hoping—that this time she would actually state a preference for one activity over another.

"Well?" Trent prompted teasingly, realizing that Vanessa was half-asleep, the result of good food and the gentle swaying motion of the swing.

"Oh, anything you want to do is fine with me, Trent," she said lazily, and sat up, stretching. The casual action strained her popcorn-knit sweater over her pert breasts, and for just a second Trent could see their nipples clearly delineated. Sweat suddenly broke out on his forehead. He swallowed hard, trying not to think about touching those delicate nipples.

"C'mon," he urged. "Tell me something you'd really like to do."

Her slim arms dropped to her sides. "Anything is fine," she repeated plaintively.

"Vanessa, you're bound to have some preferences," Trent argued.

"Well, I don't, Trent. These islands are still so new to me that I think everything here is just fabulous."

Why wouldn't she make a single simple decision? Why did she force him to make every one? Unaccountably Trent felt frustrated, probably because he was trying so hard not to think of the way her breasts had been so perfectly outlined and how badly his fingers wanted to caress them.

Immediately he felt ashamed of his flash of resentment. "We might go over to Isle Royale," he suggested thoughtfully. "You'd enjoy that, I think."

"Why? What's there, Trent?" Vanessa asked.

She managed to shift in the swing just enough for her bare thigh to rub insinuatingly against his. Since the weather had warmed, Vanessa wore shorts almost every day, and the sight of her slim, sweetly curved legs and shapely bottom were enough to elevate Trent's blood pressure.

Now, almost without his being aware of it, his arm slipped around Vanessa, tightening on her narrow waist.

"Isle Royale is a national park and wildlife sanctuary," Trent answered automatically. "The only drawback is that it's also a very big tourist attraction. At this time of year we might find hordes of other people there."

"Oh," Vanessa said, her disappointment evident in her voice.

How good she felt simply sitting next to him! She stirred again, moving against Trent just enough to set his pulse racing and making his skin alive with excitement. She gets me hotter faster than any woman I've ever known, he realized, for now his whole body felt aroused.

Nervously he cleared his throat. "On the other hand, it might be more fun if we went to visit some friends of mine who live in an old lighthouse—"

"A lighthouse!" Vanessa interrupted eagerly.

"Yes, it's quite picturesque, although the lighthouse is no longer in use. Peg and Paul Johnson live there. They're a young couple about your age, and they have a two-year-old toddler. They always welcome company—"

"A boy or a girl, Trent? The baby, I mean," Vanessa said, sliding even closer to him.

Trent was wearing shorts, too. Now he felt Vanessa's thigh brush his own again, tickling the hairs of his leg. "Oh—a boy. Well, which would you rather do?"

"Either. Both. I don't care, truly."

Truly, he knew she *did*. She didn't really want to rub elbows with throngs of people on Isle Royale. She wanted to go visit a stir-crazy young couple at a lighthouse who had a cute little kid. But why did she hesitate to tell him so?

Sometimes Trent got the idea that Vanessa was trying much too hard to please him. "We'll go to the lighthouse," he decided quickly.

"Great!" In her delight, Vanessa glided over him like a warm, welcome tide. She stopped with her lips poised mere inches from Trent's, and he blinked, trying to see her more clearly. He had not turned on the porch light earlier, so the swing was illuminated only by the reflected glow of lights from inside the house and the spasmodic flash of fireflies. In the dim light Vanessa was hauntingly, glowingly beautiful, and this was the first time she'd ever deliberately invited a kiss from Trent so early in the evening.

God, she's got me jumping through hoops, Trent thought, and wondered if that was Vanessa's intention. But he certainly wanted to kiss her too much to resist nobly. Swiftly he turned, burying his face in the fragrant cloud of her hair. Then, while his tongue outlined the delicate little ear he found there, with its shell-like contours, his fingers squeezed her waist lightly. Slowly his hands moved up Vanessa's arms to caress her shoulders and explore the sensitive column of her throat.

He felt a tremor run through her body. Ah ha, so she wasn't unaffected by him, either, he realized with a surge of wild joy.

"Umm," Vanessa breathed in husky approval. "You do that just right, Trent."

"Good," he whispered, and then his tongue dipped inside that small and perfect ear.

He felt her twist against him. Then, suddenly, Vanessa had crawled all the way over him, letting her breasts crush flat against his chest and her thighs strain against the rigid muscles in his. She set Trent on fire as he drew her face slowly toward his. Her lips quivered very slightly in readiness for his kiss, and she made no attempt to evade him.

Slowly Trent's open mouth pressed on hers, and he felt Vanessa give a convulsive shiver. Then Trent was aware that her small hands were beginning to climb his chest.

Gently he let his mouth glide back and forth over hers; then his tongue drove past the newly softened barrier of her lips. God, she was so sweet.

For a few moments he simply savored that warm, irresistible sweetness, gripping her tightly. He couldn't have allowed her to end the kiss even had she wished. When he finally tore his mouth from Vanessa's, she gazed up at him as if she were stunned.

His own head was reeling and his hands twitched, aching with their need for tactile contact. Never had he so yearned to caress a woman's skin. "Vanessa, I want to touch you," Trent warned, too aroused now to simply stop and draw away from her. *She* must call a halt to this sweet madness if she didn't want more of his kisses or feared his touch.

When his thumb dipped lower to brush her collarbone and the soft skin just above her breasts, he heard her inhale shakily. A part of her must want to tell him to stop, Trent surmised, but still another part of Vanessa obviously wanted him to go further. Slowly Trent's hand slid beneath the scooped neck of her knit sweater and cupped the warm swell of one tender breast. Immediately he felt its rosebud tip harden in sensitive, responsive perfection. The sensation was exquisite, and Trent breathed raggedly.

"I've wanted to touch you like this since the first moment I saw you again—that moment when you stepped off the ferry," he told her, and the unsteadiness in his own voice surprised him.

"Have you, Trent?" Vanessa's own voice wavered dangerously.

Again his mouth tasted the honey of her lips, but the kiss was tentative, still allowing her to decide. Now she could draw back like an innocent schoolgirl, just as she did at a certain point every night when their good-night kiss began to make her nervous, or—

Or tonight she might give in to more, allow his kisses and caresses, then kiss and touch him in return like the warm, aroused woman that he thought she really was.

Nothing had prepared Vanessa for the explosion of sensations she felt when Trent's hand cupped her breast. Now his firm, strong palm continued to rest there, warming her skin until she was sure he must hear the frantic pounding of her heart.

She leaned closer while his hand continued its erotic invasion. Her lips, already heated from his, sought to be kissed once more. Oh, he was making absolute mush of her brain and common sense, but how good it felt not to think of anything at all for once, just to relax and *feel*.

Now Trent's other hand glided slowly down her back. It outlined the curve of her hips, then pressed her lower body tight against him. Vanessa heard her own spontaneous gasp. She could feel every throbbing inch of Trent, and his obvious masculine need aroused longings inside her—new longings of the sort she had wondered if she was even capable of feeling. Her bones seemed to yield and melt against the unyielding strength and rigidity of his until she yearned to arch and stretch, catlike, against him. Since she was accustomed to acting on her feelings, and since she was no longer thinking very clearly, Vanessa's arms slipped up around Trent's neck. Silently she pulled his face even closer to hers, while her mouth opened beneath his in wordless, hungry invitation.

"I want you so!" she heard Trent breathe. Then his lips were crushing hers, almost bruising in their desperate urgency.

Wild thrills seized Vanessa, shooting through her like arrows of fire. She felt herself dissolving in this new, unaccustomed heat. Felt herself yielding to the fierce commanding strength and sheer masculinity of the man who held her. *Let go, just let go,* her senses urged, and for a giddy moment or two she did.

Trent. He was all she could think of, all she could feel. His overpowering appeal to her senses. His overwhelming assault on her heart. Trent, with the clean fresh scent of pines and herbs and soap-scrubbed skin. Vanessa absorbed him through her pores, drank in his essence with her lips and tongue. She loved him—she had always loved him! There had never really been anyone else for her in the past, and there could never be anyone else in the future. Because no other man could ever make her feel like this—a creature of flames, wanting and needing, alive and exhilarated by desire.

She wasn't quite sure how long the intense moments of abandon lasted. One moment Vanessa felt as if she'd grown wings and was soaring to paradise with Trent, and the next she felt his taut hand on her hips, grinding her against him. She knew that particular and urgent male touch, and abruptly Vanessa's passion dissolved in fear—not the fear of actual lovemaking, but the fear of the inevitable disappointment it had always entailed.

She could not bear to experience that sort of disappointment with the man she had always loved! Later, perhaps, when she felt a little braver, a little stronger, but not quite yet.

Vanessa went rigid in his arms, and a little whimper escaped her. "Trent, please—" she managed to say against his avid lips, which were hungry to claim hers again.

"Don't say no!"

It was an aroused man's heartfelt groan, but even as Trent uttered it, Vanessa could feel his arms start to loosen from around her. Suddenly a lump rose in her throat, combining relief, profound emotion and deep love. How many other men would—or could—release her at such a fervid point of passion? How many other men would care enough to protect her that way?

Slowly Vanessa drew back. Her senses were still swimming, and her own aroused body clamored, resisting its separation from the tall, strong one on which she'd been stretched almost full length. Trent's heavy breathing echoed her own. And now? Oh, Lord, what in the world could she say to him?

As it turned out, she didn't have to make any explanations at all. For suddenly, from the back of the house, came a crash so earsplitting that they could hear it even out on the porch. Vanessa leaped out of the swing just one second before Trent.

"What's that?" she gasped.

"Mrs. Pushka!" Trent cried, and for a moment their eyes met in mutual consternation. Then he darted for the door, Vanessa following fast on his heels.

Chapter Six

In a pile of broken dishes, haphazardly dropped silverware and upended pans, Mrs. Pushka lay, miraculously unhurt. She glared at Trent and even at Vanessa, whom she usually adored, when they dropped down on either side of her. Clearly the old lady was furious with herself.

"Mrs. Pushka, what happened?" Vanessa asked urgently, her fear changing to relief as she saw that the old woman was able to sit up and move all her limbs.

"She fainted," Trent supplied, one of his hands closing around Mrs. Pushka's bony wrist.

"I did not!" Mrs. Pushka snapped. "I tripped and fell."

"Sure you did," Trent retorted in a mildly sarcastic voice. "That's why your pulse is so thready. You've been working much too hard lately, and you know it!"

"I've just been doing my job the way it oughta be done," Mrs. Pushka shot back, casting a resentful look at the comforting arm that Vanessa had slipped around her shoulders.

"She's had a few spells of heart failure before," Trent informed Vanessa, and she gave a distracted nod.

"Heart failure, my eye!" Mrs. Pushka sniffed. "My heart's as good as it ever was—and I don't care what you or that young quack on Catt Island say to the contrary."

"Every once in a while I make her visit Dr. Evans. He's the only medical doctor in the islands," Trent explained, and Vanessa nodded again.

"You mean you drag me to see him!" Mrs. Pushka said accusingly.

"You're darn right I do," Trent responded. "Tomorrow we're going to pay him another visit, too."

"Over my dead body, Trent Davidson!"

Trent went right on speaking, just as if Mrs. Pushka had not made her objections known. "Right now I'm going to carry you back to your cottage, and I know Vanessa will be glad to help you undress for the night."

"I certainly will," Vanessa murmured. But her soft words were drowned out by Mrs. Pushka's emphatic "Like hell! I'm gonna clean up this mess."

"*I'll* clean up this mess when I get back," Trent went on, slipping a sinewy arm beneath Mrs. Pushka's knobby knees. Slowly and carefully he stood up with the old woman in his arms.

For a second Mrs. Pushka raised a bony hand as if to ward him off. Then her hand dropped slowly and she sighed aloud.

"Trent, I can clean up these dishes in a flash," Vanessa offered, but neither of the other two appeared to hear what she said.

Well, at least I can be useful, whether they notice me or not, Vanessa decided. She opened the back door for the burdened Trent and restrained Boots, who came bounding up to greet them. Then Vanessa followed Trent and Mrs. Pushka down the stone path in the back, the terrier barking at her heels.

"Hush, Boots," she scolded gently, straining her ears to hear what Trent was saying to Mrs. Pushka.

"You've been working too hard, and it's not necessary at all. Vanessa and I don't need such elaborate meals. We're also perfectly capable of getting our own breakfast every morning and fixing ourselves a sandwich at noon. Now you will consider yourself absolutely grounded until Rys Evans says differently. You're to rest, take your digitalis and regain your strength."

"I hate those pills and you know it, Trent. They always make my head feel funny," Mrs. Pushka complained.

"And I've told you that's probably the filler which was added to the digitalis. An allergy or inability to tolerate fillers is a common problem with prescription drugs. Vanessa can tell you all about it." Trent glanced back over his shoulder, obviously checking to see if Vanessa had followed them.

"I sure could," she muttered.

Trent continued to issue orders to Mrs. Pushka. "Now I don't care if you take the pills Rys Evans prescribed or the tonic I made you from fresh foxglove, but—"

"You wanta know what your fresh tonic tastes like, Trent Davidson? It tastes—"

"Watch it," Trent interrupted quickly. "There's a lady present, and at this moment I'm not referring to you, dear Frieda!"

"You've got no respect for a sick old person at all!" Mrs. Pushka wailed. "Oh, sometimes, Trent, when I see what you've become, I feel like I've wasted my life!"

Trent threw back his head and laughed. Vanessa might have laughed, too, if she hadn't still been so worried about Mrs. Pushka. At least the old woman's acerbic tongue was intact.

Trent led the way into the small, neat cottage where Mrs. Pushka had lived for almost half a century. Vanessa paused momentarily on the doorstep to bar Boots. "Sit," she said, and the terrier reluctantly responded.

By the time she entered the living room, Trent had already borne Mrs. Pushka into the bedroom just beyond. Gently he laid the old woman on the bed; then he turned away to open one of the bureau drawers.

"Get out of there!" Mrs. Pushka screeched, sitting up indignantly. "I don't want some man poking around in my underwear drawer. Now shoo!" With an emphatic wave of her hand, she indicated quite plainly that Trent had better leave.

He hesitated, then glanced back at Vanessa. "The fox-glove tonic is there on the nightstand. Make sure she takes a dose." He left hastily, just in time to forestall another holler from the clearly irate Mrs. Pushka.

Once the door had clicked shut behind Trent, the old woman grew much more obliging. She directed Vanessa to a clean white nightgown and to her robe and slippers. As Vanessa responded to Mrs. Pushka's bidding, she noticed that the old woman's thin lips had a distinctly bluish tinge.

"Trent's really a very dear, kind man," Mrs. Pushka said with a conspiratorial wink at Vanessa.

"From the way you talked to him, I wouldn't have guessed you felt that way," Vanessa replied in gentle reproof.

"Oh, Trent knows I care." Matter-of-factly, Mrs. Pushka began to undress, and Vanessa averted her eyes in deference to the older woman's modesty. "I've stayed here with him all these years, haven't I?" She paused for a labored-sounding breath, and Vanessa used that moment to drop the nightgown over her head.

"But I won't be here forever," Mrs. Pushka sighed a moment later. "My body's wearing out—"

Just the mention of death set Vanessa's heart fluttering. "Trent's right, you work much too hard," she scolded.

"Not that I really mind dying," Mrs. Pushka said, smoothing down the bodice of her nightgown. "Actually, I kinda look forward to it, being reunited with Myron, my late husband, you understand." She chuckled warmly. "Poor Myron's been waiting for me such a long time now. Good thing I still wear his ring—he probably wouldn't recognize me without it." Briefly she held up a brown-spotted hand on which a wide gold wedding ring still gleamed.

"It's rough being a widow," Vanessa said consolingly. "I'm one, too."

"I know. Trent told me. But you're sure not hankering to join up with your dearly departed." Mrs. Pushka spoke with a harsh honesty as she reached resignedly for her tonic bottle.

A little choked sound escaped Vanessa's lips. She still wasn't quite used to what she could only call "blunt Yankee truth," although she'd already met up with some of it, from Trent and Mrs. Pushka both. In the South, nice little hypocritical lies were usually allowed as a matter of politeness.

"No, I must admit I'm not eager to join Bailey," Vanessa said, dropping down to the spotless floor to draw off Mrs. Pushka's old-fashioned stockings and orthopedic shoes.

"No reason a young girl like you should want such a reunion," Mrs. Pushka agreed readily. "The thing I'm curious about is whether you're willing to marry Trent and live with him here. It would sure set my mind at ease if you are."

Vanessa felt her eyes widen with surprise but there was no hesitation to her reply. "You bet I am!" she blurted. "But I've hardly dared to think—much less hope—that Trent might be interested in marrying me."

"Do you really love him?" Mrs. Pushka demanded.

"Oh, yes. I've loved Trent all my life," Vanessa went on forthrightly. "Why, I can't even imagine not loving him."

"Then how'd you come to marry someone else?" Mrs. Pushka asked.

"I thought Trent was gone...lost to me forever. He'd been living here with Helene for almost two years. I waited, hoping they'd break up, which was probably very wicked of me. But finally I just gave up. I needed someone, and there was Bailey Ashton, vowing he'd always take care of me and make me happy."

"So that's how you came to marry the congressman," Mrs. Pushka mused, her black eyes fairly snapping with curiosity. "How'd you happen to stay with Bailey, especially after you found out that Trent didn't marry Helene?"

"I'd made my commitment," Vanessa said softly, gravely. "And Bailey was as good to me as he knew how to be—he needed me. And, anyway, you know how strong and independent Trent is. He doesn't really need anyone else—why, he's even said as much! That's why I've been afraid to hope that...well, that Trent could ever love me back."

To her surprise, Mrs. Pushka dropped back against the pillows of her bed, grinning like the Cheshire cat. "Oh, he needs you, little one," she said, reaching up to stroke Vanessa's face gently. "I just hope I live long enough to really see it, to see the look on Trent Davidson's face when he finds out he *isn't* complete all on his own. Yes, ma'am, I'd sure give a lot to see that look!"

Vanessa returned the old woman's knowing smile kindly, but privately she couldn't help but think that Mrs. Pushka was surely wrong about confident, competent Trent.

"I sure hope you can bring him round," Mrs. Pushka said. "I'd worried about Trent's not ever finding the right person, so you don't know what a relief you are, Miss Vanessa."

"But how can you be sure that I'm the right person?" Vanessa protested, even as her heart longed desperately to believe Mrs. Pushka.

"Because if you aren't, then there won't ever be anyone," said the old lady with finality. Her eyes closed, and a tired sigh escaped her. "And soon it *will* be too late for him. Yes, without you, my sweet, Trent will be lost."

She didn't really believe Mrs. Pushka, Vanessa thought as she walked silently back to the main house. The poor old soul was just weak, sick and maybe not altogether possessed of good sense after her faint. Vanessa couldn't conceive of Trent's actually needing anyone else.

Her mind flew back across the years. Again Vanessa saw herself as a girl barely in her teens, so appalled that Trent was all alone in the world without parents or siblings. Again she saw his calm face telling her the circumstances of his elderly father's death. Trent had so obviously been prepared for and adjusted to that inevitable separation in a way that Vanessa could not begin to understand. Years later she had sometimes envied his understanding, acceptance and composure, especially on those nights when she awoke crying for those whom she had lost: her father, her mother, even Bailey.

No, Mrs. Pushka was dead wrong. Because Trent was one person who was wholly complete in himself, content and at home with his own company.

"Go to bed now, Vanessa," Trent suggested gently. In the brutally bright light of the kitchen her face looked pale and stricken. He knew that the knowledge of Mrs. Pushka's heart condition had been a shock to her, and Trent was impressed with all that Vanessa had nevertheless managed to do. She'd really been a help to him.

"No, Trent, I'm going to help you clean up first," Vanessa announced firmly.

"That's not necessary. I can do this in a flash," Trent objected, and opened the utility cabinet where the mop and broom were stored.

"Then the two of us together can do it in a twinkle!" Vanessa retorted, seizing a dustpan and snatching the broom from his hand.

Trent couldn't help smiling. What a wonder she was, lovely little Nessie, with her chin jutting out at that stubborn angle. It was a look he'd seen a few times before in years past when she'd had her adorable little hard head clearly set on something. Now it jibed rather incongruously with the sweet, docile "anything *you* want to do, Trent" attitude that she'd displayed these past few weeks. He knew she was strong willed, even hell-bent at times. Now Trent observed the contradiction and wasn't surprised that his old "something's wrong" feeling returned like a nagging toothache.

But, working together in easily synchronized motions, they soon had the kitchen restored to order. Vanessa even measured coffee and water into the coffee maker so that the first person who was up tomorrow morning had only to plug in the machine.

Trent found himself both surprised and impressed by her—by her cool, thoughtful manner in an emergency, by the efficient and almost effortless way she had controlled Boots and worked by Trent's side.

They went upstairs just a few minutes apart, and tonight the massage Trent gave her weakened arm was more perfunctory than usual. When Vanessa lifted her face to him, he bent down swiftly, but the kiss he gave her was gentle, tender, almost brotherly.

If nothing else, Mrs. Pushka's faint had reminded him that Vanessa was still something less than wholly well. She continued to recuperate, and she was a beloved responsibility that Trent had promised her brother he would tend with care. He must keep hands off from now on.

Earlier, alone with her in the porch swing, he had completely forgotten about her illness in the passion of the moment. But now he remembered.

In retrospect, Trent knew he should probably have expected what happened next. But even fortuitous memory wasn't enough the following week when they finally went to see Peg and Paul Johnson at the lighthouse.

Of course, Trent knew that Vanessa had been keyed up. Also, with Mrs. Pushka abed, Vanessa had probably been doing too much work—oh, not that it had seemed so either to Trent or to her as they moved around the kitchen together, preparing their own meals and fixing trays for Mrs. Pushka. But Vanessa had also insisted on helping the old woman bathe and dress, flying back and forth between the main house and the cottage.

Trent had continued to play hooky from the lab, leaving Olga smoldering with resentment. But trying to keep a careful eye on both Vanessa and Mrs. Pushka had definitely proved time-consuming. Not that he minded, since he cared so deeply for both of them. But as the sixth day of Mrs. Pushka's confinement ended, Trent was chagrined to realize that for entertainment he and Vanessa had only taken a short bike ride with Boots barking behind them, watched one movie on TV and picked a lot of fresh vegetables from the garden, adding fresh herbs and making quite a tasty pot of soup. That had been the extent of their recreation. Although Vanessa was unfailingly cheerful and had made quite a game out of cutting up all the vegetables, Trent felt certain she was just being a good sport. At this rate, she would soon find some excuse to leave the island and escape back to Atlanta—dreary prospect for him indeed.

He could not bear to have her leave quite yet.

"How would you like to visit the old lighthouse tomorrow?" he asked as they sat in the swing after dinner. As usual, Vanessa had managed to curl up against him. And as was also customary during these very busy days, Trent was about to suggest they stroll down to the bridge to see if any new flowers had bloomed. It was a feeble device that he employed each time he feared that his control might be slipping and that he was liable to make a mad, wild grab for the gorgeous woman beside him.

"Umm," said Vanessa noncommittally. "What about Mrs. Pushka while we're off sight-seeing?"

"Olga can make sure she's all right," Trent said. "She can take Mrs. Pushka a sandwich and a bowl of soup for lunch."

"But Mrs. Pushka and Olga dislike each other!" Vanessa protested.

"That's their problem," Trent replied, not even caring if he sounded heartless. "I want to spend some time with you, and I want us to have fun, too. Besides, you'll like Peg and Paul and their son."

He saw Vanessa's mouth soften and curve into a smile. "Yes, I'm sure I'd enjoy meeting them," she admitted. "I really like children."

"I'll bet they like you, too," Trent responded.

"How about you?" Boldly Vanessa leaned up against him. "Don't you like me anymore, Trent?"

"You ought to know better than to ask," he said in a mock growl, even as he felt the involuntary stiffening of his body.

"Now there you go, pulling away from me again," Vanessa said reprovingly. Although her tone was light, a hint of dismay lay beneath it.

"Lady, I have everything I can do not to throw you down in this porch swing and pounce on you!"

Trent spoke emphatically, then jumped up and tugged Vanessa to a standing position beside him.

"Well, you don't act like it," she said, pouting prettily.

"Don't be a flirt!" Trent said, more sharply than he'd intended.

"Is that what you think I am?" Vanessa asked, sounding stunned.

"Well, isn't it? You must realize what you do to me, Vanessa," Trent said reasonably.

"Oh, God!" He watched anger flash across her face, then saw her huge, haunting eyes start to fill with tears. "Why in hell does sex always have to be such a major problem between a man and a woman? I wasn't asking for sex! I wasn't even *thinking* about sex."

Now Trent was the one who felt stunned. "Then what did you want, Vanessa?" he inquired.

"Affection! Have you ever heard of that? Maybe I just wanted to be held and hugged a little! Maybe I just wanted to be treated like a woman, not a basket case!" she wailed. "Is that so hard to understand?"

"Well, you have to understand that I don't want to hold you and hug you a little. I want to do a whole lot of it—and not stop at hugs and kisses, either! If I really treated you like a woman you'd be spending the night in bed with me!" Fiery images rose up in Trent's mind as he uttered the words, but he didn't miss the fact that Vanessa recoiled just a little at his bluntness. And now those sparkling tears were beginning to spill down her cheeks.

Remorse struck Trent like a savage bite. Oh, damn, now he'd made her cry, and all because every time he was alone in the moonlight with Vanessa he started aching with desire like a teenager. But didn't she understand at all her effect on him? Or was she still such a stranger to passion that she honestly didn't know?

A soft sob escaped her, and she turned her head away. The little sound slashed through Trent like a knife. He muttered a profanity under his breath and caught her close.

Vanessa tried to hide her face from him, but Trent wouldn't allow it, pressing her head over his rapidly pounding heart. "Just feel what you do to me, Vanessa," he urged her softly. "Then see if you believe I'm really trying to reject you." He tilted her chin upward, bent his head and caught her lips beneath his, kissing them until they flamed and burned. Erotic needs set Trent's nerve endings sizzling, and almost unconsciously he felt himself rubbing his lower body against hers insinuatingly. Lord, how he wanted her!

Abruptly Vanessa drew back, her eyes wide with surprise. And suddenly Trent was the one more surprised, despite the physical torture of having to release her. Why, she honestly *didn't* know what her mere presence stirred him to—which brought up another matter entirely. Since Vanessa had been married for several years to Bailey Ashton, why the hell didn't she? What on earth had the physical side of their marriage been like to have left her so young and innocent still?

"Let's take that walk now," Trent said, his voice not quite steady as he reached for her hand.

She was uncommonly silent as they strolled along, and they had almost reached the bridge over the sparkling stream before Vanessa apparently could think of a single question to ask him.

At breakfast the next morning they were careful to talk only of mundane things, but the previous night was still very much on Vanessa's mind. Somehow she must change herself into the sort of woman that Trent really wanted—a very sexy woman—and it didn't promise to be easy.

In a way she was dismayed that Trent was so much like other men—in this respect, at least. All of them overestimated sex, she thought reflectively, but apparently that was simply the nature of the male beast.

On the other hand, when a woman wanted a man in the way that Vanessa wanted Trent, as her very own husband for the rest of her life, then he was worth some effort and accommodation. Actually, what Vanessa hoped for most was more than mere accommodation. She really hoped she might awaken and bloom for Trent as she never had for Bailey.

But first she had to conquer her own squeamishness and reluctance, she thought as she trailed Trent and Boots down to the dock. She had to frankly face her deep fear of disappointment and be willing to risk it. Why, the possibility existed that she might not be disappointed at all, Vanessa thought hopefully. Just look at how she'd responded to Trent's kisses and his touch. She was always left with a sense of breathless excitement that seemed somehow unfinished, and an intense longing for something more.

"Stay, Boots," Trent commanded his dog; then he held out his hand to help Vanessa aboard the cruiser.

"Thank you," she whispered.

"You looked like you were a million miles away," Trent commented as she moved off toward a deck chair. Suddenly his arms swung over, catching her from behind, and he nuzzled his face in the softness of her neck.

The sensation felt wonderful. "Umm..." sighed Vanessa in contentment.

"That's more like it," Trent breathed. Then he planted an achingly tender kiss at the sensitive juncture of her neck and shoulder. Wild thrills shot through Vanessa, and she swung around impulsively to fling her arms tight around Trent's neck. As he kissed her throat once again, she began to fill with happiness. This was a beautiful day, golden with sunshine, and the handsomest and most exciting man in the world was taking her away for another adventure, this time to visit a couple who lived at a lighthouse, of all places. And she'd have a baby to play with, too. Enthusiastically Vanessa planted a kiss on Trent's lips, then drew away quickly lest he again brand her a tease.

Instead he caught her close. "Sometimes I think I'm like Rip Van Winkle. Remember him, Nessie?"

If only Trent wouldn't call her by that odious childhood name. "Sure. Didn't Rip sleep for twenty years?" she responded, letting her body yield a little against Trent's. There! Did it kill her to relax a bit? Curiously she added, "But how are you like Rip Van Winkle?"

"I feel like I've been sleeping for years and didn't really wake up until you got here. It's been wonderful having you with me, Vanessa . . . only sometimes I don't quite know the right things to say or do. Sometimes I also forget you're a gently nurtured Southern belle. Please be patient with me."

Vanessa understood then. Trent was apologizing for his words and actions the night before. "Oh, that's all right," she said generously, granting him instant forgiveness. For a minute they simply hugged each other warmly, allowing the memory of the previous night to fade.

"Ready to go visit now?" Trent asked, drawing away.

"Yes," Vanessa replied emphatically. "Look, are you sure I'm dressed all right, Trent? I mean, jeans and a sweater are pretty casual attire."

"You look fine, honey," he assured her.

"What's Peg like, anyway? How long have she and Paul lived at the lighthouse—?"

Vanessa stopped, seeing Trent's amused grin, and knew she was doing it again—asking him a jillion questions. Oh, well. They were having to adjust to each other, and no one had ever said that particular process was easy.

The tall white tower of the lighthouse rose from a rocky promontory and was visible for several miles. Looking at it delighted Vanessa, who had never seen a lighthouse before. This one might have come straight out of a storybook.

"It's so tall!" she exclaimed. "Oh, look, Trent, there's the flag fluttering in the breeze."

"You look at the flag—I'll watch for the pier," he called back teasingly.

The lighthouse stood on a glacier-gouged granite island covered with gnarled trees and shrubs, miniature hills and green grass. Vanessa exclaimed over everything as they cruised slowly in.

"Herring gulls use this place for nesting sites," Trent yelled back to her. "Herons and ducks, too. Peg's been studying them for—"

He stopped abruptly as he began to wave, and Vanessa swung around to see who had attracted Trent's attention. Now there were three figures on the rocky island, all hurrying down to the pier to greet them. One, a tall, bearded man, trotted from the direction of the lighthouse, while the other adult, obviously a woman from her smaller and more curved figure, moved more slowly to accommodate the little boy by her side. He was running as fast as his short legs could carry him.

The two adults waved, whooped and cheered as Trent eased his boat up against the pier. The young woman actually leaped aboard to give him an exuberant hug. "Trent, how marvelous to see you! How marvelous to see *any* living human being! Why didn't you call us on the radio and let us know you were coming today?"

"You mean he didn't?" Vanessa gasped. Then she found herself the recipient of a brief hug, too.

"Hi, I'm Peg," said the laughing young woman who caught her around the waist.

"Vanessa Ashton," Vanessa replied breathlessly, "and I can't imagine why Trent didn't—"

She turned, actually ready to glower at the man she adored, only to find him laughing as well. "It's always more fun to surprise Peg and Paul," Trent explained. "You see, when they first came out here about four years ago they were escaping from civilization. All they asked for was quiet and peace. In this tranquillity Paul would write a great novel and Peg would continue to study wild fowl. So they were polite but distant and discouraging to anyone who happened by. That lasted for—how long, Peg? Three whole months, I guess. Then cabin fever set in, and now they're totally nondiscriminating about their guests."

"Paul, you'd better come help defend us," Peg called back to her husband, who was holding the still-waving toddler. "Trent's gloating again."

"Oh, I'll forgive him, 'cause just look what he's brought," said Paul, pretending to leer at Vanessa.

"Ignore my lascivious husband, Vanessa. He drools easily. And this other character is Chad, our joint contribution."

"Hi, Chad!" Vanessa called to the little boy.

She found herself swept along a cement walk that ran from the landing up the hill. The Johnsons lived in a small house built alongside the lighthouse, she discovered, although Peg said that Paul wrote in the lantern room at the very top of the tower. Inside the cozy house Vanessa was soon seated at a round wooden table, warming her hands around a mug of steaming tea.

She and Peg laughed and talked as if they'd always known each other, and in the plain, wiry, freckle-faced woman, who was also dressed casually in jeans, Vanessa knew she'd found a friend.

Lunch, served a half hour later, consisted of pooled offerings, since Trent had brought a basket overflowing with fresh vegetables and fruit. Peg set out cold cuts, a leftover ham and a loaf of her own freshly baked bread for sandwiches. After Vanessa tossed a green salad, they sat down for the simple but tasty meal, the four adults drinking strong dark beer from a keg while Chad had a cup of milk. Dessert consisted of fruit and cheese.

Little towheaded Chad managed to stay awake until his mother passed around a tin of chocolate fudge; then he fell asleep in Vanessa's lap still clutching a half-eaten piece. Laughing, the women carried him off to bed.

"I'll stay with Chad. Why don't you let Paul show you the lighthouse, Vanessa?" Peg suggested, and Vanessa eagerly agreed.

She had no warning of what was coming, absolutely no warning at all. In fact, had anyone asked, Vanessa would have said that she was feeling perfectly all right as she and Paul set out for the lighthouse.

Trent didn't accompany them. Immediately after lunch he had settled in a worn armchair in the Johnsons' small living room to read the latest chapters of Paul's novel, which a publisher had asked the author to rewrite. Trent looked up as Vanessa and Paul went past him. "Do you two want me along?"

"Of course not!" Paul retorted.

"I shouldn't have asked *you*, Romeo. Just belt him, Vanessa, if he gets out of line."

"I will," she flung over her shoulder, knowing it was all a great joke; Paul was clearly smitten by his small, freckle-faced wife.

As Vanessa and Paul walked over to the lighthouse, Vanessa began her usual barrage of interested questions. "How tall is this thing, Paul? When was it built?"

"Built in 1890, and it's fifty-four feet high."

"Why isn't it used anymore?" Vanessa asked, following Paul inside the lighthouse where, in the empty, cavernous white space, the temperature seemed to drop at least ten degrees.

"There are other navigational aids available now that warn of rugged coastline, dangerous shoals and such," Paul replied. "Radar is one. Another is radio beacons on buoys."

"Seems a shame, though," Vanessa said wistfully as Paul led her over toward the circular iron stairs.

"I agree. This light was phased out about fifteen years ago," Paul went on. "The buildings were sold to the highest bidder, which in this case was the College of the Upper Peninsula, where Peg's father is a biology professor. The college now operates this isle as a sort of living lab, and lots of students come here on field trips every year."

"Interesting," said Vanessa, starting to climb the stairs behind Paul. "Is there still a light at the top?"

"No. It was removed to the college for safekeeping. I wish you could see it, Vanessa. It's a real beauty. Has a Fresnel lens that came from France."

Vanessa climbed higher. Then, suddenly, without any warning, her head began spinning. The steep spiral staircase going up and up made the dizzying white walls begin to revolve like some crazy merry-go-round.

Paul, climbing high above her, threw something back over his shoulder.

Vanessa couldn't make sense of his words. Now her legs began to tremble uncontrollably, and her hands were sweating on the railing. The lighthouse smelled dank and moist, making her stomach queasy.

Panic struck then, for Vanessa knew what was coming. "Paul!" she managed to call desperately before the whole world dissolved into a whirling, swirling maelstrom of white glare and blowing snow and her own circular steps, which led her back again like a doomed soul to the crashed airplane and the broken bodies sprawled within.

"Mother!" Vanessa heard herself scream. Then: "Bailey!" And finally she remembered one last name and cried it desperately at the top of her lungs before the vivid flashback crashed down on her so terribly and remorselessly: *"Trent!"*

Chapter Seven

Her limp hand lay on top of the coverlet, and now that Trent knew she was fully aware of him, he couldn't resist reaching over to squeeze it. Such a frail and delicate-looking little hand—so pale and smooth, small-fingered and slim. Fragile, just like Vanessa herself, he thought, and he made his squeeze very gentle.

After a moment her long black eyelashes fluttered, then rose reluctantly. She looked at him somberly out of narrowed and wary eyes.

"Vanessa, I phoned Dr. Zellar," Trent said softly.

She sighed, and a long moment passed before she replied. "So what did ol' Dr. Z. have to say?"

Involuntarily his hand tightened over hers. "He said you'd obviously had a recall episode or flashback. That it could have been triggered by any one of a number of stressful things—or maybe by all of them in combination. You've been doing extra work and worrying over Mrs. Pushka. And—and that little scene with me last night probably didn't help, either." Trent bit his lip to stop himself from apologizing to her all over again, although he continued to blame himself fiercely. Slowly he continued. "Today was pretty hectic and stressful, too—"

"Funny, I was enjoying today."

At the dry irony in Vanessa's voice, Trent's thumb began to stroke up and down her soft hand in gentle consolation. "Well, you probably shouldn't have drunk the beer. That homemade stuff of Paul's is potent as hell, and I—I just didn't think to stop you, either. Then there's the business of your tonic, the one I made up for you. That last bottle doesn't look like you've taken very much of it."

"I forgot." Abruptly Vanessa's eyes widened, meeting his frankly. "Oh, I may as well tell the truth. I didn't really forget, Trent. I just didn't think I needed it anymore." Her eyes closed, but not before he had seen their bright sheen of tears. "I thought I was completely well."

"Not quite," he said, trying to speak casually, although his own heart felt wrung in two. "Dr. Zellar says...says this isn't completely unexpected because you've...well, apparently you've had some of these recall episodes before."

"At first, right after the wreck. Mainly it happened while I was in that grim little hospital in Alaska where everything was white—walls, floors, even the people in white hospital uniforms." Vanessa's eyes opened again, huge, dark and tear-streaked. "But Trent, I swear I haven't had such an episode in seven months. Seven whole months!"

Her haunted look was like a hand gripping his heart. "I know, darling. Dr. Zellar told me."

Tears began to glide down Vanessa's cheeks. Oh, the hell with keeping a proper distance—he had to get closer to her or explode! Carefully, very carefully, Trent raised Vanessa's hand to his lips and pressed a kiss there. Then he turned it over and dropped another lingering kiss in the small pink palm.

What he really wanted to do was bang the wall, yell and curse. He felt like crying, too. Dammit, she'd been doing so *well*! That was why Vanessa's collapse had been so utterly unforeseen, although Trent continued to feel, guiltily, as though he should have seen it coming.

"I guess the inside of the lighthouse just brought it all back," Vanessa began to explain. "It was so—so very white inside, Trent, and the steps winding around went up so high, and suddenly I was dizzy. Then it was like what happened after the crash where everything was so *white* and I was running around in circles and—and bleeding all over the snow."

Pain closed Trent's own eyes now, and his heart banged much too rapidly against his rib cage. "I should have gone with you to the lighthouse," he muttered in self-accusation. Again he thought of that spine-chilling moment when he'd heard Vanessa screaming his name, followed by Paul's hoarse shout for help. He thought of finding Vanessa crouched in a corner, her head huddled in her arms. Thought of how she'd shaken and screamed for so long—so very long, it seemed—her eyes blind with panic. Actually, it had all been over in less than a quarter of an hour. But by the time Trent had finally calmed her, he had felt as if he'd aged twenty years. If his hair had all turned white from the experience, he wouldn't have been surprised.

Shock still continued to rumble through him like an internal eruption as he let his lips caress her hand once again. God, how he wanted to fold Vanessa in his arms—cover her with kisses, give her comfort and reassurance—but he didn't dare. Anxiously he wondered how to broach the next sensitive subject.

"Trent, what are you trying to find words to tell me?" Vanessa asked him, and Trent marveled anew at her intuitive powers and the way the light touch of her hand sent a painful throbbing straight through his heart.

"Dr. Zellar thinks you should go back to Atlanta," Trent blurted out. His words filled him with enormous desolation. Although Vanessa had only been here with him for three weeks, already he was unable to imagine life without her. "Nessie, what do you think of that idea?"

"I think it sucks!"

At the inelegant expression, which was voiced so fiercely, Trent blinked with surprise. It was the very last thing he might have expected such a sick little girl to say. But the glint in Vanessa's eyes was something less than docile, even though fear and despair were stamped there as well.

Now, as he watched her, despair seemed to get the upper hand. "Please, Trent, *please* don't make me go back to Atlanta!" she begged.

"Well, Vanessa..." Stalling, he stopped to clear his throat. His desire to hold her and protect her, to keep her safe by his side, kept swelling stronger with each passing moment.

"Of course, I will if you say I have to, Trent. But I don't want to leave here! I don't want to leave *you*! Oh, I've been having the absolute best time of my whole life!"

That Vanessa could say those words with such utter conviction touched Trent deeply.

Actually, though, he couldn't quite say the same. The past few weeks had *not* been the best time of his life—not if the best time was measured in effortless pleasure. They had been beautiful...and they had also been dreadful. He couldn't remember ever worrying quite so much over anyone as he had over Vanessa—or being so sexually frustrated, either. But, perversely, at the same time there had been a new light in his world, and a constant sense of wonder and enchantment as well.

Each day had been stamped indelibly on his mind, even as he had hungered and burned for this lovely woman who lay pleading with him now. Trent knew he had never wanted a woman so much, and that he had never before felt this fierce protectiveness.

He wouldn't have missed a minute of it!

"Trent, do you want me to go home? I'm sure I've been a big bother to you—"

Hoarsely he interrupted her. "No, I don't want you to go, Vanessa. And you haven't been a bother. But I'd never forgive myself if—"

His voice trailed off at the despair he saw on Vanessa's face. "Oh, Trent, please let me stay!" she pleaded again. "I'll never forget my tonic again! I'll do all the right things—I promise."

She gripped his hand more tightly, propping herself up on one elbow, speaking earnestly and fervently but without much hope that Trent would agree. The sheet covering her began to slip back, but Vanessa didn't notice.

Trent did, and when he saw her baby-blue nightshirt clinging to her lovely slender form, his own control simply snapped. Before he knew it he'd swept down and swooped Vanessa into his arms. Only then did he realize he might have alarmed her—but, fortunately, he felt her arms go tightly around his waist, returning the tight embrace.

She was so light! Trent was able to hold her and pluck a blanket off the bed at the same time. Then, wrapping her in it, he carried her over to the chaise longue by the window. There he sat down with her and contented himself simply with holding her close.

But as they sat, as always, her body set a fever boiling in his blood. Her satin skin gliding over him, Vanessa lay against his heart. Even as Trent warned himself to go slowly and move gently, he began fervently kissing her cheeks and forehead and those delightful little ears that were so like dainty seashells.

He hadn't intended to touch her delicious lips, but they sought his out and clung, warming rapidly. Nor had Trent ever imagined that such small, curvaceous arms could grip him so tightly. But what did Vanessa honestly feel for him? Trent simply had no way of knowing, he realized. Gratitude too often could mimic love, even passion. But, as her lips left his, he knew only that he could not send her home.

"All right," Trent breathed, succumbing to both her pleas and his own heart's desires. Emotions were still tearing him up, but at least the surge of physical desire he felt was distracting him. "All right, Vanessa. There's a risk in your staying, and Dr. Zellar didn't mince words about that. But if you want to stay so badly, then—then I guess we can face the risks together."

She buried her face in his shoulder, sagging with relief. And as he held her so close, felt her so near and dear, Trent was sure of one thing, if nothing else. He loved her, not in the sentimental way he'd felt at first, but with a man's fierce, unyielding and everlasting passion.

The feeling hadn't come easily, and he was still far from comfortable with it. But now he loved her so desperately, so hungrily, that he wanted nothing more on earth than just to see her safe, whole and well. He loved her so much that he could die for her—or even do without her in his arms, in his bed, which seemed to him infinitely worse. And so, when Vanessa leaned back and gazed up at him in near-adoration—as though he was her savior, the one and only person who could rescue her and always pull her through—Trent tried not to let it bother him.

But it did. For now, at last, he knew just exactly what was wrong. That adoring expression in the dark, glowing eyes of a young, immature, overly romantic girl of thirteen had been charming. But to see the same eyes, exactly the same expression, on the face of a supposedly grown woman when she gazed up at an all-too-human man—no wonder it had frightened the hell out of him!

Lord, what a mess!

Vanessa still lay on the chaise where Trent had left her, staring blindly out the window into the gathering dusk. Usually she loved to lie here and enjoy the view of blue sky and rippling blue water, watching birds as they wheeled and dived between the two. But today she was scarcely aware of the view on which her eyes focused. She was still aghast and chagrined over what had happened to her at the lighthouse.

Poor Trent, she thought. Poor, darling Trent! The look on his face had been absolutely ghastly. Suddenly she'd seen exactly what he would look like in twenty or thirty years. Fortunately, by the time he'd left her room a few minutes ago, he had looked a little less terrified and a lot more hopeful about the future.

But now he had a kitchen full of bickering women to face! Vanessa didn't envy him the confrontation with Mrs. Pushka, who had just pronounced herself well and taken up residence once again, or with Olga, who was already seething with quiet fury, or even with Peg Johnson, who had insisted on coming along with her husband and Trent when they'd brought Vanessa back. Peg was now trying to keep peace, tend little Chad and brew up a soothing drink that Trent had prescribed for Vanessa. She'd already lost her temper once.

Talk about walking into a veritable hornets' nest!

What have I done to Trent's settled and serene life? Vanessa wondered—other than turn it completely upside down, that is.

Did he mind terribly? Or did he really want to put her on a plane that would take her straight back to Atlanta, Dr. Zellar and big brother Clark? He'd sounded so vehement when he'd said he didn't want her to go.

For Trent's own sake, Vanessa hoped that he had meant it.

She knew, of course, that he wanted her physically. Even if he hadn't said so last night, his body's intense response to her had revealed the truth.

Before Vanessa had married, many men had chased after her. But, since she'd loved only Trent, she'd always swatted them off as though they were pesky flies.

What she hadn't understood before, but certainly knew now, was that various affectionate gestures on her part—which had barely even stirred Bailey—could fully and completely inflame Trent.

Last night Trent had been angry with her, obviously thinking she was deliberately trying to torment him. But earlier today, on board the cruiser, he had appeared more understanding. Now, in the wake of Vanessa's recall episode, he had held her and kissed her as though she was someone infinitely precious to him, completely vital and necessary for his happiness. Remembering the way he had suddenly scooped her up and crushed her so tightly against him still made Vanessa's head reel happily.

She knew something very important was happening to her with each and every one of Trent's kisses. Every glide of his hands on her skin, every contact she had with his long, strong body kept increasing her feelings. The lean, muscled strength of him, the sinewy male perfection of broad chest, flat belly and limbs, limbs that lifted and held her effortlessly, kept working continuously on Vanessa.

At first she'd simply been warmed and stirred by the glory of having her dreams come true at last: finally she was here with him and grateful just to snuggle close to the dear man she loved.

But gradually her feelings had been changing. Now, more and more, Vanessa had found herself actually responding to Trent and beginning to want more—much more—from him. She ran her tongue over her mouth, savoring again the taste of Trent that still lingered there. And when she happened to glance down at her freshly laundered Atlanta Braves nightshirt, she was surprised to see that the tips of her small breasts were standing fully erect. Deep inside her body, a slow, unfamiliar fire had ignited and now began to glow.

Trent Davidson just happened to be the most wonderful man in the whole wide world, Vanessa thought extravagantly, so no wonder he was having this effect on her!

A knock on the door interrupted her train of thought. "Come in," Vanessa called, drawing the blanket up to her shoulders.

Olga entered, carrying a tray on which a steaming bowl was set. When her cool, pale eyes met Vanessa's, the younger woman felt her newfound courage start to waver.

Obviously the delegation in the kitchen had decided that hot soup and soda crackers were the best things for someone who'd just experienced a traumatic recall episode, but Vanessa certainly wished they'd deputized someone else to deliver the tray.

Moving slowly and carefully, Olga turned and set the tray on a table near the chaise longue. Vanessa glanced at it without interest. She detested soup and crackers, grim reminders of her prolonged stay in various hospitals. There was also a banana on the tray, and at the sour look on Olga's face, Vanessa flashed a cool little smile. How she would enjoy telling Olga just what she could do with that banana!

"Thank you," Vanessa murmured politely instead.

"You do not fool me, you know," Olga replied, and for a moment Vanessa heard only the words without digesting their startling meaning. Sometimes Olga used a quaint old-world way of speaking.

Then Olga's meaning penetrated, sending the hot blood of combat rushing into Vanessa's face. "What do you mean by that?" she demanded.

"I know you're not sick. You just observed how Trent treats Mrs. Pushka when she has one of her spells, so you decided to have one of yours."

The cool, precise words sent a wave of fury rushing through Vanessa. So Olga thought that she was feigning illness just to worry Trent and keep him solicitously by her side.

At another time she might have told off Olga at the top of her lungs. But right now Vanessa was still feeling too drained and exhausted from the merry-go-round of emotions that had seized her. Anyway, why bother? Olga wouldn't be likely to alter her opinion.

Vanessa's lip curled contemptuously, and she averted her eyes from the stocky, colorless blond, choosing instead to stare out the wide window, where she could see water birds flying against the darkening sky. Sometimes it was better to frankly avoid a scene, as she had learned from group therapy last year. This certainly seemed to be one of those times.

"You may go now," Vanessa said, dismissing Olga with exaggerated courtesy.

Olga started for the door, then stopped and turned back. "Now that you know I'm on to you, I could tell Trent the truth," she threatened.

"Be my guest," Vanessa invited, her voice at its most frigid.

"But I won't. Because I feel sorry for you. I know you think that if you can just manage to stay here long enough, he will marry you. But you're mistaken."

Now Vanessa felt fiery wrath flood her whole body. "Are you into mind reading, Olga?" she inquired sarcastically. "Or do you listen at keyholes?"

Olga's broad shoulders shrugged. "There is no need to do either. Your intentions are evident, but it's actually pitiful to see you launch such a futile campaign."

"You may keep your pity to yourself!" Vanessa snapped.

But Olga continued as if Vanessa had never spoken: "Trent will never marry you, because Trent will never marry anyone. Oh, he probably deludes himself about that—and possibly he has deluded you as well. But I've known him all my life. He's completely independent and self-sufficient. Once he's had all he wants of a woman, Trent always finds a reason to reject her. He thought Helene was too demanding and didn't adjust well to the island. He thought I was too plain and—"

"Wait a minute, Olga," Vanessa interrupted. "Are you telling me that you and Trent had an affair?"

Olga's white eyebrows rose. "You mean you didn't know?"

Vanessa looked back at Olga skeptically. She knew there had been something between Trent and Olga, but a full-blown affair? Probably it had only happened because available women were scarce during the long winter nights when storms blew and the weather was brutally cold.

Meanwhile, Olga warmed to her topic. "Trent will always find a reason to reject a woman, even a beautiful woman like you. He simply does not want to share his life and his home, Vanessa. I understand that now, although it was hard for me at first. But you should at least be warned so you'll know what is coming."

"Oh, I do so appreciate your kindess in informing me," Vanessa said, her voice making a mockery of the courteous words.

"You are jeering. You don't believe me," Olga countered.

"Now why on earth would I disbelieve you?" Vanessa asked. "Although I'm sure Trent and I will have a good laugh when I tell him what you've said."

Olga looked at Vanessa calmly. "I really do not believe you will tell Trent . . . any more than I would tell him you're a fake."

"You're mistaken," Vanessa said challengingly.

"I don't believe so. Because, if you think about it, you will wonder if what I've said isn't true. Trent is a very handsome and well-educated man. He's also become quite prominent in his field, and if the herbal tonic that helped you should also prove a help to others, he could wind up with a drug patent worth millions! Of course, he is already wealthy, since this island and its assets are quite valuable."

Briefly Olga paused for breath. "Women have always chased Trent, yet he is now thirty-six and still hasn't married. Why not?"

"Well, Olga, I can certainly see you've given this a lot of thought," Vanessa remarked. "Now will you please just leave? Whether you believe it or not, I'm exhausted and want to be alone."

Silently Olga turned and trudged out. Vanessa sank back on the chaise, knowing that in a way Olga had already won. Vanessa would not tell Trent about this scene, not because she wanted to protect Olga but to protect herself in case any of what Olga had said might actually be true.

Vanessa's strength soon returned, and in the next few weeks she began to feel as well as she ever had in her life. Gradually the episode at the lighthouse began to take on the distant, unbelievable quality of a nightmare. Her mirror gave back a welcome image of a pretty woman with smooth, clear skin and glossy, thick hair.

Vanessa had now gained five and a half pounds, and as a tan crept gradually across her face and her body firmed up from exercise, energy and vitality began to course through her. In her newly happy and optimistic frame of mind, it was easy for her to dismiss anything Olga had said. The woman was jealous and unwittingly had played on Vanessa's own fears about Trent. Well, no longer! Vanessa determined to believe Mrs. Pushka's version instead and to hope for the brightest and best future possible for them both.

She arose each morning to fix breakfast with Trent, an operation he usually directed, requesting that Vanessa perform a few menial tasks such as setting the table, slicing oranges or hulling strawberries or blueberries. Then, over their meal, they talked, laughed and made plans for the day.

As Vanessa's recovery continued to progress, Trent returned to his laboratory, where he worked through the morning hours. After he'd gone, Vanessa would rinse and

stack their breakfast dishes, then retire to her room to read
or write letters. Trent had loaned her a couple of books on
herbs and plants, written specifically for the layman, and
Vanessa especially enjoyed learning about various species
Trent raised and studied. When she met him for lunch she
usually had enough questions to last through their meal.

Mrs. Pushka had seemingly recovered as well, although
Trent warned Vanessa that, because of the old woman's advanced age, her total recovery was too much to expect. At
least Mrs. Pushka had finally agreed to take life easier. She
allowed Trent to hire a cleaning woman, who came over
once a week from Catt Island, and although Mrs. Pushka
constantly found fault with the maid's cleaning techniques
and results, she did so out of earshot of the woman. Apparently Mrs. Pushka was resigned to the fact that her own
days of hard work were over.

Shortly before noon each day Mrs. Pushka arrived at the
main house, and she and Vanessa fixed a casual lunch. Trent
returned to eat between twelve-thirty and one. Then, while
Vanessa rested—which was Trent's idea, not hers—he returned to his office briefly to read his mail and dictate re-
plies to letters. Then, like a kid happily released from
school, Trent would be back at the house by two-thirty or
three, and he and Vanessa would set out on whatever excursion took their fancy.

Sometimes they cruised out into Lake Superior, visiting
various deserted islands nearby where Trent would show
Vanessa a waterfall or natural caves formed from limestone
cliffs. But mostly they bicycled over various parts of Davidson Island, then struck off on long, challenging hikes.

"How very boring," Clark drawled when his sister related some of their outings; Clark now phoned Vanessa
regularly every Sunday afternoon, but this particular crack
prompted her to respond furiously.

"You're a clod, Clark!" Vanessa cried, for she thoroughly enjoyed her hikes with Trent.

Trent was constantly pointing out things to her that she would otherwise have missed, Vanessa thought one sunny day as they clambered up a particularly steep trail. Trails springy with pine needles and damp moss frequently led past beaver ponds, and glades were often purpled with wild iris and orchids if one knew where to look. Other flowers peeped from beneath underbrush while ice-age plants grew by fallen logs. Pits deep in blueberry thickets marked where ancient Indians had mined native copper long ago with fire and hammerstone.

"I've never seen an Indian on any of these islands, Trent. What tribe were they, and what happened to make them leave?" Vanessa panted, having motioned to him to stop so she could pause and catch her breath.

"Supposedly they were Chippewa," Trent replied. "Anthropologists think they lived on most of the Prophet Islands. As to what happened to make them leave, that's a grim, bloodthirsty legend I'm not sure you want to hear."

"I *adore* grim, bloodthirsty legends," Vanessa shot back.

Trent laughed. "Okay. Apparently they lived here for generations, tending their nets and harvesting corn, squash and beans from vast gardens. But then a famine struck, and the Indians were forced to practice cannibalism until, as the legends say, the spirits of the dead began to walk at night and globes of fire supposedly danced high above the marshes. Believing the islands were cursed, the frightened Indians ran away."

"Oh, I've heard lots worse stories than that," Vanessa scoffed. "Anyway, cannibalism and various penalties for it are themes that recur in the legends of many cultures."

Trent threw her a startled look, and Vanessa almost laughed at his expression. "Well, I do know a few things, Trent Davidson," she chided him.

"Sure. Anybody who asks as many questions as you do is bound to learn a little," Trent agreed teasingly, and Vanessa stuck out her tongue at him.

Trent pointed out signs of long-ago glaciers that had scoured the islands eons before, and he showed Vanessa old fire lines where the forests had once been ablaze.

"What started the fires?" Vanessa asked, her incessant curiosity getting the better of her, as usual.

"Lightning," Trent replied, extending a hand to help Vanessa ford a small stream.

"I know lightning causes fires in the Pacific Northwest and Canada," she remarked, frowning a little as cold water splashed onto her leg. "I heard about it when Clark, my folks and I were in Montana. In fact, I nearly drove our guide crazy asking questions—"

"Hard to imagine," Trent said dryly.

"Oh, gosh, I guess I'm driving you crazy, too!" Vanessa wailed and, unaided, leaped a stream that was virtually a twin to the previous one.

"Never fear," Trent answered encouragingly. "Since you're obviously bound and determined to wind up the best-educated woman in America, who am I to stand in your way? Anyway, there are still some virgin white pines left in various areas of Michigan, but most of the forest here covers previous burns. Nature tends to obliterate mistakes, and man's scratchings, too, if given the chance."

"Good for Mother Nature," said Vanessa as she bent down to pluck a violet. "What else did she obliterate?"

"Scars left by lumberjacks," Trent answered promptly. "They cut off all the truly big timber, but today it scarcely shows. Now the forests are covered over with a second lush growth of mixed hardwoods and pines—and the granite quarries that once provided the brownstone fronts for New York City's buildings are overgrown and forgotten, too."

"Gives one pause, doesn't it?" said Vanessa, starting up a hillside behind Trent. "If you were to leave, this whole island would be wild and overgrown in a generation or two."

Trent nodded his agreement. "See, you've learned a few more things today. By the time the summer is over, you'll probably know as much about Michigan as anyone." His discourse on Vanessa's educational potential ended abruptly when something new caught his eye. "Oh, look—"

As Vanessa clambered along gamely after Trent, she gave no hint of the fear stirring inside of her. What exactly had Trent said? *When the summer's over?* But what then? Vanessa wondered. Trent had spoken as if he didn't plan on having her around after that. Or was she just being too sensitive and too quick to infer the worst? Vanessa wondered.

Ever since that terrible episode in the lighthouse, Trent had scrupulously avoided giving her anything but the most casual of kisses, and Vanessa was definitely yearning for more. Even at night, after he'd massaged the wintergreen lotion into her arm, his kiss was always brisk and light before he almost bolted from her room.

Damn Olga, anyway! Vanessa thought almost violently as she continued scrambling along after Trent, Boots a nudging presence at her heels. She knew that having had her own fears confirmed by Olga—fears that Trent really was a wholly confirmed bachelor—was what frightened her now.

She caught up with Trent as he reached the shoreline of Lake Superior, which was restless and pounding today. There Trent pointed out various colored pebbles along the shore and told Vanessa that she might even find semiprecious greenstones if she was willing to wade out into the lake and sift through the sand.

Vanessa, of course, had to try it, but when an hour's hunt yielded nothing except a chill she felt all the way to the knees, she declared that she would leave the greenstones for others to find.

Slowly they rode back to the house on their bicycles. One more day's adventures had ended. How rapidly the days flew by, Vanessa thought, and apprehension gripped her once again.

In just a few weeks the summer would be over. Fortunately she still had a trick or two up her sleeve, but the item most urgent on Vanessa's private agenda was getting Trent to make love to her.

A prospect that didn't promise to be easy, considering the way they now spent their nights.

Chapter Eight

Evening activities had become as varied as the days were routine. Vanessa never knew exactly what Trent was likely to spring on her, except that she probably wouldn't be thrilled. No longer did she feel that keen edge of excitement and anticipation as she showered, shampooed and dressed in clean clothes.

Usually, in the evenings, Mrs. Pushka was allowed to fix a fairly elaborate dinner of the sort she dearly loved to serve, and Vanessa and Trent would eat a gratifying amount, their appetites whetted by all the exercise and fresh air.

Then, following dinner, Vanessa and Trent might stroll down to the dock, pausing at the bridge that spanned the merry little stream. Vanessa would usually comment on various flowers that were newly appeared while Trent made mental notes of what next to request from the landscaping team. But quiet, uneventful nights spent at home grew increasingly rare.

As word spread through the insular island community that Trent Davidson had a summer visitor, the invitations began to pour in. And now Trent rarely declined a single one, Vanessa thought in annoyance. Oh, sure, she enjoyed herself most of the time. The Fourth of July party was fun, and she and Trent had square danced at the Tabors' place on Thorn Island until their feet were tired.

Then there were barbecues held in various backyards, as well as porch parties, patio parties and beach parties. There was a "burn the mortgage" party, as well as various "surprise" parties at which the recipients were rarely surprised. Privately Vanessa thought the partying had gone quite far enough on the night when she found herself staring into the hostile eyes of the cranky four-year-old Rhys Evans, Jr., who didn't appreciate the fact that his birthday party included strange adults. Nor did Vanessa exactly appreciate that young Rhys's father, the island doctor, kept her under close scrutiny all night and asked her far too many questions about how she felt.

But when Vanessa prevailed on Trent to decline a few invitations, he responded by becoming a gracious host himself. Sally Hedlung's sixty-fifth birthday was approaching, and nothing would do but that Trent see her properly honored. Of course, Trent and Sally had been friends for a long time, Vanessa thought grudgingly as she set places at the long picnic table that Trent had put up in the front yard. Nor was it Sally's fault if her daughter Olga insisted on being so cold. At least Sally's other daughters, Kristen and Karen, were nicer. Still, Vanessa found the entire evening difficult. Everyone was so polite to everyone else that it was all quite a strain and left her with a headache.

She enjoyed the visits of Peg and Paul Johnson with their sturdy young son considerably more, yet Vanessa still felt rather embarrassed in their presence. The Johnsons had seen her at her worst—terrified, cowering…shrieking. Of course, Trent had seen her that way, too, but he had been so understanding about it all that Vanessa had long since ceased to feel embarrassed with him.

If Trent and Vanessa did happen to find themselves with a rare quiet evening alone, Trent always had plenty of other devices to keep them at arm's length. He often challenged Vanessa to a game of Monopoly, using a set that dated from his boyhood, and sometimes he proposed Scrabble. Although Trent pretended to love Scrabble, Vanessa simply didn't believe him; he was an erratic speller, which surprised her, and consequently a lousy player, so she always won.

If she did decline to play some silly game, then Trent always suggested dropping a videocassette into the VCR. For a while Vanessa was patient with that, because she'd always liked movies, and Trent had recently joined a video club and acquired some really good older films with an emphasis on musicals and westerns. So Vanessa obediently watched *The Sound of Music* and *Funny Girl*, as well as *True Grit* and *Butch Cassidy and the Sundance Kid*. But then came a "bonus offering" from the video club that Trent had not ordered.

"No way!" said Vanessa emphatically. "Absolutely no way am I going to watch *The Texas Chainsaw Massacre*!"

"This is on its way to becoming a cult flick," Trent protested. "Besides, I thought you said you adored grim, bloodthirsty yarns."

"A bloodthirsty *legend* can be retold with subtlety and finesse," Vanessa said, flashing her eyes at him indignantly. "But there's certainly nothing edifying about watching a cinema bloodbath!"

"Sorry. But I fail to see the distinctions that elevate legendary Indian cannibalism over the contemporary fictional kind." He folded his arms across his chest. "You'll have to enlighten me."

Vanessa could tell Trent was teasing her by that revealing glint in his eyes—and by the fact that the corners of his mouth turned up ever so slightly. "You go right ahead and watch here in the family room," she offered sweetly. "I'll just get a book and read in Clarissa's formal Victorian living room."

"That room? With all that ghastly gingerbread and Clarissa's horrible horsehide? Boy, talk about grim!" he said mockingly as Vanessa went up the stairs for a novel she'd been picking up and putting down for several weeks.

She came down again, the book tucked under her arm, to find Trent sitting before a silent TV set. "What, no guts and gore?" Vanessa asked, raising her eyebrows in inquiry. "No Leatherface—or whatever his name is?"

"I guess I'm more squeamish than I thought," Trent said, laughing up at her.

It made Vanessa's heart skip just to look at him. With his thick black hair tumbling over his forehead and his twinkling navy eyes, which exactly matched the navy knit shirt he wore belted inside clean jeans, Trent made Vanessa's breath catch. His raw strength and rippling muscles weren't off-putting when coupled with the magnetism of male grace and beauty. To Vanessa he seemed to radiate the very essence of virile masculinity. Dark hair dusted his strong arms and the backs of his long, wonderful, slightly rough hands. She could see more dark hair in the vee opening of his knit shirt. His eyebrows were long and heavy, his eyelashes thick and black but too stubby to belong to a woman.

Longing and wonder, hunger and fire all knotted together in the pit of her stomach.

"I think I'll sit in the porch swing instead," Vanessa said, her eyes meeting Trent's evenly, although her voice sounded nervous to her own ears. "Want to come join me?"

It was a challenge—as well as an invitation. Trent knew it as well as Vanessa did. His eyes darkened, the expression in them one of significance as well as concern. But he replied mildly. "You won't be able to read on the porch. Too dark."

"Oh!" Vanessa's hands balled up in frustration. "Then maybe I'll just sit out there and wish I wasn't all by myself. I mean...oh, what the hell, Trent? A person's got to try something! Otherwise you just go creeping through life like a meek little mouse!"

She knew she'd said enough. Actually, she'd probably said far too much. Knowing when to shut up isn't exactly one of my greatest talents, Vanessa thought glumly, letting the screen door bang shut behind her.

The night air on the porch felt cooler than she remembered. The swing seemed wider. Of course, she'd always had company when she'd sat out here before. Defiantly Vanessa rocked the swing back and forth with a forward kick of her foot. Meanwhile the one she wanted to be kicking sat alone in the family room before a silent TV set.

"Wimp!" she accused Trent under her breath.

The screen door opened, and she saw his long shadow outlined there. Her breath caught in her throat. It was always this way. Just about the time she thought Trent would surely fail her, he came through like the trouper she knew he really was.

His body followed his shadow out onto the porch. "You know, creeping around like a meek little mouse has never exactly been my style," he contradicted, his voice quiet.

"I know, Trent," Vanessa replied, and now she was the meek one, reminded suddenly of all the things he did for her every day. She knew she'd had a lot of gall to criticize him.

"Sometimes people get...uh, bound by promises." Trent dropped down beside her as he finished the sentence.

"Maybe they made the wrong promises to the wrong people," she said huskily, and felt yearning like liquid fire in her veins. Instinctively Vanessa's hand crept out to touch Trent's arm.

She felt a little tremor run through its rock-hard strength. Did she actually affect him that much, just with a touch of her hand? she wondered.

Then his arm moved quickly, firmly around her shoulder, and the next thing Vanessa knew she was nestled over his heart, exactly where she wanted to be.

"You know, I would never forgive myself if I hurt you in any way," Trent said unsteadily, and she felt his warm lips graze her forehead.

"But you wouldn't hurt me. You couldn't!" Vanessa protested, turning so that he could kiss her properly.

He did, at long last, ending several weeks of torment for them both. His lips burned on Vanessa's, yet for all their blazing hotness they were soft, too, setting her body to an aroused tingling. Oh, his hands felt so wonderful and he smelled so good and she had missed him so much! His kiss awakened her, reminded her again of that first kiss they'd shared, at the ferry landing. She hadn't known even a touch of fear in that perfect moment. She hadn't known the dread of disappointment or the driving concern for self-preservation. She had only known ecstasy. Perfection. And rediscovery of the one person she'd always known, deep in her heart, was the only one for her.

Slowly Trent raised his head. Vanessa wondered if his eyes would hold that hazy look of passion she'd seen before, but it was too dark out here on the porch for her to tell. She snuggled up against him, finding his touch irresistible.

Trent's hold on her arms loosened slightly, but only so his hands could glide over her skin, moving up and down her arms even as his tongue found curves and hollows to caress along her neck and throat. His touch was so warm! Vanessa's whole body came alive with fire. Internal flames began to lick at her, and she swayed closer to Trent, wanting more than just the feel of his hands.

"Vanessa." It was a sigh of helplessness from a man completely unused to feeling helpless. He stopped stroking her arms and pulled her taut against him. She clung all the tighter, wanting never to stray far from these arms again. As if driven by the same frantic hunger, Trent's lips brushed her eyes, her cheeks, her ears. His mouth caressed hers more lightly now, but his kisses only fueled her own hunger with impatience and need. Greedily Vanessa clung to Trent's lips, pressing back fervently with her own. She had dreamed over and over of Trent's ecstatic kisses, wanting them, needing them as much as she needed air to breathe. Her lips parted invitingly for him and his tongue slipped over them.

Abruptly he drew back. "No," he said hoarsely.

No? Vanessa wanted to yell in frustration. She wanted to beat on his chest, kick him in the shins and then kiss him into total submission—but she knew better than to try any of those things.

Instead she gave a low, slow laugh, and the throaty sound hung in the air.

"You little devil," Trent growled in frustration. "You knew just how badly I've been wanting to kiss you and hold you."

"I'd hoped," Vanessa replied softly. "I knew how badly I wanted you to."

"Whatever am I going to do with you, Vanessa?" Trent asked breathlessly, springing up out of the swing.

"Oh, I have a few ideas." *Make love to me. Marry me. Keep me here with you forever and ever!* Yes, those would do nicely for starters. Later she would want babies, too— and maybe some kind of work to occupy her part-time, although Vanessa hadn't given much thought to a career in several years. The struggle to simply get well had consumed her time and thoughts.

"C'mon, let's go for a walk," Trent said, tugging her up out of the swing.

"We did that bit this afternoon, remember?" she reminded him laughingly. "Frankly, I'm all tuckered out from walking."

"Come on!" he insisted. "No arguments. We're going down to the dock where I just may throw myself in to cool off. But I'm not letting you trip me into bed, lady, however much I might enjoy the experience."

"Shy!" she said accusingly. "Oh, Lord, why do you modern men always have to be so *shy*?"

But she wasn't entirely displeased, either, with tonight's developments. At least she'd gotten Trent to stop thinking of her as either a poor little sick girl or a basket case. He had just been adequately reminded that she was a very desirable woman instead.

"Tell me more about your parents," Vanessa said to Trent the following afternoon.

"My parents? What do you want to know about them?" Trent asked in surprise.

"Anything! Where they came from. How they met. That sort of thing," Vanessa explained, gingerly lowering a bare toe down into the deep, crystalline waters of Lake Superior.

Today they'd chosen to walk along the beach, not on the island's gentle sheltered side, which was washed by small waves, but here on the opposite shore, where the water was deep and cold. They had sprawled on brownstone rocks that were well hollowed and chewed from the great storms that had swept over them in the past.

"Well, my father grew up in Lansing," Trent explained. "He was a farm boy, so he was familiar with plants and herbs from childhood. In high school he took a botany course or two, but after he graduated he had to go to work. All the children in his family had to become self-supporting at an early age."

"I see." Vanessa listened with interest while she drew her foot up out of the lake and gave a little shiver. Cold enough to freeze your toes off, she thought.

"So Dad went to Detroit to work in one of the auto factories," Trent continued. "But he always hated cities. Hated being on an assembly line and closed up in a building all day.

He told me once that the whole ten years he worked in Detroit he felt like he was in prison."

"Ten years! That's a long time to be unhappy," Vanessa exclaimed.

"Well, he wasn't just sitting around stewing." Trent laughed. "Dad saved every cent he could and invested his money conservatively. He went to night school and acquired several college degrees. He also spent a lot of time with his hobby, growing herbs in window boxes and in the backyard of the boarding house where he lived. He was already beginning to concoct various commercial herbal preparations when he met and married Clarissa. She had some money of her own—not a lot, but after she and Dad pooled their nest eggs, they started investigating places to buy. They had both enjoyed vacations here in the Upper Peninsula, so when they found this island they moved up here. The previous owner had gone broke trying to mine copper, and he was glad to get rid of the place. Of course, the amount Dad paid for the island sounds ludicrous today."

"Do you think your dad really loved Clarissa?" Vanessa asked, her romantic nature making her more concerned with love than money.

Trent hesitated. "I think Dad *liked* Clarissa. They seem to have lived in a pleasant state of domestic tranquillity until she died from cancer. But I think the only woman he ever really loved was my mother... Tracy."

"I've gradually sifted through all the things in her trunk," said Vanessa with a little smile.

"Oh, so that's what you do in the afternoons when you're supposed to be napping," Trent teased. His face had tanned gradually from all their afternoons in the sun, and Vanessa approved his new bronzed hue. She had acquired only a light tan and a spattering of freckles.

"Sometimes I've skipped a nap when I haven't felt sleepy," Vanessa admitted. "Anyway, Tracy's trunk was

fascinating. Binoculars and boots. Jodhpurs and slacks and
a pair of bright *red* jeans. A couple of crinoline petticoats.
Dresses with full skirts and tight, low-cut bodices. Thick
botany texts, all well thumbed and underlined—''

"Yes, Tracy was a learned botanist." Abruptly Trent
laughed. "I wonder what got the old boy interested, all her
book learning or those bright red jeans?"

"I'm putting my money on her baby-blue dress with the
tight, low-cut front," Vanessa said wisely. "It looks innocent, but must have shown off a hint of cleavage."

"Is that an expert opinion?" Trent teased; then his face
sobered. "Or is that really the way a woman catches an older
husband?"

"Well, I certainly didn't flaunt my cleavage at Bailey,"
Vanessa retorted, wondering a little at Trent's suddenly
rather grim expression. Was it possible he could be *jealous*
of Bailey? Hastily she asked, "How much older was your
dad than Tracy?"

"Thirty years. He was fifty-eight when they met." Trent
stared off at the horizon. "It still seems unbelievable to me
that they were so happy. With such an age difference, I've
often wondered if their marriage could possibly have
lasted."

Maybe. Maybe not, thought Vanessa. Both pity and guilt
had kept her tied to Bailey; he'd been so crazy about her and
so terrified of growing old and being all alone. Had he ever
known that she hadn't been able to truly love or want him?

Aloud she asked Trent, "How did your parents happen
to meet?"

"Well, by that time my father had acquired quite a rep-
utation for his extensive knowledge of herbs. His neighbors
called him the 'medicine man' because of all his various
remedies. Tracy was from Ohio but finishing her master's
degree at Auburn in the south. That's where she first heard
of John Davidson. So she wrote him and asked if she could
come confer with him on her master's thesis. Apparently she

posed enough interesting questions in her letter that Dad invited her here for the summer. Personally, I suspect he was probably lonely. But here's the real kicker: Dad didn't dream she was a woman! He thought of Tracy as a man's name.''

"Uh-oh." Vanessa laughed and unconsciously dropped her hand down on Trent's arm. After a moment his hand moved up to cover hers, and his warmth radiated through her palm. "Tracy's arrival here must have been quite a scene!''

"Well, apparently they found out pretty fast that neither was exactly a conventional person," Trent went on, "and their mutual interest in herbs and love of nature seems to have superseded everything else. So Tracy managed to scandalize the nearby community twice. First by staying all alone in the house with a man to whom she wasn't married..."

"Oh, yes, those were quite traditional times," Vanessa noted, letting her fingers curl around Trent's hand.

His answering squeeze told her he was as aware of her touch as she was of his. "...and secondly by marrying Dad less than three months later. Naturally everyone believed the marriage was doomed. Dad had always seemed rather dour, while Tracy was lively and high-spirited. Folks were sure her elderly husband would soon become a bore..."

Vanessa nodded feelingly.

"...or else they predicted that Tracy would grow to hate the loneliness of the island and the long cold winters when she'd be stranded here," Trent continued. "Apparently everyone had a reason for why it couldn't last. But, according to Mrs. Pushka, Tracy and the medicine man were blissfully happy right up until that last day, when Tracy boarded the ferry that sank on its return trip."

"I wish I could have known your parents," Vanessa mused.

"It's safe to say they were an unusual couple." Trent laughed, then held out their linked hands to catch a flash of cooling spray that came in along with a wave.

Abruptly he sobered again. Attuned as Vanessa was to him, she noticed immediately. "You know the winters up here can get pretty long and dismal," he said quietly. "Life on this island sure isn't all picnics and flowers and basking on rocks in the sun!"

"I know," Vanessa assured him. Hadn't Trent written her all about the frigid winters years and years ago?

"'Cabin fever' isn't just a trite and overworked phrase," he went on warningly. "Even for someone like me, some-one who's used to the ice and snow and the months of being cooped up, I've still found I can go a little wacko at times."

Trent's mouth tightened. He looked positively grim, Va-nessa thought, and her heart gave a little warning knock against her rib cage. What sort of memory could have brought such a look to Trent's face? But before she could wonder longer or think of something to say to ease his sud-den tenseness, he resumed talking. Gradually his voice re-turned to normal as he discussed the dark, gray, rainy days that led into winter's storms. Then he described the frigid, bone-chilling wind that whipped the surface of Lake Supe-rior and lashed at these very rocks. Then traffic on the Great Lakes was at a virtual standstill until the ice began to thaw with spring, creaking and groaning like the awakening of a fierce monster.

Vanessa heard Trent out in perfect equanimity. Years ago she had considered all of this and had read quite exten-sively on the weather patterns of the Great Lakes. Even then she had known that Trent was the only man she wanted to be snowed in with, and where he was concerned, nothing in her heart ever changed.

Was Vanessa even listening to him at all? Trent won-dered. The winters here in northern Michigan were quite a serious matter, but he'd already discovered that Vanessa didn't always take things seriously.

It was a small flaw, but, he realized uncomfortably, it troubled him nevertheless. Apparently Vanessa had the same sort of bubbly enthusiasm and lively spirit that had characterized his own mother. But did she also have his mother's maturity? When Tracy Trent Davidson had married an older man who lived on a storm-swept island, she had apparently known exactly what she was getting into. But did Vanessa—who was Southern-born and had always been protected and indulged by doting older men—really have the least idea?

The concern about his beloved worried Trent and kept him waffling on the subject of marriage. Once again his mind and his heart were at war. He loved Vanessa as he'd never loved any other woman. Consequently he was willing to accept the various risks involved in wedlock to her. In fact, Trent thought about marriage with Vanessa more all the time. But that was his heart talking.

His mind, accustomed to cold scientific thought, told him quite a different story. His mind said that emotionally Vanessa was not ready for a mature marriage between equals. Just look at her, squealing like a kid as she held out her feet to the cooling spray striking the rocks. She wore shorts and a halter that outlined every detail of her body and displayed enough of her smooth bare skin to definitely incite any man not made of stone.

"She's a beautiful doll..." In his mind Trent heard Olga's knowing voice once again. No, Vanessa was not a doll, but she was still a lovely girl. She was charming and delightful, but she had never entirely grown up.

That was certainly evident by the way she gazed at him as if he were God Almighty. Even when she quarreled with, contradicted or cajoled him, that worshipful look never quite left her eyes.

Many men would find it a heady experience, Trent knew, being the subject of such idolatry. And he, too, often felt tempted to accept it, enjoy it. But that wouldn't be fair to either of them.

Trent knew he would only be sure Vanessa had fully matured when the worshipful glow was gone from her eyes.

Which raised another, especially poignant question: would Vanessa love him then?

"Why?" Vanessa demanded indignantly later that night. They had exchanged a few flaming kisses, and Trent's hand had gradually stolen beneath her sweater, teasing her soft breasts in a little uninhibited petting. But now he drew away from her resolutely and walked over to stand on the edge of the porch.

"Because," he muttered, although Vanessa could hear the indrawn sound of his ragged breathing.

"Because?" she repeated, her voice growing increasingly irate. "What the hell sort of answer is 'because?'"

"Because quite recently you were very ill, and I don't want to do anything that might harm you, Vanessa. I'd never forgive myself if I did."

How pious he sounded! "You'd make a marvelous candidate for sainthood, Trent," Vanessa snapped, flaring into outright wrath. "Why, that dumb crack alone ought to win you a halo!"

She'd forgotten that Trent could exhibit quite a temper, too. His promptly ignited with hot words. "Vanessa, if you think for one minute that I enjoy denying myself, frustrating myself—"

"Me, too, fella. You haven't exactly been sitting here in the dark kissing yourself!" She paused for a breath that only fueled her anger. "Good Lord, Trent, I'm beginning to wonder if you don't have more problems than Bailey did!"

Vanessa spoke rashly, before she'd thought, and her slur made Trent seethe with quiet fury. Although she had never *felt* a glare before, she could definitely feel this one. Maybe she had been insulting, she thought angrily, but he deserved it!

When he continued to remain silent and brooding, Vanessa wondered if he was just digesting her words, or if he was worried she might discuss her marriage and didn't want to hear the particular details.

"Vanessa..." His voice was calmer, quieter. "You know I promised to keep my hands off you."

He'd mentioned that promise before, but she hadn't pursued the subject then. Now she came soaring out of the swing and charged over to Trent. The next thing she knew, Vanessa was stabbing him in the chest with a taut, furious finger. "Just who issued the chastity orders for me, I'd like to know? Was it Clark or Dr. Z.? Oh, don't tell me some stupid, awkward lie! It must have been that mouthy big brother of mine, though I haven't exactly seen him denying *himself*, now or ever!"

"Vanessa..." Trent's voice emerged midway between placating and firm. "Neither Clark nor I want you to be harmed—"

"I wasn't harmed by making love, for God's sake! I was injured in a plane wreck!" she cried.

"Okay, maybe I'm being overly careful. But you certainly don't want to have another recall episode," he pointed out.

"Sex doesn't trigger those," Vanessa hissed, totally exasperated with Trent, Clark and all men with their overly solicitous and patronizing attitudes. "What triggers the recall episodes is being in small, confined, bright white places. Anyway, I'm never *ever* going to have another one as long as I live—"

"That's wonderful," Trent said sincerely. "I hope it proves true."

"Well, you know what I think you're proving, Trent Davidson? How to be an absolute clod! Oh, you make me mad enough to pack my bags and go home tomorrow!" She stormed toward the door, but already she was regretting her stupid threat. Fortunately, Trent spoke in time to stop her.

"If that's what you want to do, Nessie," he said heavily, his voice fairly throbbing with sadness.

Momentarily Vanessa heard only her hated nickname. *"Don't call me Nessie!"* she shrieked.

"I'm sorry. Sorry I've hurt your feelings. Sorry I've made you mad."

Vanessa stopped. The sadness she heard reverberating in Trent's voice was like a pin pricking the balloon of her anger. Lord, what was happening to her? And what was she doing to him? But didn't Trent understand that she, who had arrived here still so fearful of lovemaking, was now eager for his? That between the warmth of his company, with his vigorous, healthy body rarely more than arm's length away, and the warmth of his affection and compassion, she'd now grown to want him in a wholly new and exciting way?

Their kisses, which had always been heated, had grown sizzling, and emboldened by their blaze, the last of Vanessa's fears had gradually dropped away. When Trent actually caressed her, when he stroked her breasts, he amazed Vanessa with the fever-pitch hunger he awakened inside of her.

She knew that, unwittingly, Trent was now denying her a victory, a victory she needed badly to feel whole and complete, alive and well. But he didn't seem able to understand and appreciate that.

Still and all, Vanessa loved him much too much to go storming back to Georgia in a huff. Why, when that somber note resounded in his voice she felt as though a knife was cruelly slicing off a piece of her heart.

"Oh, Trent, I'm sorry, too," she sighed, wanting to see an end to their argument. Reluctantly Vanessa decided to settle for peace. "I don't want to yell and be mean and—and I sure don't want to go back home to Atlanta!"

"That's okay." She saw obvious relief cross Trent's face. He came several steps closer, but he didn't touch her; Vanessa wondered if that was because he didn't really trust himself to. "It's been a long day, darling," he said after a moment. "Why don't you go get ready for bed? I'll be along shortly to massage your arm."

He'd called her "darling" once before. But since that had been under extreme stress, when Trent was almost visibly fearing that she was a permanent candidate for a well-padded cell, Vanessa hadn't let herself put much credence in the endearment. But this "darling" was spoken so honestly and spontaneously that it brought her close to tears.

It also sparked an answering honesty in Vanessa. "You don't have to rub my arm anymore, Trent," she sighed. "It quit hurting completely about a week ago." Her nose started to run, and she gave a loud, unromantic sniff. "So I guess you've cured me. Again . . . you've done it again, dammit!"

She knew she would miss the familiar bedtime ritual, the comfort of Trent's warm, wonderful hands stroking her skin and, always, their good-night kiss.

Trent laughed aloud in delight. "Well, no wonder you've been feeling so frisky if you're all healed up," he said, his voice holding its familiar teasing note. "But if you don't mind, I think I'd like to keep on treating that arm. Just call it preventive medicine."

So he didn't want to give up the ritual or their good-night kiss, either. Suddenly Vanessa felt a lot better.

Later, as he was gently massaging her arm, Trent introduced a new topic. "Hey, did I happen to mention that a couple of visiting scientists are coming from the mainland on Friday?"

"No, you didn't," Vanessa replied carefully, her voice casual. "But I heard you tell Mrs. Pushka to have a pot of coffee and a plate of sandwiches made, since they'd probably stay for lunch." Actually, it had made Vanessa feel terrible to think she'd been excluded from the gathering. Although she'd tried to psych herself into thinking that Trent simply didn't want her intruding on a work-related matter, still, not being included for lunch seemed quite something else.

"Oh. Well, I'd certainly meant to tell you. My main concern has been with Olga and the lab crew, making sure they had everything set up for Drs. Landry and Garrett." Trent spoke so frankly and honestly that Vanessa believed him. "Anyway, you'll probably find both men crashing bores, but please do be my hostess at lunch." Trent flashed Vanessa a smile that made her heart turn over. "You'll definitely brighten our meal."

Chapter Nine

Rarely had Trent been quite so surprised. For the past five years he'd had regular visits from the two scientists who'd arrived today. Both Dr. Landry and Dr. Garrett were specialists in herbal medicine—pharmacognosists like Trent—so their common work was naturally the topic of the day as well as their reason for coming to Davidson Island.

Food for them had always been minimal and its service strictly utilitarian. No serious researcher liked a heavy noon meal, and usually the visitors and Trent talked shop nonstop and were scarcely aware of what they put in their mouths for lunch.

But not today. With a surge of surprise and delight, Trent saw that his picnic table had been moved onto the front porch, covered with a long, snowy cloth that he didn't remember having ever seen before and set with casual but attractive dishes rather than paper plates. Today there were cloth napkins in a bright color to match the dishes and better-than-everyday silverware set at each place. Tall goblets had replaced the ordinary glasses that usually serviced Trent's table.

But the real eye-catcher was the centerpiece: a large straw basket brimming with an amazing assortment of fresh flowers and herbs in bloom.

"Well, my goodness!" exclaimed Dr. Landry.

"Doesn't everything look nice," echoed Dr. Garrett. "And how pleasant to sit here and see Lake Superior while we eat."

"Perfectly wonderful day for it," Dr. Landry agreed. "Doesn't lunch look good?"

Trent didn't have to ask who had wrought this miracle, but he also couldn't help staring at Vanessa in some astonishment. He'd feared this occasion might be a bit much for her, and here she was not only greeting two middle-aged scientists with perfect aplomb, but she'd absolutely transformed their usual luncheon setting as well.

When had she found time to do all this? Trent wondered, staring around curiously at fat red tomatoes stuffed with chicken salad and set on a bed of lettuce, fresh from Trent's own garden. A side dish featured crisp cucumber slices floating in thick yogurt.

There was a wide assortment of cold cuts and various cheeses, a variety of crackers, and three kinds of bread—light, black and wheat—were attractively displayed along with appropriate condiments and relishes. But Trent knew immediately that a basket of fluffy hot rolls would prove irresistible.

On a smaller table nearby Trent saw dessert, a large bowl of fresh fruit garnished with coconut and studded with fat, juicy strawberries, as well as a light, high, delectable-looking lemon soufflé.

Loveliest of all was the hostess herself. Vanessa wore a simple peasant blouse, bright with embroidery, and long matching skirt, and she looked cool, poised and beautiful. On closer scrutiny, Trent could see that she wore a modest amount of makeup, and her long dark hair, which usually flew free with the breeze, had today been deftly twisted into an upswept hairdo that was both flattering and sophisticated.

Pride swelled in his breast when he saw how deftly and graciously she moved through the group, making certain that everyone felt welcome, was guided to a chair and received the beverage of his or her choice.

As Vanessa captivated the guests with sweetness and charm, Trent did not dare look at Olga. Earlier the large blond woman had stared at him as though he was crazy when he'd said that Vanessa would be their hostess. But he certainly hadn't dreamed his darling was capable of this sort of one-upmanship.

Actually, she was being especially gracious to Olga, as if sensing that the older woman had found yet another of her previous positions being usurped.

But as they all settled in their chairs and began to eat, Vanessa fell wisely silent, although she kept a careful eye on her guests. Occasionally she started the basket of rolls around again, and once Trent saw her whisper something to his lab assistant, Timothy. It elicited a smile from the young man, who was naturally shy and had been rather obviously uncomfortable when out of his customary lab coat and milieu. What a wonderful gift it is to be able to set someone like Tim at ease, Trent thought.

Instinctively the men and Olga returned to their earlier discussions of various herbal compounds presently being used to treat cancer patients, with the most dramatic recent example, which had produced two leukemia drugs, coming from a decorative plant called the rosy periwinkle. A quarter hour later they were all still talking animatedly over the dessert and coffee that Vanessa had so unobtrusively served. Trent glanced up and flashed her an appreciative smile.

As they finished dessert, both visiting scientists began to cajole Trent to install HERBALERT. ''You know, Trent, you're going to be left languishing in the backwaters of pharmacognosy if you don't,'' Dr. Landry warned.

"Also, your information and input is vitally needed,'' Dr. Garrett added. "Both you and your late father worked with plants that many of us know absolutely nothing about, because they're unique to these particular islands.''

Trent heard Vanessa's soft question to Timothy. "Just what is HERBALERT?'' she asked him.

Trent couldn't hear Timothy's reply, but guessed that the young man was defining HERBALERT as a mammoth computerized data base that contained information on thousands of plants growing in every corner of the globe.

Olga immediately came flying to Trent's defense. "We manage to do our work quite well without HERBALERT,'' she asserted. "After all, it is usually you gentlemen who come to visit us, if you've noticed.''

"Of course we've noticed, Ms. Hedlung.'' Dr. Landry's voice was gracious, even slightly apologetic. "All I really meant is that since you're partially computerized anyway, as any modern laboratory is, it should be a simple enough matter and require relatively little new equipment to hook into HERBALERT.''

"Look, Harry—'' Unconsciously Trent used his visitor's first name. "While I'm certainly not averse to updating my system, I just don't have the time or expertise to do it. I've been hard at work for months on an especially promising compound, H-320B—''

"Yes, I've heard a little about that,'' Dr. Landry said, and leaned forward curiously. "I understand it may be of some slight use in treating clinical depression.''

Trent glanced down the length of the table and saw that Vanessa was listening intently to the conversation. "I've found it to have considerably better than 'slight use,''' Trent replied. "But back to the topic of the computer, I've already checked around Catt Island and talked to dozens of other folks who live up here as well. I can't find anyone who knows much about computer programming."

"You may have to hire someone from the mainland," Dr. Garrett suggested.

"Yes, I know." Trent sighed, for he had often considered the various alternatives. "But that presents so many other problems! Accommodations here on the island are limited—and our life has various hazards as well. I found one male programmer who was quite keen on tackling HERBALERT, but he has a wife and four lively children. That meant six people who would need to be housed and fed, not to mention problems of the kids falling into the lake or the old copper mine—"

"Maybe I could help you, Trent."

Vanessa's voice was soft and low. Trent stared up at her in complete surprise, wondering if possibly she'd learned a word-processing program somewhere and thought that would suffice. Fortunately Vanessa spoke again before Trent could respond.

"When I was in college, I debated a long time between a major in computer science or meteorology," she said. "But while I was making up my mind, I took a lot of computer courses and learned how to write various programs."

Trent hoped his mouth wasn't hanging open in astonishment. Once again he dared not look at Olga.

Old Dr. Landry turned to Vanessa with a smile. "Where did you graduate, my dear?"

"Georgetown University in Washington, D.C.," Vanessa answered quietly.

"What was your final choice of major?" he asked interestedly.

"Oh, meteorology. Computers are useful but all too predictable. Weather, of course, is anything but predictable."

"So you will presume to try to predict it?" Dr. Landry laughed.

Vanessa shrugged her slender shoulders. "I guess I've always liked a challenge."

Trent was stunned by the developments the day had revealed. Vanessa a meteorologist? No wonder she'd brushed off his remarks about the Great Lakes' weather—and, thank God, he hadn't tried to enlighten her!

As he reveled in Vanessa's triumphs that afternoon, the very last thing Trent expected was that he'd be talking long-distance to Dr. Zellar in Atlanta before another twelve hours had passed.

After the visitors had gone, Vanessa seemed to think that Trent was making too much of a fuss, exclaiming over lunch and praising her so effusively. "My goodness, what's a little ol' luncheon?" she said negligently. "But I can tell you that a formal sit-down dinner in Washington, D.C., for thirty guests is a real production that practically has to be choreographed!"

For some reason, Trent had never been able to conceive of Vanessa coordinating an event such as that. Obviously he had underestimated her. Certainly he hadn't dreamed that Vanessa had managed to finish college, another matter over which he apparently exclaimed too much.

"Want to see my diploma, Trent?" Vanessa teased him impudently.

"No. It's just that I never imagined—I mean, after you married Bailey, I guess I thought—"

"That the congressman's little woman would just sit around on her little duff all day?" Although Vanessa spoke lightly, Trent heard the edge in her voice.

"I guess so," he admitted. "The funny thing is I've never thought of myself as being a chauvinist."

"Me either. But, of course, I was conditioned to the 'me Tarzan, you Jane' attitude all my life. Southern men are still about twenty years behind the times! Or at least the ones in my family are. Bailey and Clark both thought my education was sort of amusing. Mother kept wondering why I bothered with classes when I'd 'married well.' But I wanted to graduate for me, so I did.''

''Well, I think it's wonderful,'' Trent said sincerely.

He soon found he'd also underestimated Ms. Ashton when it came to computers. Right after dinner that evening, Trent and Vanessa headed over to his office in the lab. The large personal computer that Vanessa wanted to examine sat on a workstand at the far end of the large room.

''Oh, Trent, this one's a piece of cake,'' Vanessa crooned after he'd demonstrated some of its various features.

He felt his eyebrows shoot up. He'd had hours of struggle and frustration learning to operate the damned thing. ''You think so?'' Trent said skeptically as he moved aside to let Vanessa take over.

Good Lord, she might have been born using one! She input commands with lightning speed, executed changes so fast he couldn't keep up with them and printed out the results while Trent was still trying to figure out exactly what she'd done.

''If I say so myself, I'm a real whiz on PCs,'' Vanessa remarked to Trent's astounded praise.

God, if she was this good at computers, which hadn't been her major, what in the world would she be like in meteorology? he wondered.

''Actually, I hardly know,'' Vanessa admitted reluctantly in answer to Trent's question. ''I've only had three months of actual experience. I worked as a 'weather girl'— and believe me, that's exactly what I got called, too—on a yahoo TV station in Atlanta. Then Bailey got reelected to Congress and headed back to Washington, so I had to make a choice of marriage versus a career. Actually, it was a pretty hard decision—not that I really wanted to stay a TV weather girl, but at the time it looked like I might soon be hired by the national weather service.'' A frown was etched between her brows. "Trent, do you think I chose a too-trivial occupation?"

"God, no!" he said feelingly. "Here in the Great Lakes we need and depend on people like you."

Momentarily Vanessa looked pleased. Then she turned back to the computer, muttering, "Now, just let me try this—"

Trent found himself staring at her rather than the computer screen. Even as he admired Vanessa's delicate features and small, firm chin, he wondered why she hadn't booted Bailey out of her life when she'd had the opportunity. Was it affection? Habit? The prestige of being a congressman's wife? He couldn't really believe it had been love.

"Now show me the sort of stuff that you'd contribute to the HERBALERT program," Vanessa said, obviously feeling at home already with Trent's computer and its present program.

"Okay." Trent pulled out a few files and handed them to her, then watched as Vanessa left the computer workstand and moved over to his comfortable sofa.

Studiously Vanessa zipped through the files, muttering an occasional "Uh-huh" and "Umm", all of which sounded affirmative. Trent sat next to her, inhaling her clean, sweet scent. Soon he was staring at Vanessa longingly.

"None of this should present problems to an experienced programmer, Trent." Vanessa closed the last file firmly, set it aside and looked up at him. Obviously she intercepted his heated look before he could alter the expression on his face.

"Oh, Trent!" she exclaimed, reaching up to offer him a firm, hungry kiss that further unsettled him. Losing control, he swept her into his lap, burying his face in the midnight glory of her hair, which lay loose and soft again, the way he preferred it.

He kissed her longingly, avidly, his tongue thrusting past the sweet, delicate lips and plunging far inside. But rather than startling her or scaring her, his actions drove Vanessa to lock her fingers around his head, holding his mouth fused to hers. Trent felt the tips of her taut, youthful breasts tantalizing his chest, felt the soft, luscious length of her searing through him like fire, leaving his loins aching. For a terrible moment Trent was afraid he might not be able to stop himself from claiming what he wanted so desperately, what Vanessa seemed to be offering him so willingly, longingly, lovingly.

Gritting his teeth, Trent leaned back and closed his eyes. His hands knotted into fists while his deprived body ached relentlessly.

He heard a soft, subdued sob and felt Vanessa sliding off his knees. Then she was gone, his office door shutting quietly behind her.

Trent cursed vehemently. He pounded the arm of the sofa. He called Clark Hamilton a variety of unpleasant names that reflected adversely on his ancestry, damning his brotherly concern and the oath he'd made Trent swear. And all the while, frustration, like bitter bile, kept rising inside Trent. His mind kept replaying that quiet, hopeless sob of Vanessa's. What other choice had he left her but to run away and cry? She had reasoned with him before, had fought with him before, and now she obviously felt herself wholly rejected when he actually wanted her so badly it was tearing him up.

Suddenly Trent found himself bent over his desk, the phone receiver gripped in one sweating palm while he snarled at a hapless telephone operator to find Dr. Rolf Zellar wherever the psychiatrist might be.

Where he was was apparently abed with Mrs. Z. A woman answered sleepily on the third ring; then a long minute or two passed, and Trent could hear her urging Dr. Zellar to wake up. "Some young man," he heard the woman say.

Dr. Zellar came on the line at a full roar. "Do you know what time of night this is?" he demanded.

"I'm sorry, sir," Trent replied politely, and identified himself.

"Is Vanessa unwell?" Dr. Zellar asked apprehensively.

"No. She's fine—very well indeed! It's a...ah...more personal matter between us," Trent stammered. He felt unable to simply blurt out the truth, but apparently truth was exactly what Dr. Zellar wanted.

"Tell me!" he yelled after a few more stammers on Trent's part.

So Trent blurted. He had long wanted to make love to Vanessa, he told Dr. Zellar, and she was certainly willing. But would it damage Vanessa's emotional equilibrium? Could it delay her complete recovery?

"That depends, of course," said Dr. Zellar in a voice that fairly dripped with sarcasm. "Do you plan to beat her and tie her to a tree? Did you have anything dangerous or kinky in mind?"

"Of course not!" Trent said, aghast.

"Then I fail to see the problem," the doctor snapped. "What two consenting adults do is their own damned business. Vanessa has healed physically, and emotionally she's a resilient young woman. She was married for several years, so sex isn't exactly new to her. Now kindly get off this damned phone and let me get some sleep!"

Trent stammered his thanks, which Dr. Zellar ended effectively by simply hanging up. Filled with sudden, buoyant joy, Trent dashed back to the house and flew into action, whistling like a happy idiot while he worked. What a day! he thought as he bustled around the kitchen hunting wineglasses that he knew were hidden in some cabinet. *And what a night to come...*

He carried a tray with two glasses, napkins and a bottle up the stairs, then balanced the tray with one hand while he knocked at Vanessa's door with the other. *Oh, yes, what a night this would be!*

Vanessa had stopped crying by the time she heard Trent's footsteps approach her door—had stopped by sheer effort, because her own tears continued to annoy her. She was fed up with crying, absolutely fed up! And she'd be *hanged* if she would cry any more over a jerk who was all talk and no action.

"Go away, Trent," she called in reply to his knock.

"Open up, Vanessa," he replied, and the new note of resolution in his voice startled her.

Like hell, she thought for a moment. But then she sighed, swallowed her pride and reminded herself that the jerk was, after all, her host. Since he'd been putting her up and feeding her all summer, she could scarcely deny him access in his own house. "Look, Trent, my arm doesn't hurt in the least, and I just want to go to bed," she called.

"Vanessa, open this door right now or I'll kick it in!" he threatened.

Vanessa looked at the door reflectively. It seemed to be sturdily made of heavy wood, and it would probably be a toss-up as to whether Trent broke down the door or broke his foot trying. "Oh, all right, I'm coming," she grumbled, and got off the chaise longue to go open the door. Unfortunately, she also loved the jerk, although she'd certainly been lying here for ten minutes asking herself why.

She opened the door, glared up at Trent and failed to attach significance to the fact that he held a small round tray with a bottle of wine and a couple of glasses.

His smile was tender, the corners of his mouth turned up hopefully. "I've come to make peace."

Despite herself, Vanessa melted—though not without a final grumble. "I'm not supposed to drink alcohol, remember?"

"This is the best nonalcoholic vintage you'll ever taste. It's sparkling grape juice, straight from Davidson's own vineyards. Am I tempting you just a little bit?" he asked.

"Okay," Vanessa sighed, dropping down on the edge of her bed. "Drag up a chair and pour me a shot." She could be a good sport; it might kill her, but she'd try.

The cork popped and the purplish liquid bubbled effusively. Hastily Vanessa thrust first one, then another wineglass beneath the erupting bottle.

"Very good," she said after a wary sip. "Please don't tell me if you actually stomped the grapes with your very own feet."

"Oh, I'm typical of most scientists and much too immaculate for that," Trent replied.

"You're telling *me*?" The bitter comment escaped before Vanessa could censor it, and along with her words came a number of bitter thoughts. She wondered what Helene Rosenni had had that she herself didn't? Or even Olga, for that matter.

Abruptly Trent halted any further thoughts by simply reaching down and hauling Vanessa up into his arms. Briefly she saw his face, tight-lipped with anger at her crack, and as she looked at the grim line of his lips Vanessa wondered how they could be so stern and yet sensual, too. Then she was jerked against Trent with such force that she gasped and the *faux* wine sloshed out over her hand and cascaded down her robe.

"What are you doing?" Vanessa cried. "You've made me spill my—"

"Tough," Trent said unsympathetically, and drew her up so close to him that she felt her back practically bowed.

"Trent, you're hurting me!" Vanessa wailed. "And that grape juice is going to stain your carpet."

"To hell with the carpet!" he said, in so rough a tone that Vanessa gasped again. But his arms loosened a trifle, obviously in response to her pleas, and she no longer felt as i her spine was in danger of being snapped. Then his hands tangled in her hair, forcing her face nearer to his, and suddenly a wild, primitive thrill shot through Vanessa at his strength, his forcefulness, his sudden relentless determination.

"Trent—" she stammered.

"I love you," he said, then stopped her mouth with his own.

How long had she waited to hear Trent say those words? All of her life—or so it seemed to Vanessa in that ecstatic moment. Then her arms were gripping him with all her strength while her mouth parted beneath the heat of his. *I love you, too,* she told him without words. *I always have, Trent. I always will!*

She kissed him in mindless, swift response. She'd wanted him so desperately and for so long! The intimate strokings of his tongue made her respiration and heartbeat accelerate while her palms grew damp. Now she knew the truth: this time Trent wasn't going to stop with kisses.

Even as the old, familiar fear struggled to rise up again within Vanessa, she knew she had asked for this, had begged for this. Now, finally, he was granting her dearest wish, and she would have to accept what happened and trust that it would be different with Trent, as everything was different with him. Trust that the act he performed would be perfect, just as he had made perfect each of their golden days together. She must trust, too, that her own reactions and responses would be unique and special, just because she was sharing this with *him*.

She relaxed, trusting, and felt Trent's hand cradle her chin, tilting it upward to receive more of his kisses. Then Vanessa was lost in the urgent, aching intensity invoked by his warmth and his wonderful manly touch. Briefly his lips left hers, but only to probe a sensitive strip of skin along her neck where he left a trail of kisses so incendiary that they made her whimper.

She heard the soft hiss of a zipper a moment before she felt the stroke of his hands within. *My robe... he's just unzipped my robe,* Vanessa realized. She stood statue-still in Trent's grasp, moving only to press her face into the strong corded neck above her. Greedily she inhaled Trent's smell—his clean skin and hair mingled with a faint herbal fragrance from the plants he'd handled during the day. No phony scents from expensive bottles and potions clung to him. There was only the fresh, natural aroma of rich, fertile earth and any number of wondrous things that grew there.

His hands... oh, what magic his hands wrought wherever they touched her! Slowly Trent peeled back her robe, cupping each of her breasts in his large, warm hands. His thumbs, marvelous male thumbs that were eager and slightly rough in texture, moved over the hardened nubs as Vanessa's nipples thrust up like blossoms for his caress. Gently Trent rolled and fondled them until Vanessa heard herself gasping uncontrollably.

Instantly her breasts were fully taut and ached to press against his flesh without the barrier of his clothes, which now prevented a more intimate contact. Guided by a newly discovered expertise, Vanessa's hands undid the buttons that held together the wall of cloth separating her from Trent. As his own shirt gaped open, she moved close enough to touch him, and the vibrant feel of his skin against hers and the intimate tickling of his dark, silky chest hair against her bare skin were sensual bliss.

She caressed his shoulders with her fingertips, letting her palms glide over the hairs below. Her fingers were almost, yet not quite, scratching him, and Vanessa heard the gratifying sound of Trent's own gasp.

Suddenly he was hurried—and hungry, so hungry for her. His fingers curved under the roundness of one breast, lifting it as his mouth descended to savor its taste. Vanessa caught her breath in a gulp. The delicate tugging of his mouth made her quiver with delightful agony. For a moment she felt dizzy from the longing and heat he was generating in her blood. His hard length pressed against her made clear his need, and her own body clamored for the heady fulfillment that she knew he could give her.

One large, hasty hand swept her robe entirely away. Then she was naked and shivering just for a moment, until Trent caught her tightly against him, his hands warming her first as he stretched her out on the bed. Hastily he finished his own undressing; then he dropped down against her and warmed her with his body.

In the glow of the bedside light, Vanessa watched her own hands glide up Trent's bare arms, saw her fingertips tracing the veins that showed through the surface. She saw her fingers wind through that soft pelt on his chest...and she waited, trusting him.

Gently, so very gently, he began to prepare her by kissing her hands, then turning them over to press his mouth moistly against her palms. Vanessa moaned, and Trent began kissing her body until she arched, weak with longing. Suddenly his mouth was everywhere, hot against her flesh, his tongue teasing and tasting. Silently he used his hands and lips to tell her what she meant to him.

His lips pushed against her navel, exploring it with his tongue, then kissed a path across her stomach while his hands began to explore daringly below.

An avalanche of emotions was unleashed inside Vanessa. She felt pleasure that was indescribable as Trent caressed her with lips and tongue and the light gliding of his fully knowledgeable hands. She felt a new and voluptuous rapture as she writhed beneath him. Vanessa clutched his waist and the back of his head and suddenly cried aloud with passion for the first time in her life.

She never even felt his weight, only his lips, burning and burning on hers until her own were aflame. She didn't know exactly when his hands parted her legs, but suddenly he was close, warm and hard between them. Yet the lovemaking that followed was not fierce but slow, gentle, delicate. Trent gave infinite consideration to Vanessa's feelings and responses—and how could she help but respond to such consummate tenderness?

He was being careful, so careful, as if Vanessa had never made love before, as though she was still an innocent and inexperienced virgin he was claiming as his own, and her body and heart appreciated his care.

"I love you, Trent! Oh, how I love you!" she cried as her excitement began to build, an excitement that went on and on, seemingly without end, yet always spiraling higher and higher still. Then it was upon her, the rapturous glory she had often read about but had never believed in, because it had always been so utterly alien to her experiences.

Only when her own shattering excitement had died slowly away in an afterglow of love and delight, only then did Vanessa feel Trent allow himself the final pleasure of complete culmination.

He gasped her name. "Vanessa?"

"Yes, darling?" She clutched Trent's shoulders with one hand, still holding him close to her, while her other hand rested across his slim buttocks, gently restraining him from leaving her.

"Are you *crying*?" Trent asked in concern.

"Why...yes." The realization sent Vanessa flying up off the pillow to cover Trent's face with grateful kisses. "I guess I am. All happy tears."

"You're sure?" he said dubiously.

"Good Lord, Trent, couldn't you tell?" she demanded almost indignantly; then she heard the warmth of his chuckle.

After a moment he stirred. "I'm too heavy for you."

"I don't care!"

"But I do. Here." Still holding Vanessa wedged against him, he rolled slowly over onto his side. After a moment he reached out a hand and snapped off the bedside light, plunging the room into darkness. Sighing with contentment, Vanessa relaxed in the protective circle of his arms.

Earlier tonight she hadn't bothered to draw the drapes that covered the bedroom windows. Now she felt too spent to get up and go do it. As Vanessa curled up to sleep by Trent's side, she looked out and saw the sky full of spangled stars. Slowly she slid toward the world of unconsciousness, transported by their glow.

Chapter Ten

It was early morning when Vanessa awoke, and light was just beginning to slant in through the windows. Slowly, incredulously, she turned her head on the pillow, still scarcely able to believe the events of the past night. Had she actually shared them with Trent? Her first thought on awakening was that last night must have been one of her more extravagant dreams.

But Trent actually slept beside her, and his face looked peaceful in repose. Eagerly Vanessa drank in the sight of him—the high brow, the sculpted mouth with lips slightly parted, the proud, straight nose, the lightly whiskered cheeks. So she'd had him at last, Vanessa thought in triumph.

Actually, she'd had him more than once, she remembered now, blushing a little at her audacity. At some point during the night they had awakened. Vanessa remembered stirring restlessly for a moment, seeking a comfortable place on the bed, which was no longer so wide when shared. Then

Trent was bending over her. His kisses, meant only to soothe her back to sleep, had ignited them both instead. Vanessa recalled sleepily pulling him over atop her, quickly eliciting the response she'd wanted. They had made slow, drowsy, dreamy love, startling in its final intensity. She thought she'd cried out when she touched, once again, that new and startling peak, but now, in the fresh morning light of a bold new day, she couldn't exactly remember.

Now Vanessa leaned over Trent, studying him intently. The network of dark brown hair that matted his broad chest fascinated her. It grew over his upper muscles in a graceful fan design, and at the sight of that crisp smooth carpet of masculine body hair she felt the urge to comb her fingers through it and to knead the hard muscles of his chest with her fingertips.

It fascinated her further to see the way the broad expanse of his chest tapered down into a trim rib cage. His stomach below was hard and flat, his navel dimpled in the center, his hipbones prominent. What a beautiful man he is, Vanessa thought in awe and a new kind of ecstasy. And now, at last, he's mine.

At just that moment Trent frowned, and Vanessa drew back a little. Abruptly he stared up at her through his dense black eyelashes, and she saw that his blue eyes were still dark with sleep. Softly, very softly, Vanessa kissed Trent awake and watched his frown disappear while the color of his eyes brightened until they, too, seemed to be shot through with joy.

As his arms closed around her, she knew she had never felt so utterly wonderful or been so terribly in love.

Dear God in heaven, how was he ever going to let her go?
The bleak thought, which recurred several times daily, always made Trent feel as if a knife was twisting in his guts. How could he stand to be parted from Vanessa now—now that he awoke beside her every morning, spent almost all of

the day in her delightful and uninhibited company and shared ecstatic hours holding her in his arms at night?

It was *too much* to expect him to part with her now—now that they'd been lovers for almost three weeks. Trent knew Vanessa had no desire to leave him; she'd been dropping hints about marriage thick and fast.

Oh, God, why couldn't things just stay as they were right now? From where he sat on the sandy beach, Trent watched Vanessa wading out into the shallows of Lake Superior, searching again for the magic, elusive greenstones. Ten minutes earlier Trent had abandoned his own search, but Vanessa was unwilling to give up yet.

How could she be so adult in some ways and still so much an untried child in others? Trent pondered the question now as he had so often before. Of course, Vanessa's life-style to date hadn't exactly encouraged her to become like other modern, liberated young women. She had never even spent a night of her life alone, unless one counted her various hospitalizations. But then nurses, and probably doctors, too, had been only a call button away. Certainly Vanessa had never lived alone. Indeed, on several occasions she had revealed a great and innate fear of being all by herself.

So she'd never had her own apartment or held a job long enough to support herself, and the fact that Vanessa thought she didn't need or want this kind of independence didn't distract Trent from the realization that she *did*.

Vanessa waved to him exuberantly, and she looked so damned cute in her tan shorts and yellow halter that Trent couldn't help grinning. Oh, hell, maybe it would all work out fine if we married, Trent thought, arguing with himself again. Was he being overly critical? Vanessa had so much going for her—beauty, intelligence, education, even useful skills.

And, going against her, a frightening degree of inexperience and vulnerability.

Well, he was here, wasn't he? God knows he was healthy as a horse and never took stupid risks.

Sure. Tell her you're indestructible and you'll never get struck by lightning or fall off your boat and drown. Promise her you'll never get heart disease or cancer or have a stroke, his head warned him cynically.

And even if you do live to play Big Daddy to little Scarlett, Trent thought savagely, what happens on that inevitable day, old buddy, when you screw up royally? What happens when Vanessa looks at you and realizes that Trent Davidson really isn't infallible. *When the worship dies in her eyes, as it ultimately will, what will you see then?*

So, once again, Trent was back to square one.

Damn it all, why hadn't other people helped Vanessa to mature fully? Trent found himself thinking resentfully. Why hadn't her father or Bailey, Clark or Dr. Zellar helped her? Why should he now have to risk losing the only woman he'd ever loved just because she'd never paid a bill or slept in a house alone?

But Trent suspected he knew the answer to that question, too. The childlike side of Vanessa's nature, with her immense curiosity and constant wonder at the world, had been so charmingly seductive that no one had wanted to risk changing her. So she had remained emotionally hobbled.

In short, no one had really loved her enough to challenge or encourage her into a complete expression of adulthood. Her sweet and charming self had been deemed quite satisfactory by various men, some of whom had probably enjoyed her dependency on them. Vanessa herself was at least partially aware of that. She knew she was the product of a Southern society that still encouraged women to be "sweet little things," and where nobody minded if they were also cases of arrested development.

But Trent Davidson needed a full and complete woman for his wife and, yes, for his bed as well. Because, dealing with a skittish little Southern princess, a man had to be careful to mind his bedroom manners and move gingerly, expending infinite time and effort to arouse her and bring her to a state of fulfillment she hadn't known before.

Trent didn't mind. Vanessa was worth any amount of trouble on his part, and he felt so much tenderness for her, too, that most of the time he thoroughly enjoyed their love-making.

But then there were other times, too. Times when he'd enjoy some plain rowdy sex just for fun. But Vanessa's overall inexperience in bedroom matters and her emotionally fragile state, made Trent hesitate to introduce innovations to the lovemaking she presently enjoyed.

Trent now knew far more about Vanessa's marriage to Bailey, for she'd confided certain rather intimate details while lying in his arms at night. Much of it was about what he'd expected, and overall, he'd found the picture Vanessa painted of her late husband to be a pitiable one. Bailey had been a man with a shaky ego and a serious drinking problem. Additionally, Trent suspected he'd had an underdeveloped sex drive, able to respond only to very young women who would listen to his stories with wide eyes and bated breath and praise his every accomplishment to the skies. Naturally Bailey had feared Vanessa might grow up and leave him, so it had been in his own best interests to keep her dependent and immature.

Hadn't anyone ever cared about what was best for *Vanessa*?

So Trent Davidson sat alone on the beach, his feelings seesawing back and forth as he watched the enchanting picture that Vanessa made, wading through the blue swells of the vast lake. In some ways he could understand Bailey Ashton very well. Because a selfish side to Trent's own nature feared to free her, too.

Return Vanessa to a busy, often hostile world where he could no longer protect her? To a world of muggers, rapists and terrorists? And there was a whole world of handsome, eligible men out there, too. One or more might turn her head until she completely forgot about the quiet loner who lived on a Michigan island and loved her with all his heart.

If he ever let her go, he might never get her back.

And yet with each day that passed, with every night that he spent holding her, Trent also knew that he was running out of time. He had to make a decision soon. Either marry Vanessa and keep her—or take the far more perilous chance of setting her free.

Vanessa wondered at the occasional grimness she saw on Trent's face these days. That grimness usually gave way to a forlorn look of complete desolation. At those times she could see the little boy that Trent had once been inside the very adult man.

What sort of difficult problem was Trent grappling with? Vanessa wondered, dropping down beside him on the beach. Why should he look so wretched when they always made each other so utterly happy? It left Vanessa perplexed, though she tried to tell herself that those frightening expressions flickering across Trent's face did not really concern *her*. There must be some other logical explanation, she felt sure.

It could just be a work problem. Or—or he could be missing Olga. After all, Trent and Olga had worked together for more than ten years before she had suddenly and abruptly resigned.

"Good riddance!" Mrs. Pushka had said, smiling like a satisfied shark at the news. But did Trent really share the old woman's feelings? Of course, he had told Vanessa on a couple of occasions that he wished Olga would quit, and when she had he had certainly seemed relieved at first. Still, old habits were hard to break, Vanessa knew.

Trent watched her now, that stricken look still on his face, and she felt she had to do something—*anything*—to change it. She smiled. "How about a kiss?" Without waiting for

Trent's reply, she wound her arms around his neck and drew his face down to hers.

How she loved kissing Trent's lips! There was simply no such thing as an insignificant kiss on lips like these. As she pressed her own mouth to his, allowing her lips to part invitingly, Vanessa suddenly got a more heated response than she'd expected.

Abruptly she found herself flat on her back while Trent loomed over her, the fire of arousal deepening the blue of his eyes. That hair-trigger response of his! Gracious, she'd never seen anything like it, the way Trent was always ready to make love to her. Of course, it was flattering to know she had that effect on him. But, at the same time, it could also be embarrassing . . . like right now.

"No, Trent, I didn't mean—" Futilely Vanessa pushed at the strong, unyielding shoulders above her and discovered that he'd flipped up her shirt, baring her breasts. "Let me up!"

"You want to be on top?" he whispered suggestively to her.

"No, I don't . . . ah, want to . . ." Vanessa replied, feeling color rush into her face. Primly she added, "This just isn't the time or place!"

"What's wrong with the time and place?" Trent asked, a touch of belligerence in his voice, as he stared down at Vanessa's naked breasts.

"Well, it's . . . it's broad *daylight*!" Vanessa protested.

"So?" Trent asked.

"And—and someone might see us!" she cried, although, had the truth been known, the warm desirous pressure of Trent's body on hers really made Vanessa long to just shuck off her shorts and pull him deep inside her.

"Who's going to see us? We're on a deserted island!" Trent demanded, but already he had drawn back, and Vanessa could tell that her objections had snapped his sensuous spell.

Quickly she sat up, tugging her shirt down modestly. Then he dropped a gentle hand on Trent's arm. "Don't be mad t me," she coaxed beguilingly. "Somebody really could ave seen us. You know excursion boats are often out, specially on the weekends—"

Trent sighed. "So somebody might have gotten their ed-cation broadened."

At least humor edged his voice. Relief seeped through Vanessa. Thank God, Trent was as he was—so patient and nderstanding, with a good sense of humor.

Right now he was hugging her to him. "Just wait till to-ight!" he growled, and another tingle of pure pleasure ran hrough Vanessa.

All at once she could scarcely wait. More than that, she elt sorry she'd stopped Trent. Sex with him was always chingly sweet and tender. Usually, too, it was completely atisfying. So why did she sometimes suspect that there was nore—a whole lot more—that she might be missing?

If she'd let him make love to her here and now, on the hore, beneath the warm blaze of the sun, would she have ound some new, overwhelming excitement she hadn't yet ven imagined?

Unbidden, Trent's mind, too, turned to Olga as he and Vanessa were walking back to the house. She would have let im make love to her anywhere, at any time or place and in ny way he chose. But, of course, he had never wanted to nake love with Olga again. In fact, Trent still remembered he heady rush of relief he'd felt when he'd discovered Olga leaning out her desk.

"Hey, what's going on?" he'd asked in a jocular voice.

"What does it look like?" Olga demanded, tight-lipped nd tense. With each passing day she'd had increasingly less o say, and now Trent knew that she had surmised some-ow the new relationship that he and Vanessa shared. Of

course, lovers tended not to hide their feelings for eac
other.

"I'm quitting," Olga continued bitterly. "I know I shoul
have given you notice, Trent, but I've got to go now. Oth
erwise, I—I may commit murder!"

"All right, Olga," Trent agreed quietly, although h
wondered just who she wanted to kill? Me or Vanessa? Bot
of us, more likely, with Mrs. Pushka thrown in for goo
measure, he concluded wryly.

"Olga, I hope you know that I'll always give you an ex
cellent job recommendation, and I'll always value the con
tributions you've made to my own work. They ar
considerable," he said.

"Thank you." Olga's head jerked stiffly. She withdrev
the last of her personal possessions from the desk drawer
then slammed it shut with a sound of finality.

"Wait. Let me write you a check," Trent urged, plan
ning to make it a generous one.

"Mail it to me!" Olga snapped. She had almost reache
the door when she swung around to face Trent again. "Ac
tually, I'm sorry for you both, Trent—you and your littl
Vanessa alike. Maybe she did take a couple of compute
courses and read a few meteorology texts. But none of tha
will change what she is and always will be."

"And just what do you think she is, Olga?" Trent aske
conversationally, although his stomach muscles had tight
ened instinctively.

"Vanessa was born to be some rich older man's orna
ment," Olga declared. "Didn't you see her playing up t
Landry and Garrett? She could never survive a life on thi
island! She's too soft, too used to creature comforts—"

"Vanessa survived a climb down a mountain in Alask
with a broken arm and cracked ribs," Trent retorted.

Olga gave a negligent shrug. "That was self-preservation
It's humankind's strongest instinct, haven't you heard?"

Then she was gone, the door slamming behind her.

Trent wondered if anything that Olga had said about Vanessa was true. Of course he knew the blond woman was jealous, resentful, bitter. But Olga had also lived in the Prophet Islands all her life, and she had a shrewd instinctive knowledge of other people that Trent had relied on frequently.

Olga had usually been able to predict what people could and couldn't do.

No one had ever accused Vanessa of being overly cautious or reluctant to go after what she wanted. She had always lived life on the cutting edge and supposed she always would. If Trent was proving slow to propose marriage to her, then she would just have to find a method to speed him up.

At thirteen Vanessa had undertaken the challenge herself, boldly offering herself as they sat in the swing on the front porch. But the intervening years had taught her more finesse. With just a bit of thought, Vanessa had soon devised a new plan.

Lord, I've been in love with Trent Davidson almost half my life! she thought.

Clark was the instrument that Vanessa soon settled on. Big brother Clark, who was obviously thrilled to death to have Vanessa way up there in northern Michigan and out of *his* hair for the first time in a couple of years. Not that Clark would admit it. He had too much "family feeling" for such rankness. But Vanessa knew her brother well.

Clark dutifully phoned Vanessa every Sunday afternoon, and they usually had a lengthy chat. Sometimes Kitty got on the line, too, and occasionally Vanessa reeled Trent in to talk with Clark and Kitty. But mostly those Sunday calls were just between siblings.

Several times Clark had inquired as to when Vanessa would return to Atlanta. "Not for a while yet," she had re-

plied, and from the joy that filled Clark's voice she could te
that her reply had made his day.

"Sounds like you and Trent have something going or
Nessie?" Clark had finally suggested.

"Well, perhaps we have," Vanessa had replied oblique
to her brother.

"He's being... *good* to you?" Clark asked suspiciously

"Oh, yes, Clark," said Vanessa, deliberately playing th
innocent. "Why, Trent's just the sweetest man in the whol
world!" So let Clark figure out just exactly what she'
meant by that. Anyway, whether she was or wasn't sleepin
with Trent wasn't really any of Clark's business.

After another couple of weeks had passed, Clark final
got up nerve enough to inquire again. "Look, are you an
Trent actually getting serious about each other, Nessie?"

She knew the easiest way to spark Clark's interest. "Wh
won't you call me Vanessa?" she lamented. "It's a per
fectly good name. And, yes, I think I can say that Trent an
I are pretty serious."

"Has he asked you to marry him?"

"No," Vanessa admitted. She added on a hopeful note
"But he hasn't said anything about my coming back home
either."

"The summer's almost over," Clark reminded her. "I
you're not going to stay in Michigan, then we need to star
making other plans for you. Dr. Zellar's office called o
Friday. Group therapy is resuming on September 8 and the
wanted to know if you'd be there."

"God, I hope not!" said Vanessa with a groan.

But now yet another week had passed, and she was reall
beginning to grow seriously worried. She kept remember
ing the grim expression that had tightened Trent's mout
when they were on the beach yesterday. She kept realizin
that his failure to mention the future was becoming an in
creasingly ominous sign. Yet he loved her. Vanessa coul

absolutely swear he loved her! But she also felt that, for some reason, Trent wasn't very keen on marriage.

Sometimes, late at night or very early in the morning, she tended to hear Olga's words again: "Trent will never marry you, because Trent will never marry anyone. He's completely independent and self-sufficient. After he's had all he wants of a woman, Trent always finds a reason to reject her. I was too plain. Helene was too demanding—"

Sometimes Vanessa wondered why she let herself remember words spoken by a woman who had obviously hated her. But always the sharp edge of fear kept her from totally dismissing them. What—oh, just what—if Olga had been right about Trent?

"Without you, my sweet, he'll be lost." That's what Mrs. Pushka had said in a warning of her own. Now Vanessa thought she knew what the old lady had meant. If Trent didn't marry someone soon, it would be too late for him. He would gradually pull back until he became lost to warmth, tenderness and all the other emotions.

But perhaps Trent wanted a life wholly free of commitments and dependents. It was his own choice, after all—but as the calendar moved inexorably into September, Vanessa rapidly decided on a way to hasten it.

"So what's the word, Nessie?" Clark asked hopefully the following Sunday.

"Alas, there's not a single word to report," Vanessa replied glumly.

"This is really starting to get to you, isn't it?" Clark probed, picking up on the only source of his sister's unhappiness.

"Yes, it is," she admitted. "Trent and I are close, Clark. Closer all the time. So I don't know why he won't say anything."

"Now you're damned sure that Trent is what you really want?" Clark demanded in a gruff, brotherly way.

"Oh, yes!" Vanessa breathed.

"Well, you always did have your heart set on him fo[r] some reason. Listen, why don't you put him on the line? Le[t] me see if his head is screwed on straight."

"Oh . . ." For a moment Vanessa hesitated. Fear and un[-] certainty began to stir like an unsavory broth inside of her[.] Did she really want to know badly enough to risk every[-] thing—the golden days spent with Trent, the nights whe[n] she lay feeling so safe and cherished in his arms?

Yes, she did, Vanessa realized with a gulp. Then, befor[e] her courage could desert her, she called Trent's name. Whe[n] he didn't answer immediately, she told Clark to hang o[n] while she went in search of him.

There were a number of telephones in the laboratory an[d] office, but only one for the whole of the large house. A[t] Vanessa's inquiry, Trent had explained that Mrs. Pushk[a] was not overly fond of phones. So when Clark called Va[-] nessa each Sunday, Trent usually made himself scarce, ofte[n] going outside to feed or play with Boots, so Vanessa coul[d] have privacy.

Today she found Trent in the kitchen, where between hi[s] own whistling and Boots whining for his dinner, Vanessa'[s] call had obviously gone unheard.

"Trent, Clark wants to talk to you," Vanessa said, he[r] heart in her throat.

"Sure. Give Boots his chow, will you, so he'll shut up.[']" Trent pushed the bowl of dog food toward Vanessa's hand[s] and aimed a kiss at her temple before striding off to talk t[o] Clark.

Vanessa carried the bowl outside and knelt down in th[e] backyard beside Boots, stroking the dog automatically as h[e] ate. Her heart kept beating in a series of queer little start[s] and stops, and her throat felt so dry and tight that she de[-] cided to go back to the kitchen and fix some lemonade. Af[-] ter Trent got through talking to Clark, he'd probably b[e] thirsty, too.

"Hey, pal! Sounds like you and Nessie have been getting along great! She was just telling me again what a wonderful time she's had."

Trent closed his eyes and felt his long body sag into the sofa, which was still strewn with remnants of his Sunday newspaper. He knew he should have seen this coming, and dammit, the worst of it was he *had*. He'd seen that hopeful, eager look in Vanessa's eyes, as well as her occasional signs of anxiety. He knew this was his responsibility to face and to answer frankly. Just last week he had torn off a calendar page and been reminded that autumn was almost here. When had he turned into such a procrastinator?

He didn't know when. He only knew why.

Now Clark was softening Trent up for the big question. He was cracking jokes, then laughing too hard at them in a hearty male manner.

Trent gave a silent sigh of acute psychic pain and wished Clark would go ahead and get to the point.

Finally Clark did. "So what's the deal, pal? Is the little one for keepers, or are you going to ship her back to me?"

Until this moment of decision had actually arrived, Trent hadn't known. Now he drew an unsteady breath. "Clark, she's got to go back. She's just not ready yet—"

"Not *well* enough?" Alarm resounded in Clark's voice. "I know she had that recall episode a couple of months ago, but has she—?"

"No, Vanessa has been well," Trent sighed.

"Then I don't understand."

Trent tried to enlighten Clark. Certainly it all made sense enough to *him* but maybe, hurting as he did, he didn't explain things very well. Obviously not—for in less than a minute Clark was saying huffily, "Now hold on! Now you just hold on! Are you saying that my sister, who's a twenty-six-year-old widow and been into, God knows, every kind of counseling and therapy that Freud could dream up, still hasn't 'found herself'?"

"I just think Vanessa needs time, Clark. She needs space. She needs the opportunity to become more independent and resourceful, not less so," Trent added almost desperately. "She shouldn't be tied down, with her horizons limited to this little island. She's like a bird who likes its cage because it's never even seen the sky!"

"You sound pretty sure of yourself," Clark said. His voice had cooled perceptibly. "No chance that she's been trying to push you into something, is there, Trent? Y'know, most guys your age were married long ago. You ever thought you might be allergic to marriage or something?"

"Yes, I've thought about it," Trent said wearily. Was there any angle or aspect of this particular topic that he hadn't thought about?

"And?" said Clark, his voice heavy with irony.

Trent didn't feel like either arguing or defending himself. "Maybe you're right, Clark. I don't know."

The attempt to pacify Clark was a futile one. "You're damned right you don't know! Why, I don't think you'd know your a—"

Some instinct, a slight prickling along the hairline at the base of his skull, caused Trent to turn around. Vanessa stood there in the doorway, staring at him in shock. Oh, damn! Trent thought sickly, wondering just how much she had overheard. Or had he deliberately planned for Vanessa to hear? Right now Trent was so confused he couldn't even be sure of his own motives anymore.

Wordlessly they stared at each other. Her face was paper white, and she held a tray on which were set two tall, frosty glasses. Lemonade, he realized. My God, what a ludicrous touch to interject into this scene!

Or maybe not so ludicrous, after all. For even as Trent's eyes met Vanessa's squarely he was also aware of the tray starting to slip from her shaking hands. His yelp of warning appeared to break her spell; Vanessa actually managed to catch one of the glasses in midair, although the other glass and the tray went crashing to the floor with a horrible clatter.

Meanwhile Clark was raving, going on and on in hot defense of his sister. "God only knows why she ever wanted you, anyway, Trent. Our mother sure saw through you! She used to say you were small potatoes and Vanessa could do better than to bury herself on some dinky island in Michigan with you. And to think I used to feel guilty—yes, downright guilty—because I hung in with Mother and encouraged Nessie to marry old Bailey. Well, at least, by God, Bailey loved her..."

"Vanessa...?" Trent said, unable to speak more than her name.

For a moment her mouth actually curved into a little half smile, a single touch of coral in the overall whiteness of her face. "Still waiting for me to grow up, Trent?" she said, and he heard the biting tone of her voice, then saw the hand she raised slowly, taking careful aim.

Trent ducked just in time as the remaining glass of lemonade came sailing through the air, dead on target. He dropped the telephone receiver as the glass splintered on the wall an inch above his head. Sticky lemonade splattered over him, and when he'd blinked most of it from his eyes and looked back toward the door, Vanessa was gone.

From the phone receiver Trent had dropped on the carpet, Clark continued to shout, unaware of the events that had just transpired. "...too damned good for you, anyway! So just put her on the next plane home. The sooner she gets away from you, the better! But I'm warning you, Trent. If you've caused Nessie to have a relapse, if she breaks down again because of you and the way you've treated her, then I'll come after you and I'll kill you. I swear I'll kill you, Trent, with my own bare hands!"

As Trent snatched up the telephone receiver he heard the back door slam and knew that Vanessa had fled outside. "Clark, I've got to go now," he said curtly.

But Clark had worked himself into a towering rage and was in no mood to be summarily dismissed. "Don't hang up on me, you sanctimonious bastard!" he roared.

"Your mature and responsible sister came in and heard us talking. She just threw a glass of lemonade at me."

"Good for Nessie!"

"Now she's gone running off to God knows where!" Trent snapped, then dropped the receiver back in its cradle and went dashing out after Vanessa.

He darted through the kitchen, then down the back stairs. Wildly he looked around, wondering in just which direction she had fled.

Would Vanessa do anything reckless? he wondered frantically. Could she actually harm herself? He didn't know, of course, but he considered it an unlikely possibility.

"Oh, God, what have I done?" Trent heard himself moan in a sudden agony of self-reproach. What if Clark was right and Vanessa had a relapse because of the cavalier way in which Trent had treated her? Just a few months before, she'd been desperately ill. Was Trent pushing her too hard, too fast?

"Vanessa!" Trent called aloud. "Vanessa, answer me, please!"

Finally he calmed down enough to take stock of the situation. Boots sat frozen before him, obviously in the "stay" position, as if ordered there by Vanessa.

Trent whirled around quickly, his eyes scanning the bicycle rack, and saw that her bicycle was gone. He grabbed his own from the rack, then swiftly freed Boots with a whistle. "C'mon, boy. Let's go find her!"

Chapter Eleven

Vanessa had no idea where she was going as she pedaled away from the house. She was still in a state of shock, she realized. Only anger had broken through as yet; pain was still mercifully in abeyance. At the moment, all she could think of was putting distance between herself and Trent, and her legs pumped furiously up and down on the bike's pedals.

Without any destination in mind, she headed toward the far side of the island, as if duplicating the first day's adventure here. How out of shape she'd been that day, and how quickly wearied.

As her legs kept pumping and the narrow Indian path dropped behind her, Vanessa couldn't help but be struck by how much stronger she'd become in the past three months. Why, she could really give Trent a run for his money now!

The pain started then, piercing through her numbness, as Vanessa automatically linked herself and Trent. Then she caught herself. They were no longer a couple, a pair. Trent had decided Vanessa should go back to Atlanta rather than remain here with him.

Oh, God, she was really starting to hurt now! Vanessa bent almost double on the bike seat. Suddenly she found it hard to breathe or think or do anything except cry. Momentarily the bicycle wobbled and began skidding from side to side. She was almost blinded by tears. *Oh, dear God, I love him so!*

She reached the end of the Indian trail. Abruptly Vanessa pulled off into the brush, dropped the bicycle down behind a scrubby little tree and plunged through the edge of the forest. Still crying, she scarcely felt the undergrowth beneath her sandaled feet or the occasional briars and brambles that reached out, trying to snag her. She was scarcely even aware of the dim light here in the deep forest or of the almost spooky haze into which she fled.

I should come out not far from that little inland lake, Vanessa thought, her mind beginning to function enough to calculate her whereabouts. That was the single most peaceful place on the island, to her way of thinking. Perhaps that was why she had headed here subconsciously.

Several minutes passed before Vanessa grew aware of a wet, sucking sound beneath her feet or of the fact that the briars and brambles had increased substantially, clawing at both her clothes and her tender skin. Impatiently Vanessa dashed the tears from her eyes, glanced down and froze momentarily in horror. Her feet were covered with slimy mud. Oh, God, she'd blundered into the bog—that very bog that Trent had warned her against because it was not only an evil place of spiky thorns and noxious plants but filled with quicksand as well.

I don't care if I get sucked down into the bog and die! Vanessa thought, self-pity swamping her for just a moment.

She took another few steps, aware now of the sucking sensation on the thin soles of her sandals; aware, too, of each slurping sound made by the hungry-sounding bog. Vanessa began to step more gingerly even as she wondered why she should bother. It would certainly serve Trent right if she dropped off the face of the earth, she thought.

But that, of course, was just a desire for revenge. Vanessa was far too aware of her emotions not to know what was really going on inside of her now. She was angry, deeply hurt and bitterly disillusioned.

She burst through a last dense thicket that seemed entirely composed of thorns; then she was safely out of the bog and standing beneath the trees by the lake. For a moment Vanessa dropped down there, panting for breath, but after just a brief rest she was on her feet again. She felt too open, too exposed, here on the lake's sunny bank, and right now Vanessa's every instinct was to hide away in darkness.

She began climbing up one of the steep tree-shrouded hills that swelled over the far end of the island. Now her knees were beginning to ache from exertion, but that was a small pain compared to the sword still twisting in her breast.

Oh, Olga had been right about Trent all along. No woman had ever been good enough for him—no woman ever would be!

God, what a silly, stupid, trusting little fool I've been! Vanessa thought passionately. Then she knew her feelings had advanced into self-condemnation.

She went on scrambling up the hill, climbing higher and faster. Off in the distance she heard the faint sound of a dog's barking and felt herself freeze. Boots, of course, and Trent would be right behind him.

How could she ever face Trent when she felt swamped by embarrassment and humiliation? *Oh, God, let me die right now so I never have to look at him again!* Vanessa prayed.

It all seemed so futile, so totally useless. She had struggled so hard to get well! Had fought her way out of a maze of ghastly memories and pitch-black depression and hideous recall episodes when she'd relived that awful plane crash over and over. Her ferocious efforts seemed pointless now, because, always, Trent had been at the center of her world. But she was going to have to forget about Trent. He didn't really love her. He didn't want to marry her.

Trent was gone, and to Vanessa at that moment, it seemed as though her whole life had ended, too.

Suddenly she noticed that she stood before the entrance to the old copper mine, with no memory of how she'd gotten here. With a sigh of relief, she darted inside.

The dark mine, dank and cold, was the elusive refuge she had sought. It was the perfect place for a person with a broken heart to hide, and Vanessa no longer cared if she was sharing quarters with spiders, snakes or even a black bear or two.

Trent had warned her against ever coming inside this old abandoned mine, but now she simply didn't care. Exhausted, she sank down against a damp, chill wall and buried her face in her hands.

"Vanessa, answer me! I know you're around here somewhere!"

Trent heard his own voice escalating almost crazily, its pitch evoked by dreadful fear. Boots kept plunging onward, barking his head off, and Trent followed him frantically, hoping to God that the dog was actually tracking Vanessa.

He found a couple of footprints at the edge of the bog and felt terror at the thought that she might be lost in there somewhere. They were such tiny, delicate-looking little footprints that Trent wanted to blister the air with his curses and howl like an animal in pain.

How could I have done it? he wondered. *How could I have hurt Vanessa so?*

He'd spoken the truth, but what would that matter if she was physically hurt or if his words had shattered her once-perilous grasp on reality?

Trent kept drawing nearer. Vanessa could tell by the sound of Boots's barking. Well, at least I've led him quite a merry chase, she thought, deriving satisfaction from anything she could.

She'd had ten or fifteen minutes to stop crying, marshal her inner forces and draw about her a few tattered shreds of dignity. Cold composure now lay over her like a protective cloak.

Suddenly Boots stood at the entrance to the mine, barking his silly head off in triumph. "Shut up, damn dog!" Vanessa snapped. But, at the same time, she resigned herself to the inevitable.

"Vanessa!" Trent called, and she took perverse pleasure in hearing the terror in his voice and the way he gasped for breath. Yes, she'd definitely run Trent quite a race! "Answer me, Vanessa! I know you're in there."

She stayed stubbornly silently, but hugged her knees up to her breasts, defiantly resting her chin upon them.

Trent reached the entrance to the mine. "Vanessa—?"

"Here," she muttered in a cool monosyllable.

He crouched down and came inside, a dark figure she could scarcely see in the dim, hazy light. He was still breathing heavily, and Vanessa sensed when Trent's mood of vast relief suddenly changed into blazing anger.

"You little fool!" Although she quailed, shrinking away from him, Trent snatched her up roughly off the damp ground. For a moment he didn't seem to care whether he'd hurt her or not. A small whimper of fear and pain escaped her. Then she bit her lip, refusing to show any further weakness.

"Vanessa, don't you know what you could have blundered straight into?" Trent panted. Angrily he yanked her forward two steps and fumbled in his pocket. Then Vanessa heard the sound of a metal object, probably a coin, striking the walls of a mine shaft as it fell.

Despite her own anger and defiance, Vanessa's heart chilled when she heard the long, seemingly endless pause before the coin finally splashed in water far, far below. Despite her outward indifference, she felt shaken by how close to accidentally killing herself she had actually come.

All right, God, I didn't mean it, she thought. *I fought too hard to live and be whole again to throw it all away now.*

In an empty, drained silence, Vanessa and Trent walked back to the house, trailed by the equally weary Boots.

Trent had insisted that Vanessa listen to him. Then he'd talked to her until he was blue in the face, trying to document and explain, both with anecdotes and incidents, just why he felt she was unready for the responsibilities of marriage.

Talk about getting nowhere fast! Vanessa sat on the couch in the family room, her arms crossed and her face set in an expression so stony that it both amazed and horrified Trent. He had not known that someone as soft and gentle as Vanessa could be capable of such resolve. Although, once he stopped to really think of it, he knew he'd always suspected that a layer of steel ran beneath her delicate, silken exterior. Hadn't they even joked on the eve of her arrival about her hard head?

At last he simply ran out of words to say. Anyway, the expression on her face told him plainly that she wasn't listening and he was wasting his breath.

"May I please go now?" Vanessa said at last, like a very polite child speaking to her parent. In fact, since Trent had just mentioned the word "immaturity," he was certain he heard an ironic sarcasm in her request. "I'd like to get cleaned up."

"Of course." Trent sighed and followed her up the stairs. He knew, of course, that Vanessa didn't want him in her room, and he wouldn't have followed her in there, anyway.

Still, Trent felt jolted when, as soon as the door had closed behind her, he heard Vanessa flip the bolt that locked it.

He went on into his own room and took a quick shower, washing off the muck from the woods and the bog. Then, dressed once again in clean clothes, Trent knocked on Vanessa's door to ask what she'd like to eat for dinner.

"All I'd like is to be left alone, Trent," she replied caustically. "Do you think you can manage that one?"

He bit his tongue, warning himself not to get angry. He went back downstairs, where he discovered that Mrs. Pushka had evidently been in, since someone had cleaned up the mess of lemonade and broken glass. She had also left a covered casserole and a green salad in the refrigerator, so Trent fixed himself a plate, knowing that he needed to eat. But when he carried it back into the family room he found himself unable either to eat much or to concentrate on the TV. Even worse, as soon as he switched off the set he heard Vanessa's footsteps racing back and forth overhead. Heard her closet door open and close, then a dresser drawer slam shut.

She's packing to leave me, Trent realized, and so many emotions besieged him that he felt almost swamped by them. Despair was the strongest one of all.

He couldn't let it end like *this*! He and Vanessa had been too close, had grown too intimate, sharing bodies and confidences in the long, dark nights. No, he couldn't let it all end with her detesting him.

Trent walked upstairs again and knocked at her door. When there was no answer, he called to her quietly. "Vanessa, let me in. I won't let it end this way between us."

"Oh, Trent, just please go away!" she cried passionately.

"No, I won't." He drew a deep breath. "This is still my house, Vanessa. I have a key that will open your door."

"All right!" she shouted, and a moment later she flung the door open furiously.

Trent came inside saw her packed suitcases and shut the door with quiet firmness. He walked over to the chaise longue and sank down there heavily. Vanessa perched nervously on the edge of her bed, biting her lip. She wore her rose robe, but today its color did not enhance her own, for her face was still white with strain. Trent saw a few last items of clothing scattered on the bedspread.

"Vanessa, I do care about you...deeply," Trent began again, having warned himself not to even utter the word "love." "You and I go back too far to wind up enemies."

"Sure," she murmured, and Trent knew the words he'd planned with such care were falling on hostile, disbelieving ears. Then Vanessa looked up, meeting his gaze squarely. "Tell me one thing, Trent. Just tell me when I can leave this island and I promise you'll never see me again!"

"Oh, Vanessa..." he began softly, sadly.

She stared at him ruthlessly, but as Trent watched, her own composure began to crack. "Right now I don't know why I ever thought I loved you!" she blazed. "Where the hell do you get off with that superiority complex?"

Trent drew a deep breath, aware of a sadness that cut sharper and went deeper than any he'd ever felt—except, perhaps, for the time when his father had died. "I'm sorry you feel that way, Vanessa."

"When can I go home?" she demanded, as though this was now the single most important thing in the world.

"There won't be a ferry from Catt Island to the mainland until tomorrow morning at nine," he answered automatically.

"Well, I intend to be on it! Now, if you'll excuse me—"

She was like granite. Nothing short of an absolute explosion was going to stop her, shake her, make her listen to him.

"Damn it, Vanessa!" Trent threw caution to the winds. It was getting him nowhere, anyway. He stormed over to the bed and drew her up. Impatiently he gave her slim shoulders a shake, which made her big brown eyes widen in surprise. "Just how mature was it to run away like you did today? Or to egg Clark into asking me my intentions? You're a grown woman. Why didn't you ask me yourself?"

"Oh, shut up," Vanessa said coldly, but Trent could tell he'd struck a raw nerve, especially when she added defensively, "I don't run away from things. Why, I certainly never left Bailey no matter how many times he got drunk—"

"And he was someone you probably should have shed!" Trent shot back. "Why on earth did a gorgeous young woman like you stay married to that impotent lush? Were you that scared to be alone, on your own?"

"You don't know a thing about my marriage!" Vanessa flared.

"I know what you've told me!" Trent yelled right back at her. Then his voice fell. "So you've never completely grown up. So what? It's no crime, Vanessa. Neither your upbringing nor your life so far have offered you a lot of chances to be self-reliant and responsible. No man has ever even wanted you to be that way... until now. But *I* want a whole woman, and I want *all* of a woman! And I want a passionate woman—not a delicate, fragile girl that I'm scared to even squeeze. I've missed that, missed having a really earthy, mature woman to make love with!"

Vanessa gave a gasp of outraged pride, but Trent still wasn't quite finished. He knew he was hurting her, maybe pushing her too far, but somehow he had to shake her into really listening to him. "Nessie, ever since you came here you've been trying to hand *me* the responsibility for the rest of your life. I suppose it's a natural reaction under the circumstances. You think I saved your life, not once but twice. I'm no superman. Both times I just happened to be standing around on the sidelines with the right bit of knowledge. I sure as hell don't know everything! I'm not always right and God knows I'm not perfect. I've had some lousy love affairs. I've missed some golden opportunities. In short, I screw up like every other human being."

Vanessa swayed in Trent's clutches. She gulped and tried to break away, but he only seized her shoulders even tighter. Fantasy worlds were beginning to rock. She felt frightened by that strange, eerie light in Trent's eyes and all these astounding words she had never imagined he could say.

"Vanessa, I sure can't run your life when—when I don't always run my own very well," Trent concluded. "Why, I've made some horrendous mistakes and have had to live with them!"

Immediately Vanessa's mind flashed to Olga, so fair and cool, yet also so voluptuous with her overblown body. *Trent was talking about making love to Olga,* Vanessa realized.

She hadn't expected to feel such fury—but she did. She hadn't expected to still be tormented by jealousy, but she was. Above all, Vanessa didn't realize that she could be driven to challenge until she had wrenched free of Trent's grip and begun angrily unzipping her robe.

"You want earthy, Trent? You want mature? Okay, I will definitely take responsibility for *this*!" Defiantly she stepped out of the robe and kicked it aside. "So show me what you've been missing! Broaden my horizons. Maybe I'm just a little sick of being treated like a porcelain doll myself!"

It was worth everything to her just to see the absolute and total surprise on Trent's face. He certainly hadn't expected this, not of "little Nessie"! When he hesitated, Vanessa kicked off her shoes and hooked her thumbs beneath the elastic waistband of her bikini panties, the only other garment she wore.

As she slipped the panties down over the flare of her hips and her slim yet shapely thighs, Vanessa's face offered its own challenge.

She was magnificent! Trent marveled. How could he resist? Standing there with her hands on her hips, wearing nothing but her birthday suit, Vanessa radiated all the fire and passion that Trent had always secretly longed to see.

Captivated by excitement, his body quickening in erotic response, he stepped forward and caught her in his arms.

It was like trying to hold on to a writhing electric eel. She twisted and undulated, her passion still fueled by fury, and their mouths met in an explosion of need. Vanessa's fingernails were like talons digging into either side of Trent's neck, and she clearly didn't care whether she scratched him or not.

Swiftly Trent pinned her hands and then kissed her into gradual submission, until she was writhing less and moving more slowly, sinuously, in a slow glide up and down his body that absolutely set him on fire.

"Oh, God, Trent, I hate you—I hate what you do to me still!" she whimpered when he finally freed her mouth.

"Too bad," he said unsympathetically, bearing her over to the bed. There he dropped her, and Vanessa grabbed at the mattress for support. "I love you. I still love you. I'll always..." His shirt and undershirt, pulled rapidly over his head, muffled the last of his words.

Vanessa glared up at him as Trent tore away the rest of his clothes, but her slim body quivered. The moment he dropped down on the bed beside her, she was sliding beneath him.

He took her as he never had before—quickly, without the usual preliminaries to prepare her, and silently, without a wealth of tender words to soothe her sensibilities. Now Trent claimed her as a man could claim only one woman, the one who belonged to him utterly, the one to whom he belonged totally. His wild, mindless drive to possess her seemed to spark an answering eruption within Vanessa. Her soft body curved all around him, cushioning him, welcoming him, bathing and sheathing him in pliancy and blazing fire.

"... *want* you, Trent ... I want *you*!" he heard her murmur, and the words, emphasized with her fingernails, were like a velvet lash across his back, goading him on, firing his passions even higher and hotter, driving him deeper, farther, faster, until he felt her fall apart beneath him. Then a tremendous jolt of exploding passion rocked him, too.

"Vanessa..." Night began to creep over the windowsill, but Trent still held her curled against his side. He couldn't bear to think of what it would be like to finally release her.

For just a minute or two, he thought, she cried in his arms, and he closed his own eyes, sharing her grief that they—who cared so desperately for each other—must inevitably part. "Just for a little while," he tried to assure her, but Vanessa shook her head in disbelief.

"Don't talk, Trent. We're all through talking. Just show me—" Gracefully she rolled over until she was staring straight down at him. Her eyes were dry now, with a hard brown glitter. "You said once you wanted to have me on top. Like this...?"

Trent closed his own eyes, the better to allow the sadness to leave and his passion to come surging back. "Closer," he whispered. "Let me feel all of you next to me."

The pleasure of her slim youthful body caressing him was so exquisite that he ignited almost as fast as he had before. And this time he used his mouth and hands to give Vanessa greater pleasure, stroking her until she gasped and gripped his hips, seeking to imprison him deeply within her. Then she moved on him slowly, so slowly that he gasped involuntarily, and finally so rapidly that he cried out from sensations so intense that they almost seemed past bearing.

And later, a couple of hours later, Trent carried Vanessa into his own room and demonstrated how the full-length mirror on his door could be positioned to reflect any action on the bed. Then Trent urged her to watch while he, seated behind her, let his strong hands glide intimately over her skin.

"Trent, I can't watch! I...I won't!" Vanessa cried, but her protest was only half-horrified, he suspected.

"Then don't watch. But you said you wanted to learn. Oh, boy, does this feel wonderful...." A brief, whimsical

mood swept him and seemed to transmit itself to Vanessa,
too. Perhaps things just had to lighten up—their lovemaking was too much an affirmation of life and joy to be
drenched in grief.

"Well, I won't look because this really does embarrass
me," she protested, yet at the same time Vanessa could feel
herself leaning back farther, letting her body relax against
Trent's muscled strength.

"You shouldn't be embarrassed—you're so glorious all
over. Why, right here it's like velvet...smoothest, softest
velvet. Tell me, what does my hand feel like?"

"A little rough, kind of ticklish..." she whispered,
hearing the sudden breathlessness in her voice.

"Maybe if I touched you a little more slowly and used a
lighter touch..." His voice trailed off tentatively.

Vanessa felt the rapid reheating of her blood, felt the now-
familiar desire starting to course through her once more.
"Yes...like that, oh, just like that! Don't stop, Trent!" she
urged.

"I won't—but you really ought to look, darling. Watch
my hands playing over you..." he coaxed.

She couldn't help it; she had to take a peek—and then,
rather than expiring from embarrassment at what she and
Trent were doing in vivid, bright light and directly in front
of a mirror, she found the scene almost unbearably stirring. Something in it was evocative of true, pure love. The
man, so beautiful and powerful in his own newly acceler-
ating desire, and the woman—oh, she could scarcely identify that luminous-faced woman as herself, not as she sank
back in the man's arms, her limbs all relaxed and akimbo,
allowing him every possible liberty.

As Vanessa continued to watch, entranced at the graceful movements choreographed in the mirror, she saw her
bosom flowering under his playful touch until the nipples
jutted up, eager for the tug of his mouth. At the gentle urg-
ings of her hands on the back of Trent's neck, his dark head

bent over her, and as she lay back completely in his arms, his mouth opened, absorbing one breast. His tongue lingered over it, laving and lavishing it with caresses so intense, caresses so inexplicably sweet, that now Vanessa was the one suddenly crying out.

But Trent was only just beginning, and in the next almost endless moments her pleasure grew so exquisite that it ultimately deepened to something close to pain. Under the gentle lash of Trent's mouth, Vanessa awoke fully and learned just what her body was capable of and exactly what it could be made to do. She yielded wildly, watching the reflection of herself until finally she felt driven to return intimacy for intimacy. She allowed her mouth to travel the length of Trent's body, too, until they were locked together again and both shaking and straining with almost unbearable pleasure.

It felt like always. Like forever and ever. Sprawled in Trent's arms, replete with fulfillment, Vanessa closed her eyes for just a moment, and the next thing she knew it was a cool, gray, rainy dawn—and now she had to go home.

"Trent, wake up." A not-too-gentle hand shook his shoulder. "You have to get up now. We must leave very soon."

He never overslept, but he knew immediately that he had today. He even knew why. Before he even began to wake out of deep sleep, a part of Trent knew that this was going to be one of the most painful days of his life.

"Trent!"

Vanessa's voice was compelling. He smelled the aroma of hot coffee set somewhere close by his bed. And even as he began to stir and groan, Trent wished he could disappear back into that safe, dark world of unconsciousness and nothingness. Because he knew that he didn't even want to try living without her.

He groaned and opened one weary eye a crack.

"Oh, good, you're awake," said Vanessa, relieved.

He raised his head and looked at her, only to meet the indifferent eyes of a cool stranger. Their abandoned night together might never have happened.

She was dressed for travel, wearing the same clothes in which she'd arrived, but her present almost glacial expression bore utterly no resemblance to that eager, excited girl he had met at the ferry landing.

"I've left some coffee and toast by the bed for you, Trent," Vanessa said briskly. "Can you be ready to leave in fifteen minutes?"

He sat up and looked at her searchingly. He sought any signs of anger, passion, tenderness. Last night all those emotions had played like a symphony across her face, but today she was completely emotionless, her volatile emotions in deep freeze.

Suddenly the ghastly thought occurred to Trent that, in relentlessly pushing Vanessa toward womanhood, he might have, he might have slain that eager, curious, delightful person he happened to love most in all the world.

No, he wouldn't believe that. He couldn't let himself believe *that*!

Vanessa had already swept out of the room. Trent reached for the coffee and made himself choke down a few bites of toast, then he headed for the shower.

It was drizzling by the time they were both ready to leave for Catt Island. Trent made two trips down to the dock with Vanessa's luggage. She followed him on the last trip, her canvas carryall over her arm and Boots at her heels.

"Did you tell Mrs. Pushka goodbye?" Trent suddenly thought to ask.

Vanessa gave a curt shake of her head. "I couldn't," she said after a moment. "Give her my love. And tell her I'll write her... later."

Then they were at the pier, where the whining terrier sought to accompany them onto the cruiser. "Stay, Boots," he heard Vanessa whisper. When the dog paused obediently, she bent down and gave him a quick hug. Then she stepped aboard, automatically reaching for the hand that Trent extended to her. For just a moment he thought Vanessa might be close to tears.

If she was, the moment quickly passed. She sank down into a chair on the lower deck and stared straight ahead while Trent warmed up the engine, then backed slowly away from the dock.

The weather was miserable, providing a fitting end to a love story gone awry. Drizzle obscured his visibility; a gray pall lay over the entire lake. Far away, Trent heard the doleful wail of a foghorn.

He wondered if Vanessa was too cold. If she was getting wet from the drizzle and ought to cover her bare head. Trent wanted to call anxious inquiries to her, but wouldn't allow himself to do it. If he started acting like a worried parent she would probably just get furious all over again.

At least the trip to Catt Island was short. There Vanessa waited silently while Trent made arrangements for her luggage with a young man who was also waiting to take the ferry. The guy promised to help with Vanessa's three big bags when they got to Copper Harbor. Vanessa led the way down to the ferry landing.

Soon, much too soon, the ferry appeared as a speck in the haze. Rapidly it gained visibility. Trent glanced again at Vanessa's face, which was closed off, shuttered completely against him.

Have I lost her utterly? he thought, and felt the agony of self-reproach wrench his heart. Things had been so wonderful between them once, why hadn't he just left well enough alone? He'd had to go stirring up trouble, and now look what had happened!

A blast from the ferry's horn warned that it was coming straight in. Trent knew he had only a minute or less left to be with her.

He caught her close, unable to stop himself, even though he felt Vanessa stiffening in his grasp. "Oh, Nessie!" he whispered against the soft, damp veil of her hair. Frantically Trent fumbled for words. "I—I guess if you can survive having spent the summer with me, you're a very resilient lady indeed!"

"Oh, I can survive it, Trent," Vanessa informed him, her voice at its most remote. "Believe it or not, I've actually learned to survive quite a lot of things. And by the way, I absolutely despise that nickname. Never call me 'Nessie' again!"

Numbly Trent nodded, wondering how he could have failed to see before the depth of strength and character she possessed. Had he been completely wrong about Vanessa? he wondered. Had he made a horrendous mistake that was about to cost him the only woman he had ever loved?

He forced her face up to his, even though she tried to resist. Then words were torn from him. "Think anything you want about me, Vanessa...that I'm a sanctimonious bastard, like your brother said, or—or have a superiority complex, like you said. You can even think I make love like a barbarian, I don't care! But don't ever think that I don't love you, because I *do*, even if that's the only thing I'm really sure of right now."

With that Trent leaned down and kissed her, not a light, polite, proper, public farewell kiss, but a kiss so full of his passion and his pain that it was guaranteed to keep all the residents of Catt Island gossiping for a month.

He savored those lips he'd adored parting beneath his, cherished the tenderness of her soft mouth one last time, and finally drew back only when he couldn't bear a moment longer the anguish that was now an inseparable part of his love.

He saw her staring up at him, wide-eyed. Then, for just a moment, Vanessa's small, delicate hand clutched at his sleeve. "Trent I don't believe what you said about me was true. But if I'm wrong, and you're right—if I've been that weak—then I guess this is the only way to find out," Vanessa said, her own voice trembling.

The ferry had docked now, and passengers were beginning to get on. "I don't think you're weak anymore, Vanessa," Trent said rapidly. "So find out if you really do love me or...or if you've just been grateful to me all this time. And if it's really love, then come back. I'll be here, waiting. I'll always be here, waiting for you."

It was the best declaration Trent could make on the spur of the moment. But he saw her eyes darken again with anger or pain. Obviously he'd said something that she was taking the wrong way, even if Trent couldn't for the life of him figure out what it had been. But Vanessa knew. She tore away from him and dashed blindly up the gangplank.

"Write to me!" Trent called after her. But Vanessa gave no indication of even having heard him.

Yes, he'd very effectively destroyed what they'd had—all they'd had. Regret tasted like ashes in Trent's mouth as he turned disconsolately to go home...alone.

Chapter Twelve

She had never been quite so miserable in her entire life, Vanessa thought. Nor did it help to know that mostly she had only herself to blame. "Southerners have too much stiff-necked pride," she remembered her father having said once; it was a sentiment with which she was presently in agreement. Yes, she was proud, and she'd been deeply angered and hurt. Since she didn't really think she had the chance of a snowball in hell with Trent Davidson anymore, she saw no reason to stay in touch with him.

So Vanessa's method of dealing with her pride and her pain was to withdraw completely from the person who had caused it and quietly lick her wounds.

He hadn't even believed she really loved him! For some reason, that was the most galling discovery of all.

She didn't really have to be so utterly cut off from Trent. Already he had written her a couple of letters that were casual yet friendly. It was Vanessa's own choice not to reply except with the curtest of notes reporting her safe arrival home and thanking him politely for the summer.

Trent might have phoned her, too, except that Vanessa had chosen to get an unlisted phone number.

Another reason Vanessa didn't want to hear from Trent right now was that the mechanics of sheer survival occupied her totally. It was enough to put one foot after another, to live through one grisly day and then the next.

She had rented a small apartment, but she hated it. Cold, sterile, impersonal, *empty*, it made her dread coming home at night. She especially hated its bright white walls, and she'd immediately bought several cans of paint to cover them. But then, seized by a sudden mood of daring and courage, Vanessa had decided to tough it out. If she could learn to live in this little white box, then surely she would never have to fear white, confined spaces again.

Of course, she could have moved back in with Clark and Kitty. At first her brother had been insistent that she do so— and Vanessa knew she'd left Clark astounded and probably with hurt feelings of his own when she'd vehemently cried, "No! I won't! Please quit asking me!" But she'd only said that because she was so tempted to weakly agree.

By God, she could live alone and she would, even if she died from sheer loneliness...and sometimes Vanessa thought she just might.

She also had a job, but unfortunately it was back at the same small Atlanta TV station that had once employed her for a summer. The station manager, a redneck who'd been plenty miffed when Vanessa had quit, had been completely pragmatic about why he would risk hiring her again.

"You're a looker," Deke Copeland said frankly. "We had lotsa guys phoning up, howling, after you cut out."

Then, as Vanessa sat shaken at the idea that her physical appearance was seemingly all that mattered, Deke added the capper. "You won't be the weather girl this time around, though. We recently hired Julie Molina away from this station in El Paso, and she's been doing a great job for us. Helps us look real New South, too, since she's a member of a minority."

"But—but what will I do, Deke?" Vanessa had stammered.

Deke shot her an uneasy glance. "Since you've had on-camera experie.ice I'm assigning you to work with Lion Danvers in news. He'll probably give you the donkey stuff for a while—cover the jail and churches, the society events and the local politicians at City Hall. You know..."

Vanessa knew. She would have to do every dirty little job that no one else wanted to touch. She, a trained meteorologist, had just acquired the garbage detail!

What Vanessa wanted to do was get up and walk out of Deke's office right then and there. Once she would have, too, but now the cold hand of caution held her back. She had already tried every other television station in town; this was the only one to offer her anything.

Also, Vanessa discovered to her horror—now that she was dealing with all sorts of grubby little details—that she just didn't have the kind of money that would allow her to loll around. Her parents had always spent every cent faster than her father could make it, living up to Mrs. Hamilton's exacting standards. When their estate had been settled, Vanessa and Clark had felt lucky that the assets had actually managed to cancel out the debts.

Of course, Bailey had made money. But his will had left a lot to the ex-wife he'd dumped when he'd gone seeking younger women and to his children by that previous marriage. Additionally, Bailey had provided for his elderly parents, who lived in a nursing home.

Vanessa had still inherited a considerable amount, but few people could truly appreciate how an illness like clinical depression could absolutely soak up money. And Clark, of course, had insisted that his sister receive the best of everything available to improve her emotional health.

Clark had spelled it all out gently for Vanessa, and she, who had never before worried about money, was frankly appalled.

"Why—why, I *have* to work now," Vanessa had said.

She left Clark's office feeling more frightened and alone than she ever had before. Stopping at a red light in her flashy new sports car—a car she now regretted buying—she dropped her head on the wheel. If this was growing up, it was certainly a difficult and painful business indeed!

Vanessa went home, crawled into bed and cried herself to sleep.

So now she rolled out to an alarm clock five days a week, fought traffic on the freeways as she drove to work, and once there put up with the grouchy news manager, who hadn't been nicknamed "Lion" for nothing. Mr. Danvers, as he insisted his subordinates call him, could roar and he could bite; Vanessa often heard the one and felt the other, since Danvers obviously considered her among the most useless of females. He seemed to take particular delight in dishing out all the unpalatable location stories to Vanessa.

He regularly tried to needle her into quitting. "You don't like that, huh?" he'd say if he caught Vanessa wrinkling up her nose at some assignment. "Well, Ms. Ashton, if this one is too dirty for your dainty little hands, then maybe you ought to quit."

Vanessa quickly developed a pat answer. "No, not today, Mr. Danvers," she would say very softly and politely. But she promised herself that one happy day she would certainly tell him where he could shove this job.

So was she to write Trent about all of *that*? Not hardly! Her stiff-necked pride wasn't about to let him know that she lived in three small, grim rooms, that she inhaled enough carbon monoxide on the freeways to paralyze her lungs permanently, that she was close to broke, or that her immediate supervisor thought she was a helpless ninny and a stupid fool.

"Poor Nessie," he might say condescendingly. Then he'd fold up her letter and step outside on his clean, quiet, beautiful island, which seemed more and more, in retrospect, to have been a paradise on earth. No, Vanessa definitely did not want Trent's pity!

All she had ever wanted was his love and to be allowed to love him in return. But Trent hadn't really loved her, whatever words he might have said to the contrary. Why, no man let a woman go if he really, truly loved her!

Surely there had never been a winter so cold and bleak, so harsh and merciless. Surely in the entire annals of meteorology—and what thoughts just that one word brought back!—there hadn't been a winter so filled with ice and snow... and emptiness. Emptiness filled him with its void. Such an awful, aching emptiness!

Initially Trent had thought that he'd miss Vanessa most during the first days and weeks. Even the first months. He had missed her then, desperately. Still, he'd found a great backlog of work to catch up on waiting on his desk. Work that Olga had once handled was there as well. So Trent dived in. He spent long hours at his office because that was the only place where he didn't seem to see Vanessa everywhere.

Still, a dozen times a day, he turned around to make some remark to her before seeing empty space and remembering that she had gone. Or else he woke up at night, thinking he'd felt her stir or turn in his arms, and reached out to pull her closer, only to find himself alone in bed.

And each morning Trent still woke up wondering what he and Vanessa might find to do today. For just a moment, he was filled with anticipation until he remembered...

His mind kept playing tricks on him, and he found himself holding imaginary conversations with her. How she would love the crisp, vivid autumn!

"See the forest, darling."

"Oh, Trent, what spectacular colors! What's that tree over there, the very bright one?"

"That's a sugar maple."

"Really? Oh, have you ever tapped the sap and then made maple syrup? Could we do that?"

Even in his imagination, Vanessa always asked a ton of questions!

His feelings didn't ebb or ease with time, either. Instead they deepened, and the ache grew relentlessly worse because she wouldn't even write to him. Worst of all was his realization that this was probably the way it would be for the rest of his life.

Sometimes he sought out Mrs. Pushka and tried to talk to her, just to feel the warmth of another friendly being's input and sharing. But the old lady was silent and obtuse, distinctly unfriendly, Trent discovered. Even after four months had passed, Frieda Pushka still had not forgiven Trent for "driving away that beautiful, wonderful girl." By now he wondered if she would ever forgive him.

Trent felt so defensive that once he was driven to try to explain to old Frieda—not that she bought his explanations for a minute. "Humph!" she sniffed. "I was seventeen when I married Myron. Hate to think how mature you'd say I was!"

"But that was an entirely different era! Things are different now," Trent protested.

"That's unlikely," Mrs. Pushka said with another sniff as she set an uninspired-looking casserole in front of him. Trent glanced down and recognized that it contained two ingredients that he hated more than any others, liver and cabbage.

"Men are still men and women are still women," Mrs. Pushka went on. "When a man really knows how to love a woman she'll grow up right beside him, strong and brave as you please. Course, I guess it takes a *real* man to do that."

She swept haughtily out of the room, leaving Trent with no doubts about just how she evaluated him.

Maybe she's right, Trent thought drearily as he made himself eat the damned casserole. Maybe he'd really get lucky and it would kill him!

Vanessa was never exactly sure when her life finally took a turn for the better. Each step forward always seemed to involve a test or trial of some kind.

On a day when Lion Danvers had been particularly scathing and sarcastic and Vanessa had fled into the ladies' room to cry, she was found there by Julie Molina. "You've been having a pretty rough time around here, haven't you?" said Julie as she dropped a consoling arm around Vanessa's shoulders.

Vanessa, surprised that anyone had noticed, much less cared, was also amazed when Julie asked her to go to lunch. Jan Triola, one of the news anchors, went along, and suddenly Vanessa had two new friends who plied her regularly with invitations for movies, dinners and shopping trips.

Next she discovered that a very pleasant man lived two doors down in the same apartment building. Vanessa met Shelby Whitson on a traumatic evening when the wine sauce she was pouring over chicken and rice caught fire; she bolted out her front door screaming for help. Shelby rescued the saucepan and showed Vanessa how to use the fire extinguisher that was mounted beneath her kitchen cabinet. Then, since the dinner she'd planned had been completely ruined, Shelby took Vanessa out for a bite to eat, where he explained that he was in the process of getting a divorce.

Vanessa knew right away that she and Shelby would never be anything but friends. Still, she enjoyed having him stop by her place regularly, even if only for a few minutes. He provided an interesting male perspective, telling Vanessa frankly what he thought of her clothes or hairstyle—and he was happy to change the occasional burned-out light bulb or fix a leaky faucet.

A couple of weeks later, Vanessa's red sports car was rear-ended during a rainstorm. When she leaped out to confront the careless driver of the big black Cadillac behind her, she discovered that he was the candidate for mayor with whom she'd been trying to get a personal interview for over a month. So Vanessa got both her interview and a repair job done on her car, although Lion Danvers said she'd looked like a drowned rat on camera with her still-wet hair streaming down around her shoulders. Still, he was pleased by Vanessa's coup.

A month later the station hired Phil Reuter, a cameraman, so Vanessa was no longer the newest employee and consequently lowest of the low. Also, some more interesting assignments were finally beginning to come her way. Nothing great, of course; the great assignments were still reserved for the news anchors. But more and more people were beginning to recognize Vanessa and commend her for her work when she went into restaurants and stores.

At the end of six months, Deke Copeland gave her a raise and told her that the station was pleased with both her work and her attitude. That night Vanessa, Julie and Jan went out to celebrate, and Vanessa drank two whole glasses of champagne without having anything more ominous happen to her than a pleasant buzz. That night, too, for the very first time, she began to consider if there might be a life for her A.T.

"A.T.?" her friends inquired.

"After Trent," said Vanessa decisively.

Yes, she was definitely getting along without him very well...except maybe for the nights. Those long, dark, lonely nights continued to plague her. Once Vanessa had only been able to dream about what it would be like to make love with Trent. But now she actually knew just how wonderful it was, and her memories, especially those last very uninhibited ones, returned over and over again to torment her.

"Damn you, Trent Davidson!" she cried out in anguish on more than one night, pounding her pillow futilely.

He had taught her too well. He had made her want him, hunger for him, burn for his kisses, his caresses and the fierce tenderness of his body merging with hers.

Even when Vanessa was able to suppress all the other memories, she could not forget those.

At Christmas Trent received a card from Vanessa and a note three lines long. Still, he welcomed each brief word. She was well. She'd recently received a raise and a promotion. She hoped that he, Mrs. Pushka and Boots were fine and would have a happy holiday season.

However unsatisfactory the short note was, it was news from her at last, and for at least a week Trent was elated by it. Then, when there was no further word, the winter doldrums crept over him once again.

He tried to stay busy. Trent knew that his father had always considered work an effective antidote to grief, but the son found it less satisfying. Still, Trent filled many hours of the subzero nights working on furniture, although nothing that he built really satisfied him any longer. Not, that is, until he began working on the very smallest piece of all, a cradle.

He poured his heart and soul into the wood, the sandpapering and stain, the designs of flowers and ferns, birds and butterflies that he carved so painstakingly. He knew the cradle represented only wishful thinking. Knew that the only woman with whom he would ever want to have a child had undoubtedly culled him from her life forever. Still, the little cradle represented the last of the hope that Trent had left, a hope that something...anything...might change this painful, prolonged impasse that kept on eating at his heart one lonely hour and one lonely day at a time.

Finally spring began to arrive. The first signs of it here in Trent's frozen north country were the icebreakers, chewing paths through the Great Lakes and opening them to travel once again.

As soon as Trent deemed it safe to take out his cruiser, he went over to Catt Island for the day and dropped by Sally's for a good hot meal. A lot of his neighbors were there, too, but what surprised Trent most was that Olga had returned for the weekend with a husband holding her arm!

His name was Jay VanderLaan, and he was blond and stocky, about as wide as he was tall, but the effect he'd wrought on Olga was amazing. She looked happy, radiantly happy, Trent thought, for the first time since they were children. He was happy to shake Jay's hand and give Olga a "best wishes" hug. But the marriage also left Trent with the uncomfortable realization of just how much time had passed. Had Vanessa, too, met someone else by now? he wondered with a new stab of pain.

The talk floating around Sally's was far from consoling, either, since the big news concerned the construction of a major weather station to be built right here on Catt Island. Like all the other residents, Trent welcomed the thought of more accurate weather forecasts for the area. But as his neighbors sat speculating on who might be hired to work at the weather station, since local residents would definitely be given a higher priority, a poignant pang told Trent that one person who was ideally suited and would have wanted such a job now lived in Atlanta.

How could I have ever been so stupid? he reviled himself as he made his lonely way back home. Frieda was right. If only I'd kept Vanessa here with me and married her when I actually had the opportunity, she would have gradually matured. Then we wouldn't have ever had to be apart.

With Boots supervising Trent's every move, he docked his boat and came tiredly up the hill. He just didn't know what had happened to his energy lately, but he always seemed to feel tired.

And that was the very day when a letter from Dr. Zellar arrived.

Trent found it on the corner of his desk, opened it curiously and read it with considerable surprise. Dr. Zellar was inviting him to come to Atlanta in May to speak to a group of psychiatrists who would hold a three-day seminar there. All Trent's expenses would be paid, as well as a professional honorarium. Dr. Zellar requested that Trent describe various natural substances in herbs and plants that he was investigating, especially those that might affect various aspects of emotional health, with clinical depression paramount among them.

Such an invitation would be coveted by anyone in Trent's field, he knew, since it indicated a wider acceptance of natural healing remedies by the medical profession. "Yes, I'll go," Trent decided immediately, feeling the first rush of real pleasure and enthusiasm that he'd felt in weeks.

But far more exciting to him than the prospect of speaking to a professional group was the knowledge that Vanessa was in Atlanta.

What a week! Vanessa thought, climbing the stairs to her apartment on a Friday evening in early May. The apartment no longer seemed like a white box to her. Over the months it had gradually become her refuge from the TV station with its shrilling phones, its pressing emergencies and the iron-willed dictates of Lion Danvers.

And what a day! A big bank holdup had sent Vanessa and a mobile TV crew racing to the bank, hoping to arrive first on the scene, which they had managed to do. So Vanessa went on live TV with a badly rattled bank president, who had excused himself quickly. Next she'd turned to interview an excited witness who had been forced to lie facedown in the bank. Vanessa shoved the microphone beneath the woman's mouth, then listened incredulously as the witness burst into machine-gun Spanish. It was the wholly unanticipated sort of incident from which TV-station legends were made.

As quickly as she could, Vanessa cut in on the still-babbling woman.

"Gracias, señora," she said hastily. "And there, for the benefit of our Spanish-speaking viewers, we have a further report on the recent bank robbery at First Federal. This is Vanessa Ashton for Channel Nine—"

Lion Danvers was waiting to pounce, just as Vanessa had expected, when she returned to the station. "*What* Spanish-speaking viewers?" he roared at full volume, and Vanessa could only shrug. Out of the corner of her eye she saw Julie and all her other friends trying not to crack up.

"Well, Spanish was my first language," Julie inserted helpfully.

Lion Danvers grumbled some more, but as Vanessa prepared to leave for the day, he paid her a gruff compliment. "I'll say one thing for you, Nesso. At least you think fast on your feet."

Smiling wanly at her new nickname, Vanessa left for the beauty shop where, twice each week, she endured an elaborate ritual that not only included a facial and hairstyling but frequently a manicure and pedicure as well. As a TV personality, she had to try to look her best at all times. Still, she couldn't help but remember wistfully the carefree days on Davidson Island when a bar of soap and a hairbrush had been all she'd needed to look acceptable.

Try as she might, Vanessa couldn't stop her mind from drifting back to the island a dozen times daily. Some part of her refused to relinquish those enchanted, golden days with Trent. Nothing could alter the fact that they had been the happiest days of her life.

Now she shifted the bag of groceries she carried, unlocked her mailbox and froze. She had a letter from Trent!

It had been so long she'd feared he would never write to her again—and who could blame him? Rapidly Vanessa flew down the hall toward her apartment, almost dropping the groceries in her haste.

What if something had happened to Mrs. Pushka or Boots or, especially, to *him*? she worried, risking a newly polished fingernail on the flap of the envelope.

She drew out a typewritten sheet of paper that seemed to contain quite a lot of information.

His words left Vanessa suspended somewhere between terror and anticipation. *Trent was coming to Atlanta.* Hastily she flew to her calendar. Oh, God, he would arrive in just four days!

Gulping, she sank down into a chair and made herself read the letter again carefully, one word at a time, until her heart quit pounding so hard. Trent would arrive on Tuesday night; the medical conference began on Wednesday and lasted through Friday. Presently Trent was scheduled to fly back to Michigan on Friday night, but he could stay over through the weekend. His entire itinerary was enclosed.

"I want to see you, Vanessa." He had written those words with an offer to take her to dinner on any convenient night.

"I want to see you, Vanessa." Again his words echoed in her mind, but suddenly a new part of Vanessa, a cautious, careful part that had been born of necessity over the past few months, felt desperately unsure as to whether she should see Trent or not.

She wanted to. Oh, how much she wanted to see him! She loved him still and knew that a part of her would love him until the day she died. But was it really wise to see him again?

She'd been hurt enough, Vanessa decided. She just didn't need any more hurt or pain, especially from Trent! Nor did she want to have to defend herself against any further accusations or hear her love for him questioned once again.

Trent was a born loner and quite entirely self-sufficient, she reminded herself. He was just not the marrying, settling-down, having-a-baby-together sort of man she needed. So her seeing him was, in effect, pointless.

Yet how could she manage to evade Trent if he was really determined to see her?

Vanessa stewed over the problem all weekend. She discussed it at length with Clark and Kitty, then with Julie and Jan. She even told Shelby when he dropped over to borrow an onion. Relatives and friends offered contradictory advice; Vanessa sighed and realized that this was one decision that was hers alone to make.

I won't see Trent, she decided at last. My life's going okay now, and I don't want anybody messing me up again. Why should she risk the strides she'd made? Why subject herself to the tug of conflicting emotions? Just hearing that he would be in Atlanta had sent her into a tailspin, so why should she risk her heart all over again? She would make up some polite lie to tell Trent.

Armed with resolve, Vanessa marched into the TV station early Monday morning. She intended to demand time off from her job, and if Lion Danvers didn't give it to her, she would quit! Then she intended to hop in her red sports car and drive in a leisurely way down to the Florida Keys, where she would enjoy a pleasant vacation—

"Nesso, go buy a toothbrush. You leave with Phil for Chattanooga in an hour. The hunt for that murderer who broke out of city jail yesterday is moving off in that direction," said Lion.

Vanessa blinked, unable to believe her ears. Why, she had just been handed the very acceptable excuse she needed on a silver platter!

On their way out of town, Vanessa asked Phil to wheel in at Trent's hotel. There she left a fairly lengthy message for him explaining where she'd gone and why. "Guess you'll have to catch me on the ten-o'clock news," she concluded. "Sorry."

Then Vanessa and Phil were off on their very biggest assignment.

For the next two days Vanessa was almost too busy to think about Trent, except for rare quiet moments. For the rest, she and Phil were constantly on the move, interviewing laconic lawmen and hysterical hostages who had mercifully been released unharmed. The escaped prisoner was already wanted for three murders, so nobody thought he had much to lose.

Late Thursday night, a few minutes before midnight, lawmen succeeded in firing tear-gas canisters into a barn where the former prisoner was hiding. The acrid fumes drove him out at last, his hands up in a gesture of surrender. Vanessa and Phil were on the scene to record the action live.

Vanessa phoned Lion Danvers after she and Phil finally got back to their Chattanooga motel. It was two in the morning by then. "For once you two hotdogs did okay," he allowed as Vanessa sat holding the receiver with one hand and picking crawly ticks off her canvas shoes with the other. "You and Phil can take tomorrow off."

I'll be back in Atlanta in plenty of time to see Trent before he returns to Michigan tomorrow night. The thought crashed through Vanessa's mind.

Of course, Trent didn't have to know she'd gotten back, Vanessa told herself as she tumbled into bed. But she was too tired to debate the dilemma; sleep soon snatched her away.

Very early the next morning, she awakened from a strange dream. For the first time in months, Vanessa had dreamed of the plane crash against that mountain in Alaska, and she awoke shuddering. But even as she crawled out of bed and went into the bathroom to splash cold water on her face, she knew something was different this time.

In this dream Vanessa had not gone fleeing and screaming down the mountain...which was just exactly what she
had done in reality. Of course, she'd been injured and in
shock. Not entirely responsible for her behavior, as every
one had assured her. But the fact remained that just as soon
as Vanessa had ascertained that her mother and Bailey were
both dead, she had run in screaming terror from the sight of
their broken, bleeding bodies and the smoldering wreckage
of the crash. What made last night's dream different was
that she had crouched down to decently cover the bodies
with a blanket and then had waited beside them for rescue
to come.

A totally impractical dream, of course. In reality she
hadn't had a blanket, as she had in her dream, and if she
had merely waited around to be rescued she might have frozen to death in the meantime.

But then Vanessa went a step beyond practical details, and
suddenly she grasped the symbolism of her dream: she had
not run away.

That was when she knew she would have to go back and
face Trent.

Chapter Thirteen

Hi, Trent, it's me."

"Hello, *you*!"

"We...ah...wound things up and just got back to Atlanta." Her voice sounded a trifle shaky, but then she had rarely felt so nervous.

"I know." Trent's voice didn't sound quite right, either. It seemed hoarse, almost husky to her ears. Maybe he had a cold. "I've been glued to the TV, watching you, just like everybody else in Atlanta. You're marvelous, Vanessa!"

"Why, thanks," she said, surprised. "Listen, right now I'm a totally grubby mess—"

"Impossible!" he interrupted.

"No, I really am. I've been stomping all around the backwoods of Tennessee, and I've got briars in my hair and unpleasant critters in my clothes. Listen, I'm awfully sorry I had to miss your talk. You spoke this morning, didn't you?" she asked.

"Yes. I really wish you'd heard it, too," Trent said. "I got kind of carried away and mentioned you...not by name, of course. Someone from your TV station was here. Jan, I think she said."

"Yes, she's a friend of mine." Vanessa paused, trying to quell the rapid beating of her heart. She wondered if Trent would still affect her like this when she was sixty. "Listen, if you don't have anything planned for the evening, Trent, why don't I pick you up around six-thirty? We could have dinner together. Then I'll drop you off at the airport and you could still make your flight home."

"That would be wonderful, Vanessa," Trent said, almost boyish in his eagerness. "Of course, I don't have to go home tonight if—if you'd have some free time over the weekend to spend with me, I mean."

"I'm sorry," she lied smoothly. "I really don't. And since you've already got your plane reservation—"

"Right," he said heavily. "It was just a thought. Anyway, dinner tonight sounds great. Why don't I meet you in the lobby?"

"Fine." Vanessa hung up and discovered that her hands were shaking rather badly. How annoying that the mere sound of his voice could still do this to her!

She'd really hated lying to Trent. But, after all, she didn't have to grant him a whole weekend. That would be too long—oh, much too long. Why, then he'd have time to hold her, kiss her and probably undo all her good resolutions.

No, this was a better way, Vanessa thought as she headed for the shower. She would see Trent tonight to prove both to him and to herself that she no longer needed to run away. And she would also see Trent because she owed him. He had, after all, done her a couple of huge favors in the past.

Heavens, it was just Trent. Why did she feel so hot and cold all at the same time? Vanessa wondered. Why was she secretly thrilled and, at the same time, absolutely scared to death?

First Trent cut himself shaving; then he dropped the bottle of cologne he'd bought that afternoon. At least the bottle proved to be shatterproof, but after the debacle he was making of everything else, Trent threw it away without even opening it.

She wasn't used to his wearing cologne, and now some deep instinct inside Trent yearned for things to be the way they'd always been between them. When Vanessa had been so natural, so totally without artifice, with her fresh-scrubbed face, her jeans and shorts, her thousand-and-one questions. Yes, more than anything, Trent just wanted things to be the way they'd been before he'd gone and wrecked it all.

Vanessa dressed three times before she was satisfied. First she washed her hair and let it dry naturally around her face in the loose, casual style she always wore on quiet weekends. Then she pulled on a bright new cotton sundress that she'd bought just the week before.

Wrong, she thought immediately on surveying herself in the mirror. Oh, she looked like her real self, all right, wrinkly sundress and all, and that's just what would happen after she'd sat in a restaurant booth with Trent for an hour or two. She'd be a seething mass of wrinkles! Anyway, the sundress made her look too much like a kid.

Grimacing, Vanessa tore it off, and then, while her curling iron and hot rollers heated, she dressed from the skin out once again. She sweated over her hair and swore fluently when it didn't behave, but finally every lively tendril had been subdued. Next she applied a careful coat of makeup and dressed again in a smart linen suit with an expensive blouse and pumps, scarf and pearls.

Wrong. This was the professional woman's image, but it had never really suited her. This Vanessa looked, to her own eyes, like the stiff and probably sadistic lady warden of a state prison. Oh, God, it wouldn't do either, she thought, scattering more discarded clothes on her bed.

Finally she wiped off most of her makeup, then bent over at the waist and brushed out her hair. She pinned the black curls high in a casual, simple style. Next she stepped into a sleeveless white silk dress and exotic sandals with very high heels, twirled around for her mirror's inspection and *there*! She looked exactly as she'd wanted—cool and even a little distant, unmistakably mature and actually even rather pretty.

Trent saw her from across the hotel lobby and practically lunged to his feet. She was breathtaking! Nor was he the only man to think so. Heads turned as Vanessa strolled toward him.

"Vanessa Ashton...Channel Nine," he heard some man mutter.

"Yeah, she does look even better in person. You suppose she's ever—"

Trent balled his hands in rage. *How dare they speculate about Vanessa like that!* Protectiveness surged through him. He wanted to swoop her up in his arms and carry her safely off with him forever!

"Hello, Trent." Then she was beside him again, after so endlessly long a time, and aiming a casual kiss toward his cheek. He felt its light brush. But she had withdrawn before he could recover enough to respond. "My car's double-parked out front, if you don't mind being rushed away."

"No—fine...not at all." He was stammering as he had once before, when he'd met her at the ferry after so long a time and had been struck anew by her loveliness. But at that time she had been frail, thin and a little wan, a woman still on the mend. Now, in this glorious beauty, Trent saw Vanessa's full potential revealed—and, dammit, all it did was make him feel even more insecure!

Nor could he think of anything to say to her, not to this fearless, self-reliant Vanessa whipping her little red car in and out of Atlanta traffic. Fortunately he didn't have to. She kept up a steady stream of conversation, telling him all about her job and her family and relating anecdotes about her recent adventure in Chattanooga.

Good God, the deafening traffic! Trent, coming from his quiet island of peace and serenity, wondered how Vanessa could endure it. He further admired her ability to treat such traffic casually. Still, at the same time he wished she were safely encased in an armor-plated tank so no careless hot-rodder could hit and kill her!

But perhaps the traffic worried her, too, just a trifle. Trent noticed that her dainty, polished fingernails trembled ever so slightly. But good Lord, whose wouldn't in the middle of this mess?

Suddenly she darted across two lanes of traffic, zipped down an exit ramp and hung a hard left into a parking lot. Such rapid, death-defying maneuvers left him gasping. "Oh, Trent, I'm sorry," Vanessa said, abashed. "Why, you're positively white! I really didn't mean to scare you, I just saw my chance to get off the freeway—"

"It's all right," he muttered, feeling perspiration pop up on his forehead.

After a second Trent recovered enough to glance around. They were parked beside a large and fairly elegant-looking restaurant. He drew a deep, steadying breath, then looked over at Vanessa, a glance that proved to be a mistake.

Had her legs always been quite so shapely? Of course, he hadn't seen her wearing silken hose and high heels on the island. Now the sight of her graceful, gorgeous legs sent heat rushing throughout his body and made his mouth fairly water. For a moment all Trent could think about was pressing his face against them, kissing a path upward from the pert arch of her feet to the apex of her thighs where he would—

Quickly he censored the rest of the thought. Otherwise he was going to embarrass himself by becoming visibly aroused. But he hadn't been able to forget making love with Vanessa, especially that last night, when she'd been so angry and yet so abandoned to passion. Did Vanessa ever think of that night with him at all?

Probably not, for as their gazes suddenly, abruptly collided in the close confines of the car, Trent saw that those fabulous huge eyes of hers were calm yet chill. His hope deflating rapidly, he opened the door of the car and got out on legs that still felt weak.

She was doing fine, Vanessa knew. *Great*...except that her hands persisted in trembling. Right now they were wrapped securely around her cocktail glass. She had already belted back her first drink and now aimed at sipping this one more slowly, but neither had had the desired effect of relaxing her so far. She still felt nervous, and her hand continued to shake.

Trent seemed equally strained, and he kept throwing harried glances around the restaurant. Who could blame him? Vanessa thought privately. It was loud and crowded, the worst possible place for a personal and intimate conversation—and that was exactly why Vanessa had pulled her zip exit, whipping across three lanes of kamikaze traffic to wind up here. Initially she'd planned to take Trent to a quieter place for dinner, but all at once she'd realized she wasn't ready to handle it.

Okay, so she wasn't Superwoman yet, and she was terribly, awfully afraid that if they got into a deep personal discussion she might break down and cry or do something equally girlish and terrible. Like...like draping herself across his broad chest and begging him to take her back home with him to Michigan where she belonged.

For that matter, how did she even know that Trent was still up for grabs? He seemed awfully nervous about some hing tonight. It might be entirely presumptuous of her to blindly assume he was still uninvolved. Initially, with his rejection of her as a potential marriage partner, it had suited Vanessa to brand Trent a freedom-loving loner, too set in his familiar bachelor's groove to be a fit partner for any woman. But, of course, she'd been mad as hell at him then.

Come to think of it, she was still mad as hell at him! Vanessa realized. But at least her once-paralyzed brain and emotions were now able to allow for the fact that she might have been wrong. Trent had made such a point of wanting to see her. Why? To gently break the news that at last he had found his right and perfect mate? After all, months and months had passed. Vanessa could scarcely assume that the man who hadn't wanted her on the island last summer could have the least interest in her now. No, he probably had some perfectly ghastly news that he was steeling himself to deliver. Why, she could just imagine how Trent would probably circle around the subject, then zero in for the clincher.

"Vanessa, I must tell you that at the last annual meeting of the Association of American Pharmacognosists I met the most intriguing woman. She's a microbiologist . . ."

Or maybe Olga had come back to him, Olga with her voluptuous figure. . . . Olga, who had worked for Trent for ten years, and whom he must have found mature and earthy on a few occasions, at least. And now I'm starting to think like a vicious cat, Vanessa thought, and she gulped the remainder of her drink.

She realized she was absolutely terrified of hearing whatever Trent might say.

Alas, she still loved him so! What did it take to finally quit loving a man when you had cared about him half your life?

And all the time that her mind kept racing in a paroxysm of fear, Vanessa heard herself chattering, chattering, chattering. Once, when she lived in Washington, a bitchy acquaintance had told Vanessa that Southern women talked more and said less than people anywhere else in the world.

Although it had been a regional put-down, Vanessa had
nevertheless recognized a certain kernel of truth. From
childhood she'd been schooled in how to be charming with
her mouth wide open; now she utilized that talent to its
greatest limit.

She told Trent all about Clark and Kitty, speaking at
length about Kitty's recent pregnancy and how excited they
all were to be having a baby in the family. Next she told
Trent about her brother and sister-in-law's new house, de-
scribing it, too, in detail.

Their dinner arrived. Vanessa said, "Oh, good, I'm
starved!" then proceeded to nibble her way around the
edges while she talked on and on. She spoke of the amusing
incident when she was rear-ended by the mayoral candidate. She described the time she'd cremated chicken breast
by igniting the wine sauce and how her very good friend
Shelby had come to her rescue. Then she laughed over the
adorable foibles of her sweet boss, Lion Danvers, and all the
while she steadfastly ignored the grim downward quirk of
Trent's lips.

Finally, Vanessa's mouth was so dry she had to pause for
a sip of water. "Don't you want to know about anyone you
met in the islands, Vanessa?" Trent asked abruptly. "Mrs.
Pushka, for instance? She sent you her love."

Desperately she took another sip, then looked up squarely
as she blotted her lips with her napkin. "Well, Trent, last
summer seems, well . . . pretty long ago," she said, implying
that her memories of that distant time had grown quite
vague, that she didn't remember lying in his arms, making
love with him, as if it had happened yesterday.

She saw Trent beckon the waitress to refill his highball
glass. Why, we never used to drink at all and just look at us
now, Vanessa thought, amazed by their mutually uncharacteristic behavior. And Trent wasn't eating his dinner
either, Vanessa noticed.

He drained his fresh drink and now Vanessa saw that *his* hands were trembling. *Good! It served him right for playing with her heart and her emotions as he had in Michigan.*

"You don't want me to discuss anything that happened last summer, do you?" he asked her deliberately.

She looked straight at him and made her voice just as deliberate. "No, I don't, Trent." *Because I can't stand it! I'll fall to pieces! I'll totally humiliate myself or, worse, I'll wind up hurting so bad I can't live with all the pain! Oh, Trent don't you understand? I've had enough of hurt and pain to last a whole lifetime!*

"All right," he said bitterly. He reached for his wallet and began scattering bills on the table. Just for a moment, Vanessa saw pure screaming misery in his dark blue eyes. And although she didn't know the cause, and indeed feared even to ask, misery was something she understood very well.

So she gulped, hard. She'd been so obsessed with her own feelings, with her pain and fear, that she'd barely considered what he might feel. "Trent, I—" Vanessa began. Then she broke off at the sight of a handsome young man, an absolute stranger to her, suddenly standing by their table.

"Ms. Ashton!" he exclaimed. "Why, it really is you, isn't it? I told my friends I just knew you were Vanessa Ashton, but they didn't—"

Vanessa smiled, automatically going into her role of gracious television personality, and a few minutes later she was signing autographs for the man and all of his friends.

Trent finally managed to pry Vanessa away from her admirers and out of that smoky, overpriced restaurant, not that it did much good.

He had lost her utterly and forever, Trent knew. She was mixed up now with some guy named Shelby, so it counted for very little that she had become the woman he had always known she could be: competent, mature and independent.

Modern man's ultimate dilemma, Trent thought grimly opening the door to her little red sports car so she could slide beneath the wheel. You finally manage to persuade a sweet blindly adoring woman that you aren't God, and you push her out of the nest for her own protection so she won't always have to hang on to a man, and she changes and grows until she completely fulfills—even surpasses—your expectations. But just as soon as she has her feet firmly fixed on the ground, she has no more use for you, your love and protectiveness.

Well, buddy, you asked for it! he told himself. Bitter self condemnation had become quite familiar to him. And now he was apparently trying to wallow in self-pity, too.

Still, letting her go had been so difficult for him, and he'd suffered so much from Vanessa's absence, that it felt as if he deserved better than this.

Old Frieda Pushka had probably had the right idea. If you loved such a woman you kept her, despite her dependency and girlish immaturity. Then, gently, lovingly, you helped her to grow. That way there was still hope she'd grow with you and not apart from you as Vanessa had.

Trent had often wondered what he would see when the worship in her eyes had died and now he knew. They were cool. Indifferent. *Nothing*—that was what he saw.

Well, this theoretical stuff was interesting as all hell, but it didn't stop the ache deep inside that felt like a raw wound had been gouged out of his heart.

"I'm really sorry about that, Trent," Vanessa said contritely as she headed the car out onto the freeway again. "Listen, I didn't mean to be so abrupt, either. If there's something you need to tell me—"

"There isn't," Trent said curtly. "Anyway, we should go straight to the airport now. I don't want to miss my flight."

Oh, Lord, he really is angry, Vanessa realized, and since the huge Atlanta airport was just a short distance away

Trent probably wouldn't have time to swallow his anger and pride even if he wanted to.

Almost before Vanessa knew it, they were gliding up before the proper terminal. Then she knew she had to say something, do something. "Oh, Trent, I'm so sorry," she blurted. "I—"

As he turned to her she stopped, stunned by the sudden wildness she read in his eyes and saw on his face. Suddenly his large hand was beneath her chin, his warm mouth covering hers in a brief kiss that was nevertheless so sweet that Vanessa couldn't speak. All the memories she'd tried to repress came flooding over her in a riptide of emotion. Oh, God, there was just no way to protect yourself when you loved someone this much!

"I'm sorry, too, Vanessa," Trent said tautly. Then, before she could recover, he had grabbed his bag from the back seat and had turned, disappearing into the throngs of people bustling by.

Behind her a car horn honked. She was, after all, blocking a passenger-unloading zone. Still, it took a few moments before Vanessa dared to drive away, her eyes were so full of tears.

She had to pass the TV station on her way home. Julie and Jan would both be there, she knew, preparing for the ten o'clock broadcast. And suddenly Vanessa needed badly to see her friends. She cast a wary eye over the traffic, then pulled another zip exit.

The station was quiet, far quieter than it was during the day, when phones rang and office machines clattered and dozens of people milled around. Vanessa finally caught up with Julie and Jan in front of one of the private monitors to which a VCR was attached.

"Hey, great!" Julie said with a clap of her hands. "You're the very person we wanted to see. Guess what? Jan caught your one-and-only this morning, and now we've got him on tape."

"Oh, God, what a hunk!" moaned Jan, a tall, attractiv woman. "He's absolutely fascinating! And what a story! just wish I could use this whole tape and not just a seg ment."

"Sit down and take a look," Julie advised Vanessa, grin ning and patting a chair beside her. "You obviously need treat. Your face looks like you just got hit by a steam roller."

"No, *I* did the steamrolling...and now I'm sorry." Va nessa sank into her seat and watched the tape rewind. She' forgotten all about Trent's speech—why, she hadn't eve thought to ask him what he'd said. Rude, very rude. Bu then she'd also been very, very nervous.

Suddenly there he was on screen, bigger than life an twice as beautiful to her, looking just as he had a few mo ments ago. Why, he was even wearing the same dark blu suit. Vanessa blinked away fresh tears as she saw that th doctors' convention had been larger than she'd expected Still, Trent appeared perfectly calm and poised as he face them from the lectern.

"Ladies and gentlemen, I appreciate the opportunity t speak to you today," he began. "I will first discuss my lab oratory in northern Michigan and the work we do there synthesizing and combining various natural ingredient found in herbs and plants. If you are interested in our spe cific methods and the various techniques we've developed you'll find a four-page handout available in the back of th room which discusses them at length."

Then, for the next few minutes, Trent talked of his wor in general, of the legacy from his father and the presen worldwide search for new and better drugs to combat th host of human ills. He was eloquent, so very eloquent, Va nessa thought.

"But your business is chiefly people," Trent said to th psychiatrists next. "Most of you in this room treat patient for depression, chemical dependency, emotional distur bances and/or mental illness. You come to know your patients quite well, and often you know their families, too.

"It is because of one of those patients that your path and mine, your work and mine, have happened to cross," Trent continued, and Vanessa never even heard the suddenly audible breath she drew.

"It was my privilege to first meet this person when she was still just a child... though she was the most delightful child I'd ever known—intelligent, inquisitive, uninhibited. Then, unfortunately, I lost track of her for a number of years, which was certainly my loss as I discovered as soon as I saw her again. She was in her early twenties then—and quite the loveliest creature in the world."

Trent paused, looking out over the audience. "I won't describe specific details. My dear friend probably wouldn't appreciate those being aired—also, some of you might guess her identity, which I wish to protect. But a few years ago she was subjected to a terrible accident when she was physically injured and two people to whom she was closely related were killed outright. In the aftermath of that wreck, she was engulfed by severe depression.

"She didn't respond in textbook fashion to any traditional drugs. Either they proved wholly ineffective in her case or they caused severe and unacceptable reactions. By a fortunate coincidence, I was already working with a compound which, in controlled drug trials, appeared to have both naturally calming and energizing effects. When my friend's dilemma was called to my attention, I naturally thought of this preparation, H-320B, and of course I prayed that it might be of some help.

"Briefly, in this instance my formula did work and proved a helpful aid in my friend's recovery. It was, of course, *only* an aid. She had the best of modern medical care as well, provided by one of your colleagues who is in the audience today. Additionally she had the support of loving family members, and we all know how valuable that can be. Most of all, she had the courage and resolution, the very *will* to be well and whole, that spring from an indomitable spirit and a loving and intrepid heart.

"Ladies and gentlemen . . . I just wish you could see what a glorious and radiant woman she is today. All of the early promise that she displayed in girlhood has been so wonderfully fulfilled. And, having said that, I realize what a ludicrous statement I've just made," Trent added ruefully, "because most of you probably have seen my beautiful lady. Her work is in the public eye, so she is often on display.

"And now I would like to offer to you the natural antidepressant we developed in Michigan for use either as an adjunct to traditional therapy or possibly as an alternative regime. I will make this formula available, free of charge, to any licensed physician or authorized institution that requests its use. Consider it my gift of gratitude for the complete recovery of a lady I have loved much of my life and now hope to marry." Trent paused briefly and looked out at the assembly. "Thank you for your attention."

The tape clicked off. The three women gathered around the monitor were silent for a moment. "Awesome, isn't it?" said Jan admiringly. "Vanessa, was Dr. Davidson really talking about you?"

When Vanessa didn't answer, Julie gave her a little shake. "Hey . . . hey, doesn't that make you feel a whole lot better? Why, Vanessa, what's wrong?" she cried, catching sight of her friend, who was clearly stunned, both hands clapped over her mouth.

Vanessa sat glowing with an inner light that was all the more incandescent for coming, as it did right now, after such crushing disappointment and bitter remorse. Wrapped in its laserlike intensity of utter joy, she felt her mind groping toward a measure of understanding.

Why, Trent must have actually meant it when he'd told her, months ago at the ferry landing on Catt Island, that he loved her and would be there, waiting for her to come back to him. At the time, Vanessa had been too angry, too hurt, too bent on ultimately *showing him* to take those words seriously. But if Trent had meant them, as apparently he really had—then that poor, dear man had been waiting for her such a long, long time!

She still didn't entirely understand him, Vanessa knew. She remained puzzled by much. If Trent had really loved her—as apparently he did—why then had he ever made her leave him at all? Why? And why had it been so important to him that she become what he considered "mature?" But it was no longer necessary for Vanessa to understand everything. Faith and trust, those inevitable components of real love, stepped into the breach.

Finally, as Julie continued to shake her shoulder impatiently, Vanessa turned to stare at her friend.

"Say something, Vanessa! Talk to us."

So she replied politely to Julie and Jan with the very first words that occurred to her. "I believe I have a plane to catch."

Chapter Fourteen

Y̶ou're acting like she's the only woman in the world,'' Trent told himself as he stomped across the island. "Well, she isn't, old buddy. The world is full of beautiful and sexy women—''

He stopped, his throat suddenly constricting until he couldn't think, much less talk. Who was he kidding? Even with Vanessa, love had not come easily to him.

No, he would never find another woman he could love.

This was it—the way things were going to be for the rest of his life—and he'd better start getting used to it instead of hacking himself up over missed opportunities and what might have been.

You need a new hobby, he told himself desperately. How about being a ham-radio operator? Yeah, that's a pretty good hobby. Get a tall enough antenna, I'll bet I could talk to folks from here to Borneo.

Suddenly he felt overwhelmed again by exhaustion. That was natural enough. He'd been unable to sleep on last night's red-eye flight. He'd been home by nine this morning and had gone straight to bed, but after an hour or two he'd awakened himself, tossing and turning. Finally he'd gotten up, feeling even more tired than before.

His appetite was shot to hell, too, and had been for days. When he'd taken off his new blue suit he'd found that it was already too loose, when it had fitted him fine a scant two weeks earlier.

He'd seen Mrs. Pushka briefly, had thanked her for the lunch she'd set out and which he hadn't eaten and had assured her that Vanessa was well and very busy in Atlanta. But he'd brushed off the old woman's further questions. He just couldn't bear to answer them . . . now.

This . . . this was the way things were always going to be, and he just had to get used to it.

Boots whined, as if picking up Trent's disconsolate mood, and pushed his cold nose into his master's palm. Absently Trent scratched the dog behind the ears as they walked along.

Another year or two and Boots would be an old dog, just as Frieda Pushka was a very old woman. *Before long I'll lose them both,* Trent thought almost morbidly.

Suddenly something flickered at the corner of his eye. Trent whirled, thinking for a moment that—Instead, through the thick underbrush, he glimpsed a small white-spotted fawn. Carefully Trent began to move away, for if too much of his human scent should cling to the little animal, the doe would abandon her offspring in fear.

"See the little fawn, darling?"

"Oh, Trent, what a sweet little thing! Why, just look at that face! But where's its mother? Why does she leave her baby—?"

It was no good. He saw Vanessa everywhere. His island was haunted by her now, and always would be.

Taking a deep breath, Trent dragged his hands down the sides of his jeans. Then he began slowly walking back home.

He went in the house through the back door, carefull
scraping his shoes as Mrs. Pushka had taught him to d
when he was a boy. The deathly quiet silence of the hous
shrouded him. How on earth had he lived so many years i
this—this *tomb*?

He climbed the stairs, leaning on the rail. Offhand, h
couldn't remember ever needing it before.

At the top of the stairs Trent stopped, aware that some
thing was wrong.

The door to Vanessa's room stood ajar.

Had he left it open? Trent wondered for a moment.

No, of course not! He couldn't bear to go in there, it wa
so full of poignant memories. Months ago he had closed th
door quite firmly. Had instructed Frieda to keep it closed
except to let the cleaning woman in occasionally.

Now, dammit, somebody had carelessly left it open and—

Trent stormed to the door, seized the doorknob and ther
froze.

Across the room stood Vanessa, pulling pins from he
hair.

Mesmerized and hypnotized, Trent simply stared, drink
ing in the marvelous sight of her. He was terrified that h
might be hallucinating.

She still wore the white silk dress that she'd worn to din
ner, but her makeup was all gone now, and her hair spilled
like a dark cloud over her shoulders, the way he'd always
liked it best. Vanessa saw him then and began to smile.

*Oh, God, that look . . . that tender, compassionate, lov
ing look he saw in her eyes!*

"What—" he stammered.

"It's about time you showed up," Vanessa replied with a
laugh.

Would a vision really talk and laugh? "How did you—?"
He choked, then stopped, his voice disappearing entirely.

"Oh, I caught the next plane after you, but then I had to
wait a while for the commuter plane to Copper Harbor. I

took a ferry over to Catt Island, where I ran into Paul Johnson buying supplies. I offered to pay him to bring me here. Well, he brought me, but he wouldn't take any pay, so I guess we'll just have to invite Paul and Peg to our wedding.''

"Our wedding?" Trent repeated numbly.

"Oh, yes!" Suddenly Vanessa flung her arms wide, her dark, lustrous eyes aglow. "I've got you this time, Trent Davidson! Oh, I've finally got you at long last!" Triumphantly she waved an oblong black object in front of him. "I've got you right here on videocassette telling the whole world how you love me and want to marry me, so I'd like to see you try and squirm out of it—" Abruptly Vanessa stopped. "Trent! Oh, darling, don't look like that! It's all right, Trent—"

Wordlessly he walked toward her, and then at last he was in her arms.

She seized him tightly and held him as close as she could when she felt his long, strong body began to shake. For a moment Vanessa's own frame held him upright; then she realized that even with the support of her arms he appeared to be sagging. "Trent, let's sit down," she whispered, and helped ease him down beside her on the soft, thick carpet.

There Vanessa caught him even closer still, her grip fierce and passionately protective. "Oh, Trent—I didn't understand! I'm so sorry, sweetheart. I really didn't understand that you do love me!"

"It was so hard to send you away!" he blurted. "I've been so afraid for months and months—"

"Afraid, darling? You?" she asked gently.

The girl she'd once been would have been incredulous, probably frightened, by the sound of his fear. Because the Trent Davidson of her imagination could always leap tall buildings and rescue damsels in distress, and he feared absolutely nothing and no one on earth. But that had been the fantasy figure she'd worshipped, not this very real man that she held, that she loved.

"Yes. I was so afraid I would always have to live without you. Vanessa, I didn't know if I could!"

She felt hot splashes against her throat where his face was pressed so passionately. "Trent...oh, my darling, don't cry!" Vanessa crooned, her own voice starting to wobble from so many intense emotions, for now she felt Trent's as well as her own.

At last she understood what had so mystified her before. At long last Vanessa finally understood why it had been so important to Trent, so crucially important, that she become strong.

It was for times like this. Times when he wasn't.

So she held him and rocked him. She combed her fingers through his thick dark hair and pressed her lips to his temples over and over until she could sense that strength was flowing into him again.

"Hey, couldn't we be making love instead of just sitting here on the floor?" she teased him lightly. "Now, I ask you, isn't that a good idea? Oh, Trent, I've missed you so desperately! And I've wanted you so badly, too—wanted to make love with you, I mean. But not in the old way—you know, when I was still scared and you were being so gentle and cautious with me...oh, not that *that* wasn't wonderful, too—and I do want us to make sweet love like that sometimes. But—oh, Trent, do you remember that very last night we spent? When I asked you to broaden my horizons, and, good Lord, did you ever! Could we make love like that again, do you think?" She paused. "Oh, aren't you even going to talk to me at all? Or are you still mad at me because of that horrible dinner at that perfectly hideous restaurant?"

Now Vanessa felt Trent start to shake again, but this time she knew he was laughing. He drew back and stared down at her, his blue eyes blazing with love.

"You're never going to change, are you?" he demanded.

"Oh, probably not very much," Vanessa admitted, winding her arms up and around his neck. "You know you can't really change a hardhead—"

"I *adore* your hard head!" he whispered.

"Good! It's always been set on you."

Then he caught her so close she gasped, and began to kiss her with lips so molten that Vanessa felt herself yielding and melting beneath them. Her heart hammered wildly, and she thought that surely she had never been so happy in her whole life.

Abruptly Trent kicked the door closed, and with choked, whispered words he was saying everything she'd longed to hear as he drew her beneath him. "Oh, Trent, I love you so!" she managed to reply. Then the glide of white silk muffled any further words as Trent rapidly pulled her dress over her head.

But now there was no need to talk at all.

Hours later they were back in Vanessa's room once again, more properly in bed this time, but still lying in a blissful tangle of arms and legs.

Beneath her cheek Vanessa could feel the warm regular beat of Trent's heart.

"Tell me..." he said after a moment. "Was I right to cut you loose last year?"

"Yes—and no," Vanessa replied thoughtfully. "Mostly yes. I did need to learn responsibility for myself. I needed to earn my own living, get myself into and out of various scrapes. I really had been too dependent on other people." For a moment she fell silent; then she went on quietly. "I'll tell you something I've never told another living soul. Do you know what I felt on that mountain in Alaska when I realized that Mother and Bailey were both dead? I felt free ... finally free of two people I had actively disliked but always been too weak to break away from before. Now

that's where my particular case of 'survivor's guilt' cam
from.''

"That's easy to understand," Trent assured her.

"So, yes, I did need the experience of being on my own
But I'd still rather be here with you."

"I'd much rather you were, too, darling," Trent replie
fervently, his arms tightening.

"Of course, you still haven't properly proposed to me
you know," Vanessa chided him.

"My God! Is there no satisfying women?" he pretende
to complain. "I've phoned about the blood tests. Phone
about the church and the minister since you said you wante
'a very binding ceremony.' Then I called your brother an
made peace with him—Oh, well. Marry me and stay her
with me forever or—" He paused threateningly.

"Or what?" Vanessa dared, laughing up at him.

"Or I really will tie you to a tree!" Trent threatened.

"Oh, I'm not going to leave you. I'm going to link yo
and your computer up to HERBALERT and the rest of th
modern world. That should take me a few months. By tha
time the new weather station will probably be finished, ac
cording to Paul Johnson. Maybe I can go to work there an
fulfill a longtime career ambition of mine. What do yo
think?" Vanessa inquired, twining her fingers in the dar
hair on Trent's chest.

"You've certainly got the best chance of anyone I know
You have a degree in meteorology, after all. So you inten
to stay a career woman?" he asked.

Vanessa smiled and tugged mischievously at a couple o
chest hairs. She had heard the very faint resonance of dis
appointment in Trent's voice. "Well, *part* of the time. I d
need my own things. I think any woman does."

"Would you really be satisfied with a part-time job?"

She raised an elbow to his chest, cupped her chin in he
hand and stared down at him. "Yes. I saw that cradle yo

built. Mrs. Pushka showed it to me before you got back from your walk. Oh, Trent, it's the most beautiful thing you've ever built!"

"Thanks," he muttered. Then: "Well?"

"Yes, I'd love to have a baby with you," Vanessa whispered. "I'd like two children at least—"

"At least?" he interrupted with mock suspicion. "Listen, I know the way your mind works. What do you really have in mind?"

"Three or four," Vanessa admitted. Then, at the expression of absolute alarm on his face, she added defensively, "Well, Trent, you know we have plenty of room here. And, speaking of that, I definitely want to pack off dear old Clarissa's Victorian antiques and furnish the living room and dining room in—"

"Oh, no, you don't," Trent laughed, although he was delighted to hear her making decisions of that nature. "You're not getting away with changing the subject." He wrestled her down until she was flat on her back while he sprawled across her. Then he kissed her warmly, thoroughly. "You can certainly decorate the house any way you want, but I didn't save your pretty hide *twice* just so you could turn into a baby machine! I want a wife who will have time to spend with me."

"Oh, I will, Trent!" Vanessa promised fervently. "And I do know what a lot I owe you—"

"You don't owe me anything!" he interrupted emphatically, running a finger lightly down her nose. "We're even now, because you've saved my life, too. Twice, at least!"

"What in the world are you talking about?" Vanessa asked in genuine puzzlement. "Why, I never—"

"When you came here last summer you saved me from settling down into confirmed bachelorhood," he told her. "I haven't enjoyed being alone a single day since! And now, by coming back, you've saved me from becoming a lonely,

eccentric old man, all set in my ways and forgetting my ta
ble manners.''

"Oh.'' Vanessa considered his words, then kissed him
enthusiastically. "Why, I guess I did! Okay, then. We're
even. But it was never gratitude that made me love you
anyway. I just did. It was always that simple.'' Her hand
glided over the planes of his face, cherishing every single
inch of skin. He was a much more complicated person than
she, Vanessa realized. It was probably the result of his
unorthodox upbringing, which had been rather obviously
deficient in love.

"Trent, why have you always had such a hard time be
lieving I loved you?'' she inquired.

"Scientists always have trouble believing in miracles,'' he
murmured, and she felt his lips beginning to glide over her
body again.

"Well, I used to harbor the dangerous delusion that you
were rather wonderful and probably walked on water,'' Va
nessa confessed. "I certainly know better than that now, O
wise and unwise one. So you blew your chance to have an
adoring and subservient wife.''

"I'll settle for a hot-blooded independent one,'' Trent
breathed, his mouth and hands moving in unison now.

"*Again?* My goodness, Trent!'' she exclaimed with a
laugh.

"I'm still starved for you,'' he admitted.

"That's okay. I'm ravenous for you myself. But
y'know...'' She stopped, finding speech growing difficult
as his lips and tongue continued their arousing downward
path. "...if we're going to act like this all the time, you
probably will wind up the father of a whole slew of kids!''

"Oh, I think that's probably destined to happen any
way,'' Trent said resignedly. "I've never been able to out
wit you.'' He glanced down at her and saw at least a dozen

questions forming on her lips and in her huge brown eyes. "Now, for once, don't ask me a *thing*, and just let me make love to you!"

And, just that once, she did.

* * * * *

ATTRACTIVE, SPACE SAVING BOOK RACK

Display your most prized novels on this handsome and sturdy book rack. The hand-rubbed walnut finish will blend into your library decor with quiet elegance, providing a practical organizer for your favorite hard-or-soft-covered books.

Only $9.95

Approximately 16" x 8" when assembled

Assembles in seconds!

To order, rush your name, address and zip code, along with a check or money order for $10.70* ($9.95 plus 75¢ postage and handling) payable to *Silhouette Books.*

Silhouette Books
Book Rack Offer
901 Fuhrmann Blvd.
P.O. Box 1396
Buffalo, NY 14269-1396

Offer not available in Canada.

BKR-2A

*New York and Iowa residents add appropriate sales tax.

Silhouette Special Edition

COMING NEXT MONTH

#427 LOCAL HERO—Nora Roberts
Divorcée Hester Wallace was wary of men, but her overly friendly
neighbor wasn't taking the hint. Though cartoonist Mitch Dempsey
enthralled her young son, convincing Hester to believe in heroes again was
another story entirely.

#428 SAY IT WITH FLOWERS—Andrea Edwards
Nurse Cristin O'Leary's clowning kept sick children happy, but her
response to hospital hunk Dr. Sam Rossi was no joke. Would the
handsome heart specialist have a remedy for a lovesick nurse?

#429 ARMY DAUGHTER—Maggi Charles
Architect Kerry Gundersen was no longer a lowly sergeant, but to him,
interior designer Jennifer Smith would always be the general's daughter.
As she decorated his mansion, resentment simmered . . . and desire flared
out of control.

#430 CROSS MY HEART—Phyllis Halldorson
Senator Sterling couldn't let a family scandal jeopardize his reelection;
he'd have to investigate his rascally brother's latest heartthrob. To his
chagrin, he felt his *own* heart throbbing at his very first glimpse of her. . . .

#431 NEPTUNE SUMMER—Jeanne Stephens
Single parent Andrea Darnell knew Joe Underwood could breathe new life
into Neptune, Nebraska, but she hadn't expected mouth-to-mouth
resuscitation! Besides, did Joe really want *her*, or just her ready-made
family?

#432 GREEK TO ME—Jennifer West
Kate Reynolds's divorce had shattered her heart, and no island romance
could mend it. Still, dashing Greek Andreas Pateras was a powerful
charmer, and he'd summoned the gods to help topple Kate's resistance!

AVAILABLE NOW:

#421 NO ROOM FOR DOUBT
Tracy Sinclair

#422 INTREPID HEART
Anne Lacey

#423 HIGH BID
Carole Halston

#424 LOVE LYRICS
Mary Curtis

#425 SAFE HARBOR
Sherryl Woods

#426 LAST CHANCE CAFE
Curtiss Ann Matlock